FOOD FOR LOVE

Whilst on holiday in Ireland with her young
friend Gillian Lechmere, thirty-five-year-old
Eira Shearme hears a young tenor sing and is
tremendously stirred by his voice. But when she
asks him if he would be interested in a musical
career, the young Welshman, Deri Rhys, tells
her he is a miner. On the way home Eira, who
is head of Shearme's Enterprises Ltd., theatrical
copyright holders, calls at Garreg Wen and tries
once more to persuade him, and again fails.
But when the mine closes down and Deri
eventually accepts her offer of financial help to
train his voice – a decision which has far-
reaching results.

Food for Love

LEILA MACKINLAY

World Distributors (Manchester) Ltd.

"If music be the food of love, play on"
Twelfth Night

This edition published in MCMLXXIII by
World Distributors (Manchester) Ltd
12 Lever Street Manchester M60 1TS

First published in Great Britain by
Ward Lock and Co. Ltd

Copyright © Leila Mackinlay MCMLX

Made and printed in Great Britain by
C. Nicholls & Company Ltd
The Philips Park Press, Manchester

SBN 7235 5131 6

1

EIRA SHEARME was not given to quixotic gestures and already she was half regretting the particular impulse that had led her to invite the girl on holiday with her to Southern Ireland. The sluggish lines of traffic out of London; the oft-travelled road across Wiltshire and a two hours' wait for the Aust Ferry to save some thirty miles, had combined to sour Eira's mood. The meal at the overnight hotel had been unexceptionable and the tide wrong for bathing along those portions of Welsh coast passed before cutting across from Haverford West to Fishguard. There they had to hang about, in dreary lack of occupation, before a sea crossing of under four hours for which quite twelve would be needed before driving off at Rosslare.

Ships aroused no excitement in Eira. She considered them cramped, comfortless and—below deck—stifling. It was only now that her companion, Gillian Lechmere, seemed to come alive. Of course, Eira remembered, the girl's fiance's hobby had been ships.

"How Alec would have enjoyed this."

The gentle, wistful voice smote Eira unexpectedly. She knew herself to have been unbearable for the past half hour or so.

"Let's go see if the bar is open, shall we?"

There was nothing, Eira thought wryly, that a stiff tot could not cure.

Later, they stood on deck, watching cars—in their rope wheel-nets—being slung dexterously on board. Eira wondered whether her own were already in the for'ard hold at present being loaded. A glance over the side did not show the car still on the platform and she fancied that cream and black Rolls had been behind them in the customs' shed.

Eira drew at her cigarette, conscious of a deep physical tiredness and disappointment that still she could not relax. It was silly, but the habits of an over-busy town life had made her that way. All sorts of nagging work—queries refused to be sublimated just because she had begun her holiday.

Gratefully she saw that Gillian, poor child, was conversing with an American couple.

Eira leaned back against the lifeboat, eyes closed; the clanking of the crane and the scream of seagulls, as someone unloaded a pail from the ship's galley, became a blur of sound, no longer disturbing but not tranquillising, either. She thought of that complicated concern of theatrical copyright holdings of which—since her father's death—she had become head. Shearme's Enterprizes Ltd. leased musicals and plays for performance all over the world. Even the ship's cook, in his galley, was humming a march from one of the Shearme successes. Her methodical mind tabulated it. "March of the Moravians" from Act I of *Lady Lovely*; fees 10% of gross; hire of band parts £5.5.0., deposit £21.

"Eira!" Gillian, cheered by her talk to the Americans, suggested they ate. "The notice did say 7.30, didn't it?"

The elder woman threw the cigarette butt into the sea. "Come along, then, let's see what they have to offer us."

The meal was a good one and made them realize it had been a long time since the thermos of tea and hotel-cut sandwiches on Pendine beach.

They shared a cabin. Gillian offered to take the top bunk but Eira said tartly that not yet being an old-age pensioner, she was quite capable of scrambling up—which she did with more dexterity than the girl could have managed. They took their particular anti-seasick-dope, despite the promise of a calm crossing, and settled down to sleep.

However that was not so easy. Even with the cabin door hooked open and the air-conditioning on, they were bathed in perspiration. People kept walking, heavy footedly, along the corridors. A recalcitrant baby howled and further away a toy dog barked.

"Are ye all right now, Bernadette?" said a voice seemingly in Eira's ear but actually in the adjoining cabin.

"Go to hell," she said darkly, rather hoping to be heard.

Several semi-sleepless hours later a steward brought tea. It seemed the middle of the night; in actual fact it was 6 a.m.

"Oh, God," Eira groaned with such ferocity that Gillian giggled.

It being impossible for both to dress at the same time in the space, Eira told her companion to go ahead and lay,

6

idly watching the slight girlish figure in shorty pyjamas run water into the hand basin.

Eira found it difficult to conceive a greater tragedy than to have had one's fiancé killed a few brief days before the wedding. He had been on his way to Gillian when his motor-scooter skidded on a patch of oil. Even the crash helmet did not save him. He was taken to hospital where they had patched his poor, broken body as best they could, but he had died before Gillian could reach him. She maintained it would have been less hard, if only she could have sat at his bedside, his hand in hers.

"People don't die in a nice convenient way, my child," Eira recalled telling her. "There aren't any tidy speeches, often not even recognition. A person always slips into un-consciousness at the last. How then can he know whether or not anyone is with him?"

"Surely instinct—"

"Perhaps. I wouldn't be sure . . . In the case of poor Alec it is improbable that he ever recovered his faculties, even for a moment."

A sleeping into silence was how Eira conceived death. It had been that way, certainly, with her father's thrombosis. Her mother had gone when Eira was too young to have understood such things.

She had not expected Gillian to believe her, then or later. The child clung to the touching idea that in some way Alec would have derived comfort from her hand holding onto his until the fingers in hers grew cold . . .

Eira shivered, annoyed at her own dark fancies. When, at the end of six months, Gillian was still inconsolable, Eira had suggested this holiday, half surprised the child had agreed to come. She had relations in County Cork whom she had never seen and was anxious to visit. The holiday was loosely planned, allowing of last minute changes and adjustments.

"I am longing to see all the leprechauns, shillelaghs and peat bogs. Not to mention sampling poteen." Gillian was putting on her shoes, as she spoke.

"Here's hoping neither of us is disappointed," Eira remarked, swinging her feet over the side of the bunk. She was sure that the only thing in Gillian's list likely to exist today was presumably the bogs.

7

Gillian vacated the cabin, to stand breathing-in fresh gusts of air through the now open porthole outside it. She was slim, with soft ash-blonde hair and rather delicate colouring. Her eyes were a very deep blue. She put her hands in the pockets of her slacks, which were of unobtrusive material and moderate cut. As long as people were around her, it was not so bad. Except when she saw young couples together or—worse still, parents with small children. Then she was stricken by her total unfulfilment.

'This is how Alec and I should have been,' she would tell herself. The thought came to her now that it was Alec, not Eira, who should have shared Cabin 70/71.

'What an ungrateful wretch I am,' she admonished herself sharply. The trip was a grand gesture on Eira's part. The least Gillian could do was to be an appreciative and lively companion.

Only it was so difficult to put on cheerfulness, as if it were a blouse to be slipped over the shoulders and tucked into a waistband. She could not help missing Alec. Thinking of all the joyous preparations they had made together. The flat, in one of those new corridor towns of London, all ready for them to go into after their honeymoon. She had not the courage to be there on her own. Letting it furnished whilst she made up her mind what to do over the future was but a palliative. In her heart she knew she would end by selling it up with all its contents.

She thought, too, of the bridal dress ordered but never worn, of the presents, which she had felt bound to return.

Sometimes she talked to Alec's memory, as it were, telling him what she had been doing and thinking, but the game was one she could not keep going for any length of time. Always there would be returning realization that there was no longer any Alec, only the little cross in a London crematorium's Garden of Remembrance.

Sighing, she moved towards the stairs and out onto the boat deck.

" 'Tis a lovely soft mornin'," a sailor was telling a passenger, who looked annoyed at the distant drizzle through which a single white building across at Rosslare was visible.

"Sure t'will turn out all right," the sailor prophesied.

"Indeed I hope so," the fellow passenger said, with asperity, as if he personally were to blame.

Gillian halted, smiling at the sailor, with his narrow-jawed Irish face, creased by laughter lines at the eye-corners.

"And will it really come out fine later on, do you think?"

"God willing," was his reply. It brought her sharply up against the important part God played in the lives of a mainly Catholic nation.

Eira had joined them, tall, rather spare, in her excellently tailored slacks and jacket. Her dark, rebellious hair was momentarily disciplined. Her even darker eyes—a little sleep weary—missed nothing.

"So that's Ireland," she observed, looking across from the quay and Harbour Station end of the horseshoe of land to Rosslare itself.

" 'Tis a grand place," the sailor's tone was reflective.

"Which, I suppose, is why you all emigrate?" and Eira smiled, the very early morning immediately kinder to the hardness that the middle thirties had given to her expression in repose.

Philosophic rhetoric was apt to occur in what at first seemed the most unlikely of Irish men and women. The sailor propounded his views upon the earthly paradise that country could become were it not for several things wrong. The barren quality of much of the land. The sloth of certain inhabitants. The fact that it was not impossible to find 32 places in which to drink in a village totalling 35 inhabitants. Fate. The Government. If one or all only had been different—

"There isn't the work in the South, is there?" Gillian forgot she had been warned not to mention the Partition, Cromwell or religion once she left English shores.

As it happened Eira was quickly bored and a loud-speaker had been reminding passengers to hurry on with breakfast even before she came to find her young friend.

"Oh, look, there's our—I mean your car!" Gillian pointed to the station platform.

"Ah, well, she is in Ireland before us, isn't she? Come on, child. I can smell bacon."

At 8 a.m. they descended the gangplank and drove the car to where a one-carriage train—very reminiscent of that which used to run from Ventnor west to St. Lawrence—was waiting. Eight cars at a time were carried behind it on an iron trailer.

"Ever done this before?" A sporty-type Englishman leaned

in at the driving window and advised Eira to use her steering wheel "like a tiller, don't you know".

Another time the implication that she was not perfectly capable of tackling any motoring emergency, however bizarre, would have annoyed her, but she heard herself thanking him in perfectly pleasant tones.

"When you've driven on, you both have to go in the train." He laughed. "Don't ask me why!"

Settling himself obstinately next to them, he proceeded to tell them that they would find many amusing things about Ireland.

"I suppose you'll be going through New Ross? There's a bridge there with a creaky wooden centre. You cross it at under five miles an hour. Then at Youghal—they call it Yawl by the way—you zig-zag between oil cans because that, too, is unsafe. But I musn't spoil *all* your fun in advance, must I?"

Having reversed off the trailer again at the far end, Eira turned the car up on to the Wexford Road. Shortly they passed on their left a place offering breakfast to hungry travellers.

"Ah! There's enterprise for you." (Only later did they learn that the owner was English!) By-passing Rosslare Strand in their ignorance, they made for Enniscorthy and dropped coastwards to Blackwater, where the appearance of "a lady drivin' " seemed to cause local amazement.

"They *must* have seen a woman at the wheel before, Gilly."

Already they had come across petrol stations with exotic-sounding brands, Caltex and Lobitos which, however, turned out to be rather more expensive than some English ones.

On the beach they relaxed to make up for the disturbed night.

"Oh, what peace!" Eira stretched luxuriously, flicking a welcoming finger at a collarless terrier bitch only too anxious to make friends with them.

Once away from London she wondered what civilised madness caused her to live there for all save two or three weeks of a year. Why was she not sensible enough to take a counterpart of one of these widely-spaced white snow-cemmed cottages they had passed on the way through Co. Wexford?

"Doesn't this make one hate town life?" Gillian evidently was feeling the same. "This is so different from—well—Brighton. We're the only people on this beach."

10

They were to find a great many beaches where the same was to be true.

"You can live where you choose," Eira pointed out gently. "You don't have to be in London or any other city."

Gillian had left home at eighteen and been in a hostel ever since, where she had been unexpectedly happy.

"I have thought about chucking the job and going far away where I know nobody and everything isn't calculated to remind me of Alec."

"I am not sure that staying on with Herbert Latter and Co. hasn't been a mistake, my dear. I mean, Alec did work there as well, didn't he? It was where you met. And every time you sit down behind your typewriter you must be remembering how he used to be only three doors down the corridor, in the junior partner's office."

Gillian made no answer. It was one thing to know the other was right and another to be in so inactive a state of mind as to be beyond making the direct break.

"I expect I could find you something in Shearme's, if it comes to that. The department dealing with our overseas commitments is always under-staffed. The work is quite interesting. Or, shall we say, no less boring than an estate agents'."

"It is very kind of you, Eira, but—"

"See how you feel by the end of the holiday, hum?"

Gillian looked relieved as she watched yet another barque of decision float past her on the seas of life. Just as she·was looking at the seas of Blackwater, collecting, spreading out and drawing back again over sand and stones.

Taking decisions had not always been difficult. Gillian had had the courage to demand a rise when sure her salary was too low. Neither had she shilly-shallied over accepting Alec, when he proposed. And when it came to choosing a colour scheme for their flat, she had been as full of ideas and suggestions as he. Since his death everything had become too much effort. Herbert Latter's had no future. That had not seemed very important at first, because, as any young girl of her age, she had felt reasonably sure of leaving there to marry.

'Now I shall never marry,' she reminded herself, with all the dramatic certainty of three and twenty.

Eira's concern would hold far better prospects. Why then

did Gillian hesitate? Looking at her benefactor, who had dropped into a light doze, head pillowed on an airways zip bag which held bathing gear, Gillian wondered if it could be an instinctive dislike of domination. In a way she was risking that already, by coming on holiday with Eira.

The latter was a keen minded woman of business. Under her direction the copyrights' concern had expanded. There was little doubt that in his final years her mild, artistic father had been content with his holdings. He had not gone all out to acquire fresh works for the list, as she had. She was not afraid to take chances, and no big concern was ever built to heights without an element of risk.

Gillian's parents had known the Shearme family, who also lived in Berkshire. When Gillian moved into London—except for those weekends she could afford to spend at home—it had been natural for Eira to "keep an eye on our youngster", as Gillian's father had put it.

She had been extraordinarily kind about Alec, placing her car, with driver at Gillian's disposal when the young people were flat hunting and when Alec died, Eira's unemotional capacity for seeing to things had been of inestimable help: in its way, worth all the sympathetic tears of relations on both sides.

Gillian supposed the older woman to be fond of her, as the outwardly hard-boiled free lance careerist sometimes could be a gentle, less efficient person. Their relationship was not that of sisters nor again of mother and child, though undoubtedly a maternal element entered into it on Eira's side. There was awareness of belonging to different generations without any real barrier because of it. Gillian never thought of Eira as being all of twelve years older than herself.

Now, as she slept, but for those tired lines round the eyes, she could have been in her final twenties instead of within more than hailing distance of forty.

'I admire her tremendously,' Gillian decided. 'She is so clear-headed and level. And, when she is in the right mood, a lot of fun, too.'

Though Eira had her eyes closed, she was not really asleep. Again she was wondering why she had saddled herself with Gillian for this holiday. The girl was such a sorrowful little soul.

'And I've had my fill of sorrow,' Eira thought, recalling the death of a well-loved father as recent enough still to hold an element of pain. Besides she always had considered other people's love lives boring, probably because she had none of her own. Whilst she enjoyed the society of the opposite sex as much as any woman did, she rather distrusted romance, being fairly certain it must exist largely in the imagination.

She had a secret impatience with Gillian for not being more resilient. No doubt the child had been very fond of Alec—a nice, rather shy boy who never knew what to do with his hands and feet—still it was by no means the end of life for Gillian. In due course there would be other young men. There always were.

'Meanwhile I have let myself in for two weeks or so of watching her wipe away "una furtiva lagrima" every time the wretched boy's name was mentioned.'

Sighing, Eira prayed:

'Please God she meets someone else in Ireland.' Never for a moment imagining that it was she herself who also was to do the meeting.

2

AFTER TWO nights with business acquaintances of Eira's who lived near New Ross, they intended to spend a day or so in Tramore, after which they planned a longer stay in Kenmare —in order to see the Ring of Kerry and Killarney—before tackling the west coast.

As it happened, Gillian's Cork relations were away just then but would be back shortly. She had extended her holiday time for this contingency by asking for a third week, this without pay.

She had all but decided to move to Shearme's and, unless she changed her mind with a fickleness foreign to her character, would be handing in her notice at Latter's on returning to England.

Eira was more or less her own mistress and could take the

extra days. It had meant seeing what could be done about altering their sailing arrangements. This was managed only on the Dun Laoghaire-Holyhead route, which would entail coming up country again from Cork. But they had been lucky in being able to re-book the car.

Having left Wexford, therefore, they came finally over the bridge on to Waterford Quay to find the town mildly *en fête* for some hurling event. Driving along by the clock-tower Eira noted a board with the words "Site for National Memorial" but when she made enquiries at the hotel where they lunched there seemed more than an element of doubt as to whom the memorial would be raised. She caught Gillian's smile.

"As typically Irish as that bel dame walking along there with a black shawl over her head," lighting a sweet Afton cigarette. "Did you ever see *Red Roses for Me?* The crone could have stepped out of the Liffey bridge scene."

But Gillian had not seen the O'Casey play. Nor *Juno and the Paycock* of which Eira was subsequently reminded by a quayside lounger they saw on their way out to the car.

Turning round by Reginald's Tower into the Mall and heading for Cork before forking left for the Tramore Road, they discussed the green "Telefon" kiosks and Gillian wondered why—though they had passed a post office of size—there were no pillar boxes.

"Because they're probably painted green too," a guess that Eira was able to substantiate during the afternoon, when they also discovered that the police were called Garda.

Tramore was like, yet unlike their expectations of it. A splendid sandy bay with few of the pleasure elements that marred the natural beauties of too many English seaside resorts. It had a promenade and shelters, but no amusement park or cafes—only sweet shops-cum postcard ones with sellers willing to make a pot of tea.

"I am glad it isn't just another Paignton, aren't you, Eira?"

"I keep forgetting you haven't had my theatregoing advantages," having harked back to the previous topic, Eira broke off to add laughingly. "It would seem that even public conveniences have intriguing names over here." Solemnly she spelt out "fir". Later she found that ladies was "mnà" but in most cases the English also was given. It had

14

taken her a little time to realise that the foreign looking names on the signposts were the same places as the English ones below and that in asking for Port Lairge she was enquiring for Waterford.

They found high tea *de rigeur* at the hotel as indeed it was at most and during the next days made the acquaintance of many delightfu' coves and strands, all within a small radius of natural beauty. Eira could not help noticing that Gillian had not even mentioned Alec, so much was there to amuse and interest her. Every visit to a shop was liable to devolve into quite a *conversazione* and characters, with a capital c, continued to delight.

"You don't know how glad I am we came, Eira."

"As the Yanks say, you ain't seen nothin' yet. Do you want to remain till the end of the week or push on towards Bantry Bay?"

On the advice of some hotel acquaintances they stayed an extra day in order to attend a local ball. Four a year was the average quota. A crack band had been engaged and tickets were not unreasonably priced. In some amusement Gillian nudged Eira to point out the term "powder room" in place of "mnà".

There was a bar, of course. An air of decorum gave the ball a sense of ritual. Yet the tone was in no way inhibited. From what Eira could see from where she stood the standard of dancing was high. No graceless rock and cha. Not even the reels that she had half expected. She saw Gillian looking sad and forlorn, as she had not done for days. Perhaps it had been a mistake for them to come.

'She must recover from Alec sometime.' Eira was not displeased with the progress in that direction. Long stretches of the day would pass without Gillian even thinking about him and his name had long ceased to be the inspiration of all she said.

This ball was, of course, the stiffest test so far.

Eira could not help feeling slightly anxious when quite a handsome young man, with a lapel badge proclaiming him a non-drinker, halted before Gillian and asked her to dance.

"I—oh—I don't think," the tones were panic-stricken. Eira gave her a little push in the back.

"Don't be unreasonable! We're supposed to enjoy ourselves here."

They stayed on the floor for two numbers then he delivered her back and invited Eira.

"What, an old fogey like me?" she exclaimed, undoubtedly pleased.

"You're not old, sure you're not."

Laughing she moved into the old fashioned waltz made a little hazardous by the extreme slipperiness of the floor.

"Your friend is very nice but she hasn't much to say for herself."

"I couldn't explain in front of Gillian but she has recently lost her fiancé."

He looked shocked and sympathetic at the same time. Did Eira think her friend would prefer not to dance again?

"Make her dance as much as possible, young man."

He smiled. "Mike's the name."

Eira very nearly said 'it usually is'.

Mike took his task seriously, introducing Gillian to his friends and at the same time ensuring that Eira did not spend too much time on her own. As soon as she saw Gillian safely in the coterie she made her way over to the bar and lost no time at all being drawn into conversation. At about midnight the first sitting of supper was announced and Mike hurried up to her, urging her to come or they would not have seats. Was it not then the usual stand-up buffet?

"Why no, 'tis a dinner."

"God bless my soul! At this hour?" Eira's stomach seemed to constrict a little at the thought but when she was seated and had begun on the grapefruit which preceded soup, cold meats and potent trifle, she found herself unexpectedly hungry. It pleased her to see that by now Gillian had quite an animated look.

Youth was indeed wonderfully resilient and not for the first time she wondered just how deeply in love Gillian had been.

'I have no yardstick against which to measure such feelings,' Eira thought wistfully. 'For myself I have never been in love. And I guess I never will be now.'

She was not aware of sighing aloud as she drank her coffee.

The ball was to go on till 5 a.m. but both she and Gillian flagged before that time and the obliging Mike insisted upon seeing them back to their hotel. Very correctly he shook hands and bowed to both.

16

"Thank you, Mike, for being so kind to a couple of lone females," Eira observed, since Gillian had become silent. He went off, humming "the Hills of Donegal" which was what the band had been playing as they left.

Gillian looked after him thoughtfully. "Eira, do you think Alec would mind my dancing?"

The older woman put her arm about the other in one of her rare, demonstrative gestures. "Life has to go on, Gilly. Mike was O.K. And his friends. No romance. No strings attached. So what are you worrying about, my dear?"

"About seeming disloyal."

"To a memory?" The words were softly spoken and the girl gave a shudder as if a weight, heavier by far than that which Atlas had borne, was on her own bared back. "You can't go on grieving for ever, Gilly. I am sure that was the last thing Alec would expect from you. Run along, child. If you are half as tired as I am, you must be asleep standing up. I'll alter our early morning tea to 8.30. Goodnight." Eira touched her cheek with her lips and the girl ran off as if she wanted to reach the sanctuary of her own room before giving way to the inevitable tears.

Eira sighed and turning saw Sean, the hall porter look at her enquiringly. There was something madam wanted?

"I could have used a Jameson but the bar is closed."

Apparently that constituted no trouble. The hotel had one of those convenient "travellers" licences which, so far as Eira could see, allowed drinks to be served at any one of the twenty-four hours.

"Sure ye travelled from the Paladian Ballroom to here, didn't ye now?" argued Sean, tray in hand.

Next day Gillian seemed restless and anxious to be moving. Was it that she did not want to run into Mike again? Eira decided that guilt complexes could be very surprising.

They set off to see the beauties of 'the Ring' and enjoyed the fresh experience of "jaunting" round the biggest of the Killarney lakes. Later they had ten shillings' worth of equestrian hazard through the Gap of Dunloe.

"Och, he'll give ye a grand safe ride," the hirer assured the timid Gillian. To Eira, who looked more experienced, he said: "Sally'll trot, if you so wish."

Eira wished—but 'Sally' did not.

17

"On this dude ranch the nags have only one pace—dead slow."

Gillian could not help laughing at her friend's expressive face.

"Come along now," their stripling guide called, giving the mare's rump a flick with a twig, but it made no difference.

"Mine's in the drink." Ruefully Gillian tugged at the reins whilst her mount lapped in leisurely fashion from a stream near the first bridge.

Nothing could equal the rugged beauty of the surrounding scenery or the fun of testing the reverberating echo of their voices amongst the rocky peaks. True it all took a long time, then time had ceased to be important. Eira tried not to think about nice, swift paced ponies as she prodded the unresponsive 'Sally's' flanks with her heels.

"Did you enjoy yourselves, now?" the guide asked, as the ladies dismounted. His employer held forth on the local beauties for quite ten minutes and only broke off because he saw a car approach. "Will ye be wantin' horses?"

"We'll drive, thank you."

"Not if you value your car," Eira warned them. "It might be possible on a scooter but the road is very ragged."

The couple in the car consulted one another then turned back the way they had come.

"Did you see that now?" and the horse-hirer shifted his cap just sufficiently to scratch his grizzled head in perplexity.

"Goodbye and God bless," Gillian called, unaware how completely she had slipped into Irish customs.

In Killarney town they came across a poster of the Bally-kenny Players, who were presenting *Princess Paula* at their local theatre. The show was one of those of which Shearme's held the copyright and they decided that it might be fun to go to this, the last night. The performance started at the usual eight p.m. favoured in Ireland, which allowed time for them to drive the fifteen miles or so in the direction of Rathmore, where Ballykenny was situated.

Like most small southern Irish towns it had its excess quota of bars, a rather ramshackle garage and very few general stores. The theatre was Victorian, with a dark plushiness not unreminiscent of the music halls of yesteryear. It also had the chipped cream façade of lost gentility.

Eira had no professional card upon her. She had not thought

18

to need one, but the lady in the box office made no difficulty about finding them seats in the balcony. Heat rose in waves from the packed stalls and the gangways were soon full of people standing.

"English regulations obviously couldn't concern Bally-kenny less," Eira observed, glancing behind her at a notice which proclaimed standing room for twenty only—she counted forty without difficulty. Her alert eye took in the empty gas brackets of the emergency lighting.

"I hope you've made a will, Gilly."

The girl looked up, momentarily startled, then saw that her companion was smiling.

"If does seem a bit crowded, doesn't it?"

"We'll just not think about the possibility of fire."

The dark green velvet curtain rose on the—to Eira—familiar scene of Cossack soldiers singing:

"Slash, slash, slash with your sabres
Fight, fight, fight foes and neighbours—"

They were joined by the girls, who did their pretty best to fake the Gopak, then the heroine, 'Paula' came on to the recitative "A Princess!" which went straight into "Heart unawakened".

"I never knew *that* was what it was from," Gillian exclaimed.

"If only that girl wouldn't let her hands hang—like hams—"

The next few minutes were unimportant and then the soldiers re-grouped, sabres in hand (some upside down) for the entrance of their Captain, 'Ivan Nicholaï'. Eira, who had found her attention straying to reflections on far better productions of the same work, closed her eyes—the ride, perhaps, had made her extra sleepy or it could have been the intolerable heat of the overfilled theatre. All at once, through the kind of haze of inattention, she heard a voice. She sat up, almost stunned by the impact, so beautiful was the quality of tone. Her glance took in the stage and the tall, not un-pleasing young man, who wore his ill-fitting stage uniform with something of awkwardness yet he was not stiff, only shy.

"Fair was your smile
My heart to beguile . . . "

It was a tenor warm, rich of timbre, free of throatiness and the vocal affections of the exhibitionist. This man sang as one who loved to sing. He gave the great beauty of his voice without stint yet with it all Eira found endearing simplicity.

'What a magnificent voice,' she thought, wondering when she last had heard anything as good.

This singer had a gift, the greatness of which he was possibly unaware.

She sat, tense, listening. Her hands were tight clasped in her lap. Once in a while shivers passed down her spine, the only infallible test she ever had known of musical beauty. She scarcely realized her own bewitchment. Had anyone spoken she would not have heard. Just now she was a woman, deeply stirred, almost for the first time, by the untutored freshness of this perfect voice.

Even Gillian, who was less musical by far, recognised that touch of the unique. And when he had finished, the entire audience seemed to rise up to acclaim him. He stood, a little bewildered by it all: uncertain once he had stopped using his voice, obviously never expecting such a reception.

Eira clapped till her palms tingled, crying "bravo" as she rarely did in any professional theatre. Tears were running unheeded down her sun-tanned cheeks. Gillian looked at her astounded. She would not have believed the other capable of such feeling. Eira, however breezy and good humoured she might be, gave the impression of one to whom all emotional displays were foreign. Gillian could not imagine Eira mopping her eyes to the Metro-Goldwyn-Mayer celestial choir in any cinema, much less crying over the direst drama ever to be staged. Yet here, in little Ballykenny, she restrained nothing, so moved was she by a man's voice.

In Eira's experience there had been no reception of a singer like this since Tauber's first night in *The Land of Smiles*. She thought, 'Tauber had mannerisms. This boy is still unspoiled.'

He took his encores and it was quite a time before the comedy couple, whose scene followed, could make their entrance.

'So this is what is meant by stopping the show,' Gillian marvelled, unable to see quite why it had happened.

There was a general air of waiting for him to sing again.

First, however, there was the dialogue which he spoke without distinction. His was the curious jerkiness of one unused to stringing long sentences together. He could not have been a voluble person in private life.

"This libretto is pretty heavy going," Eira observed.

"He certainly doesn't sound as if he has kissed the Blarney Stone," spoken with the slight conceit justified by one who had personal experience of lying, with neck near dislocated and legs grabbed for safety, in order to fulfil an old custom.

"His delivery of lines could be remedied."

"Do you think he is Irish?"

"By his vowels I would say Welsh."

They broke off as the orchestra played the opening bars of a duet for tenor and baritone, in which the young man displayed a touch of comedy. The number was a kind of double serenade where each mimicked the style of the other. The audience was well pleased but this time the conductor was not allowing encores. The act closed without further chances for the tenor.

When the lights were up Eira saw he was called Deri Gwilym Rhys and wondered how he came to be in what was otherwise an all Irish company. Could he be a guest artist? Such things were not unknown in the amateur world.

Eira lighted a cigarette, aware that she was smoking too much. "What do you think of him, Gilly?"

"It's a very nice voice."

" 'A very nice voice'! Oh, my God, have you no soul?" There was a kind of despair which replaced the previous elation. "It is the most beautiful I think I have heard in the whole of my life."

The words had the solemnity of ones spoken in a church.

Gillian flushed, wishing herself more musically informed. She had thought it just that. A nice voice. For some reason Eira seemed to be making it out the voice of an epoch. Was he all that good?

In the second act he had the love duet in three four time with the heroine and here it was apparent that in addition to his own ability to sing he was able to make others do so, too. Up to then the heroine had been undistinguished. Now she seemed to come alive and her rather cold soprano caught warmth from the emotional fire of his.

At the end he enfolded her in his arms. Eira was shocked

21

to find herself minding what was a mere stage kiss passing between them.

'Am I going out of my senses?' she asked herself furiously.

With a kind of courteous grace he released his stage sweetheart and a ballet took over from them.

He had one more song, as Eira knew; a beautiful invocation to the night. Anything he had achieved earlier was completely surpassed. This time she did not cry. She only experienced what seemed to be a much stronger beat to her heart. All the things she had ever regretted and missed in life seemed to rise to mock her. Gone was the early elation, leaving only sadness behind. She felt as though she had been squeezed through a wringer. Beads of moisture were round her hair line. The theatre was overpoweringly hot. She felt too drained to do more than make a show of clapping. There was only just so much emotion a woman could endure in one evening.

But when the curtain swung down Eira was already on her feet and saying:

"We're going behind, Gilly."

3

GILLIAN, WHO had never been backstage, found herself hurried through pass doors, along narrow passageways and up to some small, shabby rooms above the auditorium. Eira looked about her, used to such places, but here were no neatly labelled cast names. Just three rooms one of which said "Men", another "Male Chorus" and the final and largest room "Women". A member of the men's chorus came into the passage, stared at Eira and Gillian with the frank regard of the Irish who showed no false shame in natural curiosity.

"Do you think you could find Deri Rhys for me?"

He replied: "Well, now, that would be a little difficult. You see he is changing and after that we're all going to Murphy's hotel for a party."

"Just try, would you?" her tone was authoritative yet

at the same time Gillian could see she was nervous, which was not in the least like Eira.

The young man hesitated then thumped hard on the door further down the passage.

"Is Deri Rhys there? Two ladies to see him."

Eira heard an unmistakable Anglo-Saxon word hastily bitten off and hid her momentary amusement. What did she expect? Buckingham Palace manners from a miner? And that, quite probably was what Rhys would be. That she had never met a miner and had not the least idea what one would be like did not strike her. She had a confused idea of men with lamps on their foreheads, squatting on haunches in the village street down the valley, each with a whippet beside him. Though she had driven through miles of Wales for aesthetic reasons she had avoided the mining districts. To Eira slag heaps were something to be seen only on a conveniently distant skyline.

Presently Deri Rhys appeared, still in his Cossack trousers and boots but with a modern nylon shirt—a little marked by make up—wide open at the chest. His very dark curls were ruffled and gave him the air of a boy, though she guessed him to be in his twenties. He looked embarrassed.

"I must ask you to excuse me. I am rather untidy and there isn't much time—"

"So our friend here was telling me," Eira gave the Irishman a look of frank dismissal, which he did not choose to accept. Ignoring him, she explained her credentials in brief and the fact that she wanted a talk about Deri's future.

"My future?" he looked more awkward than ever and his glance kept moving past her to Gillian, who he either admired or hoped might help him in this predicament. "You would not know, but I am a shot firer in Garreg Wen South Wales Mining Company." His tone implied that he could rise to Deputy and even Overman.

"That could be taken care of," Eira spoke smoothly but her hands were not still. Gillian knew the unaccountable nervousness still present.

"I don't know about that," he answered, his voice settling into its Welsh lilt with the broad vowels that made him sound almost foreign to them.

"If you will excuse me, Mrs. —"

"Miss Shearme." She did not over-emphasise the dis-

23

tinction as if spinsterhood were a banner of pride, the way some women did. Truth to tell Eira never thought about it in that way. One married or one did not, according to choice or circumstance; that was all. In her view one state had no intrinsic virtue greater than the other.

He smiled; a warm friendly smile it was. He seemed uncertain whether or not he was expected to shake hands with them. Deciding not, he ducked his head in an odd sort of bow and shut the dressing room door in relief behind him. Someone made a remark which they did not catch but a great laugh went up after it had been said.

Eira's face reddened. "Come," she commanded.

"I don't think Mr. Rhys was very glad to see us," Gillian exclaimed, as they descended the awkward winding stairs, scarcely easier to negotiate than those of Blarney Castle.

"A man of that type has no mind of his own. It has to be made up for him."

Gillian had not received that idea at all about Deri Rhys. Her quick impression had been of a man, content with his lot, having no wish to be ordered elsewhere by an ambitious woman. For Eira's intentions were obvious. She wanted to make a professional singer out of him. Gillian was by no means certain that he participated in this desire. Probably to sing was a hobby that relieved a little the possible drabness and danger of his life. (Gillian also only knew of mining communities from what authors Cronin and Llewellyn had written about them.)

"He can't be allowed to rusticate in whatever that outlandish place was called. Not with such a voice." There was a vehement, passionate note in Eira's own, betraying the extent in which she was already involved. Her hands shook in negotiating her lighter, with its shamrock pattern. The thing refused to respond to her first flick. Swearing, she managed, after several attempts, to light the cigarette upon which she drew, as a bather air, surfacing after a swim beneath the water.

"Deri Rhys has a God-sent gift which he mustn't be allowed to waste."

"But suppose he doesn't want to be a professional singer?"

Eira stared hard at her companion, eyes hard, face set, lips compressed. "Then I must make him."

24

"Aren't you taking an awful lot for granted?" the girl ventured.

Eira seemed about to say something more then, with a quick look at her watch, exclaimed that they had best be driving back to the hotel. "We never have an early night."

Next day she made local enquiries about the Ballykenny amateurs but by the time she had disentangled hearsay from truth she was not greatly assisted. Already she knew that Rhys had been engaged to play for them. It was assumed that one of the committee had seen him playing in Wales, or at least heard of his voice.

That had been the last performance of *Princess Paula*. No doubt he would be leaving at once for Wales. Eira left Gillian to amuse herself for the morning and drove over to Ballykenny itself, only to find—after an exhaustive pursuit —that he had done precisely as expected. She located the musical director, who was a turf accountant, as popular a business concern as running a bar was in Ireland. He was willing but not altogether helpful.

Yes, young Rhys had a remarkable voice. Nice fellow too; no side, easy to work with and not one to save his singing for all the solo passages and let "the divil take the rest".

"He made the show for you, Mr. Sheehan."

"That he did."

"You have his address?"

"Ah, no, I have not. But you will find him in Garreg Wen. He was telling us that means White Rock."

"Where the hell is Garreg Wen?" Eira asked herself. The directions she had were not entirely satisfactory. It was supposed to be up a mountain pass near the Rhondda Valley.

In giving this information the musical director admitted: "I've never been to Wales. That I have not."

He fingered some Irish sweepstake tickets, wondering if the Englishwoman would like one. Eira saw the gesture, decided it might cement friendly relations to purchase one and anyway she liked a gamble.

"How much?" opening a purse and producing one of the attractive Irish pound notes. Who was the sad beautiful lady on them again? Eira had forgotten. She folded her sweepstake ticket, heard the musical director's assurance that it would turn out lucky, thanked him for his information and gave him a firm handshake across the counter.

25

Emerging into the sunlight she wondered if there was anywhere she might find non-alcoholic refreshment in Ballykenny. There really was! A corn chandler had a small notice, "Coffee". He left a sale of cattle fodder to make her a cup of Nescafe, which he set out in a kind of back parlour. An upstairs wireless was droning a children's musical of which Shearme's also had the rights.

Eira stirred the coffee, aware that her mood was one of acute restlessness. The leisurely rhythm of Irish life had begun to weary her, or should she say it had been superseded by her anxiety to start the first move in Deri Rhy's career? Had she been alone, she would have been inclined to try to get another alteration of the car-booking on the boat, transferring to any route necessary, in order to leave as soon as possible for South Wales. It was an absurd idea and besides she could not do that to Gillian.

'I brought her on this holiday and I suppose I'll have to see it through.' She sighed, wishing suddenly that those Cork relations would return more speedily and beg Gillian to stay with them at once.

'I could leave the car over here, even, and come back—'
Eira crushed out her cigarette, the tenth since breakfast. She was not normally as heavy a smoker and this showed the extent of her nervous excitement.

She drove back, no longer with any special interest in the countryside and found an enthusiastic Gillian, just in from a walk.

"It was so lovely, Eira, I wish you had been with me."

"Was it?" the elder woman repented her earlier mood and slipped an arm through that of the girl. "Perhaps there might be time for us to do it together?"

But there were no longer hours for the mere squandering. Eira was a woman with a purpose. Though she did her best to spoil nothing of the remaining days, it was obvious that for her the zest had gone from the trip. She seemed to drive more quickly, to suggest fewer stops and to take less interest in sightseeing, about which she had been previously enthusiastic.

'A week ago,' Gillian thought, 'Eira would not have dismissed the old woman wearing a real red Connemara cloak as "very fetching". Eira would have wanted to stop and talk to her and most certainly take a photograph. Not just— turn her head in the car and go on driving!'

Gillian wanted to be able to understand this new phase of her friend's:

'I suppose if one is intensely keen about one's job—as Eira is—one sort of carries it with one, all the while.'

As yet neither of them saw that the voice of Deri Rhys was just the excuse for a much more personal interest on Eira's part. Absurd as it might be it was not his singing she remembered now so clearly as the puzzled way in which he had looked at her. It was as if he had been saying to himself:

'Damn it, woman, what do you want with me?'

And not even Eira would have been prepared to give the real answer, if indeed she knew it—then.

The Irish trip went on, though its tempo had quickened. They still saw lovely places and exclaimed about them, but the enthusiasm had grown a little false. Until now Gillian had been convinced that she knew Eira as someone essentially sane and unemotional. Yet here was Eira introducing the name of Deri Rhys into conversation, even if the subject were quite different. A man humming in the street: a song on the radio: these were enough to make her say:

"I would like to hear Deri sing that."

Already it had become Deri, not Mr. Rhys. Gillian grew a little tired of the name. To her he had seemed no more than a woefully embarrassed man in a hurry, not quite sure how to rid himself of their presence without giving offence. He had wanted to be off to his party, not stand listening to Eira planning a possibly unwelcome future for him.

'She does like doing that sort of thing.'

Gillian had begun to wonder if she were wise to have agreed to working at Shearme's when they were back in London. Would it have been best to have gone elswhere? Once Gillian had decided to leave Latter's she did not want to re-consider the idea. She had begun to see that the only method of living with her bereavement would be to cut those material ties which held her closest to him. Of course she could not *forget* Alec. That was unthinkable. At least she wanted to bring herself towards a state of mind—and heart—where the happiness of every other young person could not mock her, where she could speak to a man of her own age without remembering it should be Alec.

'I can't keep his shadow over the whole of my future,' unconsciously she was echoing Eira.

As they drove due west from Galway town, Gillian took a sideways glimpse at her friend's face. Grim, tired and vaguely unhappy: yet strong even if a little sombre. It was the face of a woman at war with herself. What could have happened to bring about this change?

Eira muffed her gears and swore in a man's fashion. Gillian was used to this though once it had rather shocked her. She wished she could ask what it was that troubled Eira, why she read so late at night and wandered about the hotel garden before early morning tea. Hands in the pockets of her slacks, head forward, feet quickly moving. The first time Gillian had seen her this way it had reminded her of a fox pacing its miserably small zoo cage. No. Not exactly a fox, there was nothing whatever of the vixen about Eira. A sleek puma, perhaps; or better still, a lean-flanked lioness.

Gillian wished they could talk of this matter together. Yet, alas, there were subjects that seemed outside the scope of women's friendships. They had been able to talk of Alec, but this "feeling" that Eira had for Deri Rhys was a shy and very private thing.

'I can't go asking her if she is in love with him. How could she be? I mean, she has only seen him that once. Could people fall for a voice? Perhaps, if it were a very beautiful voice, like poor Mario Lanza's—' at that Gillian felt herself smiling. No woman, except presumably his wife, could have taken seriously that amiable mountain of a man.

Deri Rhys had scarcely looked in Eira's direction. Gillian was forced to admit that in so far as he had had 'eyes for anyone, they were for me'.

'That's just because I'm younger than Eira, I expect,' she reminded herself, unwilling as yet to think that any male—other than Alec—should express masculine interest in herself. She had not thought Deri's gaze particularly admiring. As she saw it, she had merely provided a focal point for his eyes so that they might escape Eira's appraisement.

'I expect I've imagined the whole thing. But she did seem— kind of—carried away! Quite without her usual poise.'

Gillian so wished to make her sympathy felt that she put her hand on the other's. Eira turned a startled glance upon her, asking:

"Anything wrong?"

"No. It's just I had the idea you weren't enjoying the holiday as much as you did at first. I was wondering if I were at fault."

"You, Gilly?" A sigh seemed torn from her. "No, child, it is nothing you have done. It's just this cursed restlessness of mine. I believe it is not unusual in spinsters." Her lips were drawn up in a wry smile. "Psychologists would put it down to frustrated sex. Actually, it's that I am used to a very busy life and I can't relax for more than a limited length of time."

"If you would rather go back to England earlier—"

"Of course not! Pay no attention to my damned moods. We're enjoying ourselves enormously," and as if to demonstrate the fact, she took an approaching incline of the Sheeffry Hills (between Leenane, which they had passed, and Westport, for which they were bound), at a tremendous pace. Eira was inclined to eliminate "the furies", as she called them, with her car.

They completed their tour, parting company for a few days in Cork, where Gillian stayed with her relatives whilst Eira went to see a retired director of Shearme's who now lived in Kinsale. Their last night in Ireland was spent in Dublin, where they visited the famous Abbey Theatre to see a new play by an unknown Irish dramatist. It castigated the priests and drink, became whimsy and earthy in bewildering sequence with a good measure of riotous comedy to leven what might otherwise have been a theatrically indigestive cake.

The curtain descended on an old, old man singing "The Soldiers' Song" to a half-witted child, who played at his feet.

Gillian had found the evening vaguely depressing, reminding her as it did of the poverty so clearly visible a few turnings off O'Connell Street. A poverty shaming to one cushioned by the English welfare state.

They were staying at Gresham's, because Eira always had wanted to be in an hotel with so international a reputation. As it exceeded the price of their previous accommodation she had insisted that Gillian be her guest.

"We never know when we'll be in Dublin again together and let us do ourselves proud—even to liqueur after our coffee."

29

Gillian had the idea that this revival in Eira's spirits was due neither to being in Dublin nor to having visited the Abbey Theatre. It was simply because soon they would be aboard ship. Then, when the car had been slung safely ashore at Holyhead and they were through the customs, Eira could start looking up Garreg Wen on the map.

4

It was one of those "lovely soft mornin's", in other words, wet. Holyhead looked dismal in consequence as they set off past Valley towards the Menai Bridge. Not in itself very interesting countryside, leaving as it did the more attractive coastal regions alone.

"It makes a change to see pubs with names instead of so and so's 'bar', doesn't it, Eira?"

"No 'travellers' licences' here to take care of any thirst you may have. Oh, a red pillar box again. Now we really know we have left Southern Ireland. Sorry?"

Gillian nodded. "I hope to go back sometimes."

The other smiled non-committally and began to sing, in her rather surprising husky voice, a swinging tune that promised the wanderer a welcome from the hillside when he—or she—came back to Wales.

The twenty-three miles to Bangor were entirely uneventful and, despite breakfast on the boat, they felt ready for coffee which they found at a Red Dragon Cafe. The green A. A. touring book of Ireland was now in the car's glove compartment. Eira had brought out an England and Wales map which she proceeded to spread on the cafe table.

"Our best plan seems to take the Capel Curig road, keeping on past Corwen and Llangollen. From there we'll have to cut down through Oswestry to Welshpool and New-town and so into Radnor. That may be far enough for one day, but I don't think we need book anywhere in advance."

They stayed in Llandrindod Wells, a pleasant spa which seemed over-populated after the sparser-peopled towns of Southern Ireland.

They resumed their journey after a late start, both being tired from the interrupted sleep on the boat the night before landing in Anglesey. By easy laps they reached Builth Wells and were soon in Brecknock. Once over the Brecon Beacons, with their magnificent views and compact long-tailed mountain sheep indifferent to traffic, they began to reach the mining districts, where grass now covered long-forgotten slag heaps and made them seem almost a natural part of the countryside. Here and there they could see the workings which showed the entry to some pit, perhaps no longer even one where men were employed.

Somehow it was less grim than they had expected and whatever the artistic shortcomings of the villages through which they passed, there was always the compensation of superb mountain scenery within a mile at most.

When finally they found it, Garreg Wen was no different from its sister villages. There was the same steep main street with terraced houses in grey stone with doors and windows picked out with ugly yellow bricks. T.V. antennae made weird shapes in their clustered profusion.

Eira pulled up outside Morgan's, the grocer. Deri Gwilym Rhys apparently lived in Glendower Road, a turning, so she was told, past the Ritzy Cinema. Number twenty was called "Cartref" and the knocker was brightly shining.

An elderly woman opened. She wore the usual dark dress brightened by a smock overall in chintz design. On her feet were slippers, on her head a hat. The two seemed to contradict themselves, as it were, by suggesting that she both visited the house and lived in it at one and the same time. The stairs were immediately behind her and a row of coats hung inside the front door.

She looked enquiringly at Eira—Gillian had stayed in the car.

"Is Mr. Deri Rhys at home?"

"My son is not up yet," the woman said, speaking very slowly as if she had to think of the words she was to say.

As it was then mid-afternoon, Eira's expression showed that she thought it strange. Realizing this, Mrs. Rhys added:
"From—the pit."

There seemed nothing for it but to return later, which they did. Mrs. Rhys again opened to them, gave a nod which was neither welcoming nor otherwise and led them into the sitting room. Again this was not at all what Eira had expected.

Confusedly she had imagined well worn, old fashioned furniture. Instead everything was neat and modern, with a 17 inch screen T.V. in one corner. In a glass cabinet were cups and medals which she guessed might be Eisteddfod trophies.

"Oh, it is you!" Deri exclaimed, perhaps expecting other visitors. He spoke in Welsh to his mother who, with the same unchanging expression of face and still wearing a hat, withdrew. "Mam does not speak much English."

He stood, awkwardly glancing at them. He had a clean, shining look and his hair was moist from the pithead shower.

"Please to sit."

Gillian took a low fireside seat, Eira one of the armchairs. Deri deposited himself with care in that opposite her.

"I have to mind the springs," he explained, with a very boyish grin showing his good teeth.

Leaving Eira to do the talking, Gillian took opportunity to study him. He had a strong, athletic build, broad at the shoulder and tapering off at the waist. His feet were large, his hands capable yet well shaped. His chin was a little dark, as if he needed shaving twice daily. He had a large mouth which could smile merrily enough but was usually serious. His very deep blue eyes watched Eira in an intent way suggesting that he did not quite know what to make of her.

She was less nervous than last time she had seen him. Very much—Gillian decided—the woman of business anxious to put forward a proposition calculated to interest him. She questioned him bluntly and on the whole he answered her with unfailing good humour.

Had he had any singing lessons?

"Only at school. Oh, and Mr. Pugh, our organist, takes me through some songs when he has time." Deri implied that Mr. Pugh, who also conducted the colliery band and acted as musical director to two of the five operatic societies of the valley, was a very busy man.

"You read music, of course?"

"I know tonic sol fa."

"Play the piano?"

He glanced at the upright evidently as much a feature of mining houses as a T.V.

"Alas no. At least—only with one finger. I pick out the notes, as you might say."

32

She switched to his work: whether he was content with his prospects. Deri sat forward in his chair, hands clasped between his knees, his brow furrowed.

"I never thought to be anything else but a miner. My da—" he cocked an eye towards an enlargement on the mantelpiece—a small man with bowler hat and gold watch chain to distinguish him—"was killed in a blasting accident when I was—" he indicated the height of a child of about ten.

"Yet you went into mining yourself?"

"What else should I do?"

Eira felt a kind of impatience with him. "With your voice—"

He smiled slowly. He liked to sing. It made him happy. But a man could not live by singing. Not if he came from a little place like Garreg Wen. He needed education, many things that were not the privileges of the working class. Without going into undue detail Deri made his case. A small local school and into the mine when he was old enough to be allowed below ground.

"I make good money," he added, and not defensively, either.

Rather vaguely Eira supposed that would be since the National Coal Board took over the mining industry.

"I have a sweetheart. In the Spring we hope to be married."

"Have you no *ambition?*"

"Is it not ambition enough? To have a wife and children . . . and this house will be mine some day. Mam does for me now. She will live with us, just the same. She likes Rhiannon."

Gillian smiled and he saw that she did so. His manner changed to gentle playfulness as he asked if she found the Welsh names very difficult.

"I have never heard Rhiannon before certainly."

"There are several—in the valleys."

Eira was aware how much more at ease he became talking to Gillian. They seemed to understand one another.

'He is not frightened of her. I think he is a little, of me.' It gave her a delicious sense of power. As she saw it she would soon have this large, amiable young man falling in with her plans for him. The girl Rhiannon could be dismissed. She must not be allowed to stand between him and his career.

They could marry later, perhaps, when he had made a start. For the next few months he was going to be much too busy to think of valley sweethearts. He would have to have singing lessons to place his voice properly and to teach him to conserve it. At least no harm had been done by wrong tuition, which was the important thing. Then he would need to learn a little more about acting and the manly graces of stage movement. As Eira knew a voice alone was not enough. At least he had no great initial drawbacks to hamper his chances. He was personable—

She broke off her reflections to find him regarding her with an air of amusement which, for some reason annoyed her. Why would he not take her seriously?

"Listen, Deri Rhys, what I am offering you is this. Vocal training at my—or rather at my firm's expense—together with the necessary things that go with it. Then an introduction to West End managers or, perhaps, the chance to go on tour with one of our musical releases. They are sending out shows of this kind again, despite T.V.," and she gave it the glance of enmity it seemed to her to merit. She went on more calmly: "I don't expect you to give me your decision now, but at least you will promise to think over what I have said?"

He scratched his curls in puzzlement.

"You are very generous, Miss—"

"Shearme."

"Miss Shearme. I could not settle anything without talking to my fiancée." He looked up with frankness, his initial suspicion of Eira deflected. "You see the way it is with me?"

"Don't think me unsympathetic," she answered, her voice gentling him. For a moment she was letting him see the woman behind the would-be benefactress. A woman suddenly humble because already she recognised—albeit only be instinct—his potential power over her.

'It would break my heart to leave him here, in this valley, with that old mother of his who wears a hat indoors—has she perhaps a wig? Does she even go to bed in her hat? I don't care if Rhiannon is plain or a dream of beauty. I don't mind if she has to break her heart over him. One thing I must do is to take him out of this—*milieu*. If only for the sake of posterity.'

Posterity? It was too harsh to say "my own vanity"; too soon to admit "for my own need of him".

Deri heard his mother in the passage. He did not rise as she said something in Welsh in the doorway. He turned to his visitors.

"Mam has made a cup of tea. She wants to know if you will join us."

"That would be very nice, Gillian?"

They rose and followed him into a morning room-cum-kitchen with a beautiful Welsh dresser along one wall. Beyond could be glimpsed a scullery with modern sink unit and cupboards, and, through, a door ajar, a bathroom.

"How nice this is," she observed, thinking aloud.

"Deri did it all for me," Mrs. Rhys gestured to them to draw up chairs to a tea of finely-cut bread and butter and home-made cakes.

He smiled. "Getting my hand in, you know."

Mrs. Rhys did not speak much, the barrier of language being present, but she saw to their wants.

"Miss Shearme wishes to make a singer out of me, Mam." He stirred his tea with its generous quota of sugar.

"You are to be married," she reminded him, as if that settled the matter.

"So I told them."

The old woman gave Eira a long, deep look. It was a face grooved with sorrow and adversity, yet full of rather stern character. Immediately Eira recognised an enemy. This woman would fight to the end for her son's happiness and to maintain what she saw to be his duty. She conveyed that his place was *here*, in Garreg Wen, looking after his mother and bringing to the house a bride to whom approval was already given. Mrs. Rhys lacked the eloquence to convey her sentiments in words. But her expression did this for her. It was enough to stare at this woman from beyond the valley who wanted to take Deri from his rightful place in the community and make of him what he was not.

Eira recognised the struggle ahead and it gave to her a sense of tingling excitement.

The moment of silent conflict was broken by a rattle of the knocker. Deri sprang up, nearly upsetting his chair and dashed from the room. There was a girl's bright voice mingled with his then he brought Rhiannon in to meet them, his arm proudly about her.

"My fiancée, Miss Rhiannon Maddy."

35

.She was small, compact, with dark brown eyes and straight hair, more brown than blonde. She had a buxom bust emphasised by the white blouse tucked into the wide belt of her summer skirt. She had a pretty, flute-like speaking voice and rather a shy gravity.

"These ladies are from London," Deri was saying, rather as if he were introducing visitors from the moon.

"I have never been further than Cardiff." Rhiannon emphasised the second syllable slightly making the name sound different.

Eira's face seemed to say 'is it possible?'

"But Deri has been to London."

"Only to see the football, *cariad*."

They laughed. With her he was natural and happy.

Gillian glanced reproachfully at Eira. What was it she meant to do? Destory all this?

"Miss Shearme wants to make a singer out of me. What do you think of that, now?" His tone was still half amused.

Rhiannon, however, sounded serious.

"Mr. Pugh is always saying what a good voice you have, Deri. Yet, I don't know—"

"He has a wonderful voice." Eira's tone was desperate as she cast herself upon the mercy of this girl who, perhaps, would have the greatest influence with him in the end.

"I think that, too," looking up adoringly at the young man. "All the same—" remembering, no doubt, his much safer prospects at the mine.

Eira experienced something akin to physical sickness. Almost it was as if Deri and the girl had embraced in public. Eira hated and feared Rhiannon's power over him. The power of love and of sex—about which Eira but imperfectly understood. Furiously she thought he must not be allowed to throw himself away on this girl.

'I'll have to intervene, if necessary.'

She rose, including Gillian with a quick gesture of the head.

"Perhaps you will think over my suggestion, Mr. Rhys? We'll be staying at the Gwent Arms until tomorrow. You could phone me there?" She looked round vaguely.

"We have a phone," he told her, eyes mocking again.

"The number is—"

"I can look it up, Miss Shearme." He moved to the hall to give the ladies the chance of adjournment, if they so wished.

36

"Mnà" was just outside the back door; spotlessly clean like the rest of the place. The garden was thick with well-tended vegetables and only a few flowers in the border. All this in a difficult, dry summer.

Eira and Gillian found Deri out by the car, on which he was bestowing a boyish interest in its year and model. Mrs. Rhys bowed from the doorstep; Rhiannon stood beside her.

Eira unlocked the driving side door and leaned over to open the catch of the other, scarcely noticing how Deri had moved round to open the door to Gillian. He bowed to them both a little gravely as Eira turned the car with less than her usual efficiency, bumping her back tyres against the kerb.

"That man makes me nervous," she muttered, changing through into top as they reached the main road and turned right for the hill that led out of the village.

5

THE GWENT ARMS was solidly old-fashioned with an almost archaic amount of mahogany and glass partitioning in the bar downstairs. The entrance hall had a hat rack, and leather chairs worn smooth by many drinkers. The quite modern reception corner seemed out of place. To the left was the dining room, with its turkey carpet, heavy brocade curtains and the slight miasma of past meals. But the napery was spotless and the waitresses not too matey.

The main staircase, wide and wasteful of design, led to a right hand corridor where there was a commercial room where travellers went tediously through their sales books and tapped out business lists. Over the dining room was the residents' lounge and once again there was an impression of permanence about the place.

Eira was lost in one of the very deep chairs, a neat whisky on the brass topped table beside her. Her foot swung impatiently. It was obvious to Gillian that she was listening for the phone call from Deri Rhys. Eira was out of the chair almost before the old hall porter, a seedier edition of Mr. Chips, blinked about him and said:

"Miss Shearme is wanted on the phone, please."

Gillian sipped her gin and French, a little puzzled by her friend's anxiety. After all, if the young man was happy to be a miner, why seek to disturb him by creating artistic ambitions? He was evidently anxious to settle down with that nice, sensible girl of his. If Eira had her way and brought him to London to study, that romance might be broken-up and to poor Gillian, life could hold no greater tragedy than an unfulfilled love affair.

Eira was back very quickly. It was obvious from her face that she was cross. She drained the rest of her whisky and went over to the bell. A white coated waiter took the fresh order and departed.

"The fool—the blithering young fool," she said, meaning Deri, not the waiter.

"Mr. Rhys isn't falling in with your plans for him, then?"

"No." Eira paced the lounge, which was empty except for themselves. She gave a bitter, cruel imitation of Deri's Welsh accent as she recounted the brief conversation. " 'Is that Miss Shearme? This is De-ri Rh-ys spea-king. We have talked it ov-er, yes indeed, and I am afr-aid the ans-wer is "no".' "

She said that he had thanked her for her interest and hung up without giving her a chance to speak. Gillian could not help thinking that Deri was a lot shrewder than they credited him with being. He was giving Eira no chance to persuade him against a decision he doubtless felt right and proper. Gillian wondered how much his mother had had to do with helping him to make up his mind. At the same time he did not strike Gillian as the type to submit to petticoat rule. Oh, well, that was that. She was sorry that Eira should be taking the business so seriously. Gillian appreciated that good voices were something of a rarity, but no one could *force* a man to become a singer if he simply did not want to be one, except in an amateur capacity.

"Bad luck, Eira, but I expect there are plenty of other good tenors to be discovered."

She wheeled round. "Understand this, Gillian, Deri Rhys has a voice that is possibly unique. He simply cannot be allowed to fill his lungs with coal dust and—and sing to and from the pit and, I suppose, in chapel on Sundays. I can't permit it."

Gillian goggled at her friend. Had Eira gone out of her mind? Was she trying to act like one of those ancient Greek goddesses who shaped the destinies of men to please a whim?

Eira stopped her perambulations and resumed her seat, taking a gulp of the freshly-brought whisky.

"We are going back to Garreg Wen in the morning."

"You can't force yourself on him," Gillian protested.

"I shall not see Deri. It is the girl friend with whom I am concerned—now."

So next morning, their overnight bill paid and a filling breakfast inside them, they headed back for the valley. Gillian was quiet, feeling that their visit could only be an intrusion. She had made up her own mind about one thing. She would take no part in the sorry business. Eira must seek out and interview Rhiannon on her own.

"I'll remain in the car," Gillian stated quietly, when they drew up in Talgarth Road, the main street of Garreg Wen. Eira made no reply. She went into the post office and came back almost at once.

"She works at the greengrocer's on the corner. I'll leave the car where it is," and Eira set off with a purposeful stroll.

Gillian saw her glance at the display of fruit and vegetables outside the shop, pause, light a cigarette, and wait around until two customers had emerged, whereupon Eira went straight into the shop. Rhiannon turned, a potato sieve still in her hand.

"Oh!"

"I want to talk to you. Is it possible to do so without interruption?"

"I could call Mrs. Thomas."

Rhiannon explained quickly in Welsh and a greying-haired buxom woman took over the serving as the girl rather hesitantly raised the counter flap and opened the door into the private quarters at the rear of the shop. There was a stove on which beetroots were cooking, cases of market produce still to be unpacked and used tea-cups on an enamel tray. There was one Windsor chair from which Rhiannon removed a chopped-eared tom cat then dusted the chair seat with her apron, gesturing to Eira to sit. The girl stood, hands clasped attentively before her.

"How much did you have to do with Deri Rhys's decision?" the question was blunt enough to suggest a gloves-off contest.

Rhiannon flushed. "I—not so much as all that, Miss Shearme."

"Then it was his mother?"

"You must understand. Deri is all Mrs. Rhys has. It would be a big—trouble—to her if he left the valley."

"For that he would throw away a great career?"

"We have only your word that it would be great, Miss Shearme. Besides there were—other things."

"Your wedding?"

"Is it so strange that I should wish to marry the man I love?"

Embarrassed despite her scepticism, Eira lowered her glance, and said, almost humbly, "I suppose not."

"The house is ready. Can you expect me to want him to go away to London?"

"If you saw further than just in front of you, yes. Yes." Eira's tone grew firmer. "If I loved a man I would want what would be best for him, even if it meant waiting a while longer for marriage."

The girl unclasped her hands and, as if for something to do, went across to the beetroots, which she tested with a long toasting fork.

"Miss Shearme, you are a very clever lady, I am sure. You know all about music and the theatre. You think my Deri has a good voice. So do I. So does everyone in the valley and the people who heard him sing in Ballykenny, too, I expect. But—let me be frank with you. We are working class people. And you—you are from the big city." With a kind of frightened passion in her voice she turned appealingly to Eira. "What might it not do to Deri? It could be that he met some grand lady—like yourself—and forgot all about me."

Eira was unable to feel compassion for one she felt to be wrong in her determination to stand in his way. Accusingly, therefore, she snapped:

"So you *did* use your influence."

"Only a very little," again growing scarlet. "You still don't understand. I love Deri."

"Yours is a very selfish love, then, I must say. What real future is there for him here? All over the country they are closing mines—"

"I suppose that could happen in Garreg Wen, too." Now Rhiannon was close to tears.

40

"Then where would your fine Deri be? Drawing Public Assistance to support his old mother, his wife and child—or children." There was a touch of contempt in the tones.

"You are very hard, Miss Shearme."

"Because I cannot stand criminal waste."

The mood changed. Rhiannon looked at her, eyes suddenly bright with anger. "By what right do you come, upsetting other people's lives? Deri was happy—until you interfered. Oh, yes, he has said 'no' and he means it. But just the same you have—disturbed him. If it weren't for his mam and the fact that he loves me—" She broke off, afraid to admit more.

"So all that stands between him and fame is two women!" Eira's laugh was brittle. "Two women, determined to suffocate him with their love."

"What do you know of love?" the girl whispered.

"More than you suppose," was Eira's answer, because suddenly it was becoming true. She was no longer fighting just for a man's career as a singer. The issue with her had grown obviously personal. In reality she was fighting this girl for Deri's love . . .

Even Eira herself did not realise what was happening to her. Incredible though it might seem, she was falling in love for the very first time. A state she dreaded yet wanted to experience. What did it matter that the man was practically a stranger to her? That the words they had exchanged had been of business instead of tenderness?

His eyes had mocked her. Yet his singing voice had made every bone in her body seem to melt as did snow under the rays of the sun. Oh, love was made up of many factors she imperfectly recognised. Strong physical attraction there was, however much she shrank from such admission. Then, too, the appeal of music, leading her to the sensuous excitement of the unknown.

Eira had heard people talk of "the attraction of opposites". Had she stopped to analyse her sensations she would have known the lest important of them was knowledge that he came from a different station in life to her own. Her sympathies were widely democratic. Besides she had seen nothing coarse in him. If such elements existed, he could be schooled. What she had observed of his table manners—passed.

First Eira recognised that it was going to be necessary to place him in her material power. Once he allowed himself to be assisted by her, he must come to feel a degree of gratitude towards his benefactor. He would cease to regard her then as the enemy: the disturber of domestic peace, as he doubtless did at the present time.

She was confident this attitude of mind could be helped to pass.

Eira did not wish him just to be beholden. That was a chill state of subjugation. No! She wanted him to look upon her with eyes of desire.

'As he did Rhiannon, when they all but kissed one another in public.'

She was exaggerating a harmless moment in their affianced lives, but it was then that jealousy had been born. The harsh distrust that the woman in her later thirties has for the girl who can give her ten or fifteen years. Years which often dealt harder with a woman than they did with a man. Especially a business woman with masculine responsibilities.

To Rhiannon Eira's face in absent-minded repose revealed far more than the latter ever suspected. Rhiannon was intuitive for very reason of her love; seeing the stark expression of thwarted desire and dislike of herself. She drew in her breath with pain. So this smart, sophisticated woman, was not just interested in Deri's voice! It was for more dangerous than that. She was beginning to be interested in Deri himself.

"Go away!" cried Rhiannon. "Let us be!"

With a start Eira emerged from her reverie. Her face became inscrutable again, as from her handbag, she produced a used envelope and pencil. She scribbled down her name and London address.

"This will always find me. If—either of you—change your mind." She was smiling now with a kind of banked-up warmth. Anxious to make Rhiannon like her enough to be made an ally. There was a plea for forgiveness, too.

Eira told herself she did not really hate this girl and she was too insignificant to fear.

"Don't think badly of me for wanting to help him, Rhiannon."

Very cleverly, no doubt, Eira was putting the complete onus of Deri's refusal on to the girl's selfishness. Eira played up her charm. She could summon it at will for her clients thereby often succeeding in making them agree to producing

42

a Shearme musical when they had been contemplating one published by a rival firm.

Suspicious as Rhiannon had unwillingly become, she had to admit that in the end the lady from London seemed sincere. The girl's hand lay cold and limp in Eira's clasp. The latter turned, leaving without so much as replying to Mrs. Thomas's polite "good day".

The slam of the shop door aroused Rhiannon from the momentary spell of Eira's personality. Looking at the slip of paper, the girl tore it, with sudden viciousness, and let the shreds fall from her fingers to the stale cabbage leaves on the floor.

6

GILLIAN FOUND her new job in the overseas department of Shearme's Enterprizes Ltd. no more exciting than her old one at the estate agents but at least she was not faced with the day to day reminder of Alec. She did not find it hard to know the others in the department. There were only four of them. Liz, a girl about her own age, a secretary of advanced years and a sense of humour office life provoked rather than subdued, a chuck out from one of the theatrical academies whom they called Roger the Dodger and the stern-mouthed head of the department, Mr. Birdsall. The mouth, however, was deceiving. Though he expected efficiency he was far from inhuman in his dealings with the staff and the only person to whom Eira could be said to defer.

Gillian did not see a great deal of her in working hours. Though not big, as regards office space—they had the upper floors of the Jollity Theatre—the organisation was complex and "the overseas" did not have much contact with the "G.B. and I.", as they called the Great Britain and Irish section.

Gillian never knew precisely what had taken place that morning in Garreg Wen. Returning to the car, Eira merely had said that the girl was "unco-operative in the extreme". For the rest of the journey back to town Eira had been agreeable to speak of any topic in the universe save Deri Rhys. Nor did she mention him again in London. It did seem to Gillian that Eira, personification of efficiency, was at times a little distrait. Others of the staff also remarked upon the fact. As Mr. Birdsall's elderly secretary uncompromisingly put it: "If one didn't *know* Miss Shearme one would wonder if she hadn't fallen in love."

"At her time of life?" Roger the Dodger exclaimed tactlessly.

"Come, come, Miss Shearme is a good deal younger than you seem to think."

"Oh, fortyish, I would say."

"Thirty-five." Gillian blushed at an indiscretion caused through her private friendship with Eira. This was kept very much "outside the office". In Shearme's, Gillian was just a very junior employee.

Eira asked her out to dinner once, mainly to find out how she was liking the work.

"Mr. Birdsall reports well of you, my dear."

"I am glad to be giving satisfaction." The girl sounded a shade tentative.

"Come, Gilly, my being the boss mustn't be allowed to make any difference to us in private life." It was Eira who had made the distinction. True she did her best to be re-assuring, but there was no doubt that Gillian's working for her led to an initial restraint.

The dinner was not repeated.

Gillian was not sorry. Gradually she had begun to rebuild her life again; to go about with her friends. The Cork relatives had been assiduous in putting in touch any stray Irish acquaintances going to be in London for a matter of days or weeks. Gillian was becoming quite used to finding messages for her at the hostel. She now considered leaving that, too, and Liz spoke of wanting a fourth to come in over a flat at Earl's Court. Gillian asked to be considered. She met the others concerned, they devised a financial schedule and a rota for the work and borrowed enough furniture from their respective families to start them off in the venture.

Eira heard of the new arrangement with full approval.

'Another step towards independence of Alec,' she thought to herself. Aloud she exclaimed:

"What about asking me over to see Cordelia Crescent, Gilly?"

If the girls thought Eira would be an embarrassing guest, they were mistaken. She was friendly and amusing and brought welcome contributions to the supper.

"The bottle of Jamesons," she exclaimed, laughing. "Remember how easily we went through the customs with it, Gilly?"

One of the others knew Southern Ireland fairly well and produced some good colour transparencies ·which they squinted at through a viewer. Eira left at ten and Gillian went out with her to the car. She could not help thinking that Eira looked down-in-the-mouth. However she smiled and kissed Gillian lightly on the cheek, thanking her for a "grand evening".

A few mornings later Eira buzzed through for Gillian who went into her office, a little puzzled by this departure from precedent. Eira was in her revolving chair, the usual pile of contracts and correspondence on the desk. The Waterford glass ashtray, which Gillian had bought her as a keepsake of their holiday, was full of cigarette stubs.

Eira came straight to the point.

"The Garreg Wen Amateur Choral and Dramatic Society is doing *The Girl From Krasnia* the week of the 17th. I want you to go down and see the show on the Saturday for me. You'll find a score and libretto over there," she pointed to the filing cabinet. "We try to send a representative whenever we can."

"Wouldn't you rather go yourself, Eira?"

The elder woman did not answer for a moment then, without turning her head, she observed that it would do Gillian good to become *au fait* with the Shearme holdings.

Gillian was handed her ticket—first class—and reservation at the Gwent Arms, which was the only feasible place to stay in the district. She was told that transport arrangements would be made.

When her tedious journey to South Wales ended at the branch line station which served Garreg Wen, she saw a small car with an operatic society sticker on its windscreen. The driver was evidently looking out for her.

"You'll be the young lady coming down from London? I am the treasurer of the society. Danny Ungoed is my name."

His instructions were to take her the few miles out to

45

the hotel, join her for a meal and return her to the Ritzy cinema, which also served as theatre.

Over Welsh mutton, cabbage and roast potatoes, Mr. Ungoed told Gillian that the valley was approaching a depression. Too much coal was being produced for public demand and already some of the men were working on short time. Earlier retirement was no real solution to redundancy.

"For all the Coal Board's assurances it stands to reason that the pits that don't pay will be closed down. If not this year, then next."

There was talk of opening up a fresh seam at the open cast workings three miles outside Garreg Wen.

"It is a matter of economics, you see. If they do enlarge the Pryddwed Road Mine, it would provide alternate employment for only some of our chaps."

Feeling her way cautiously she asked how it was likely to affect such people as their tenor.

"Oh, then you know Deri Rhys?"

"We heard him at Ballykenny."

"Ah, yes. A fine voice he has, to be sure. He was telling me that some woman from London was interested in making a professional singer of him."

Gillian guardedly explained that her principal, Miss Shearme, had been impressed with his possibilities.

"A man can do with a second string sometimes, can't he now?" was Mr. Ungoed's only comment.

The waitress again handed them a handwritten menu. Gillian chose steamed sponge pudding; her companion, cheese and biscuits. Talk turned to the production of *The Girl From Krasnia* which he hoped Gillian would like.

"I am sure it would be appreciated if you would come round and meet the company."

She understood that to be Eira's practice and nodded. The dining room clock gathered itself together for asthmatic recording of the hour.

"My goodness, is that the time?" he threw aside his paper serviette and she also rose.

The Ritzy cinema struck Gillian as enormous for the needs of the little community. It held close upon a thousand and was rarely full, except when the various local operatic societies performed there. People came in from neighbouring villages up and down the valley. She was shown to a seat in the front

46

in one of the South Wales papers at the hotel, Gillian gathered it was caused by "incedive arcking". A coal-cutting machine's cable had been damaged, possibly by a stone thrown up in the shot-firing.

"I was on the rescue job," Deri explained.

"Was it—very grim?"

"At a thousand feet down, bad enough." He brushed the back of his hand on his forehead. "I didn't feel in the mood for this—" making a little gesture.

"I can understand." Her sympathy was obvious.

People came and went.

Deri and Gillian could have moved but did not. She explained that she was working for Eira's concern.

"Miss Shearme is a very influential lady?" a hint of a smile showed at the corners of his mouth.

"Certainly in the theatre."

He hesitated. "You really think she was serious about being willing to help me?"

"Eira never talks for the sake of talking."

This seemed to confirm his own opinion of her.

"If I become redundant in the mine I might have to consider taking her up on her offer."

"You could do much worse, Mr. Rhys."

"Trouble is, I hate domineering women," he confessed.

Gillian's laughter seemed to make them immediate allies.

"Shall I tell you something?" she asked. "When Eira suggested that I changed my job—what I was doing before isn't important—I was half afraid to accept, because I didn't want to be in her power. Believe me, it hasn't turned out that way. I'm even not in the same department. Does that—help at all?"

He grinned conspiratorially then becoming serious a moment, confessed that he had thought a lot about Eira's wish to help him become a professional singer.

"Things happen—like yesterday—and a man is forced to think still harder about the future."

She did not interrupt.

"Mam wants me to stay in the valley. Rhiannon—for us to marry, but we've had to put it off a time. As things are it is too risky. You know Miss Shearme tried to talk Rhiannon round to her way of thinking?"

"Eira never disclosed what passed between them and I never liked to ask."

"From what I can gather Rhiannon was scared of Miss Shearme. She thought, but of course that is too absurd—" he blushed. "She thought Miss Shearme had taken a liking to me. I told Rhiannon it was just my singing."

"It was your singing," but Gillian looked down as she spoke.

"That's what I said," and he seemed to exhale in relief. Turning his head, he saw Rhiannon looking for him and beckoned. "You remember Miss Shearme's friend?"

The girl's face was non-committal as she shook hands. Gillian explained that she had been sent to report on *The Girl From Krasnia.*

"It was just a routine visit."

"I am surprised Miss Shearme didn't come herself," Rhiannon's voice was as cold as the Swallow Falls which Gillian had seen with Eira at Bettwys-y-Coed.

"My employer is a very busy person."

'Too busy to concern herself with the likes of us' was what Gillian read in the other's hostile expression. With deliberation Rhiannon laid a peremptory hand on her young man's arm. He made a comic face to Gillian, as much as to say, 'You see what a difficult life I lead?'

"Remember us to Miss Shearme," and Deri allowed himself to be towed away just as a troubled Mr. Ungoed hurried up to take care of Gillian's run back to the Gwent Arms.

7

IT WAS a morning three months later and Eira was in the middle of a telephone conversation with a London manager when Poppy, the office junior, put her home-permed red head round the door after the merest apology for a knock.

"Yes?"

"Gentleman from Wales," Poppy ran all the syllables together, which did not make for clarity.

"Again—slowly, please."

"Gentleman—from—Wales to see you, Miss."

"Name?"

Poppy put her hand to her mouth with an exaggerated gesture borrowed from someone in a T.V. farce.

"Oh! I forgot to ask." Brightening she added that he had said he was from somewhere like "Craig Owen."

Eira frowned, then her face cleared. "The name wouldn't be Rhys?" She was not aware of the fearful anxiety of her tone.

"That's right, miss."

"Show him in—no, wait. Give me five minutes." She picked up the telephone again to conclude the conversation.

Relating the incident in the outer office Poppy said it was the only time she had ever seen "the boss" what she called "all shook up". Allowances had to be made for exaggeration, of course, but even Eira knew the sphinx-like air she tried to impose on herself before the staff had let her down badly. She hurried the poor manager off the line, saying she had to be "in conference", then took her handbag out of the drawer to see her appearance in the pocket mirror. This again was against precedent. Eira made-up in the morning and did not expect to study the subsequent wear and tear before lunch-time.

"Deri Rhys," she whispered, aware of an extraordinary sense of excitement. It needed all her self control to pick up a contract and appear to be gravely studying it when Poppy knocked, this time a little louder.

Eira waited for the door to close before trusting herself to turn her head, and greet him.

"So you have come?" she observed in a quiet voice.

"Cap in hand, as you might say," and he gave his sunny smile. There was nothing subservient in his manner. He made the office seem small as he stood there, a little awkward, bareheaded and wearing what she took to be his best suit.

"Won't you sit down, Mr. Rhys?" Eira was making herself sound a woman of business but had she known it, the flutter of her hands caused her to seem to him a nervous schoolgirl. He enquired after Gillian then seated himself, glancing about him with lively interest before letting his questing glance rest finally upon Eira's face. Her eyes were held by his and the colour mounted plainly to her cheeks. Deri began to

51

wonder if Rhiannon could have been right about Miss Shearme liking him for himself. Only Rhiannon had put it with greater crudity.

"What has made you come and see me?" Eira asked, when the silence between them had grown too tense.

"Curiosity and—"

"An honest desire to be helped?" Her smile was half amused.

"I'll not beat about any bushes, Miss Shearme. I hitched a lift to London; one of the chaps I know drives a long distance lorry. I have a bed for the night at the Y.M.C.A. He returns to Wales tomorrow. I know how to contact him."

"I see. Am I to assume you wanted to test the genuineness of my interest in your singing? Make sure I wasn't—talking for talk's sake?"

He looked down at his hands. "I couldn't know in advance if you still meant what you had said."

"I don't change, Deri Rhys. My offer to have you trained and find you work stands. I am only curious as to why you have suddenly changed your mind about accepting my help."

"Garreg Wen pit closed last month."

"I am sorry to hear that."

"They mean to re-open Prydwedd Road Mine, but even if they do, they can't take us all."

"Does your fiancée know you've come to London?"

"Rhiannon was not sold with the idea. I'll be honest with you."

Eira's mouth twitched a little. "We didn't hit it off any too well. How is it you aren't married?" Her tone was brisker than it had been.

"First there is one thing, then another. Now with the pit closing—"

"Yes, of course." She looked secretly satisfied.

It was then half past twelve, the time she usually went to lunch.

"Come with me and have something to eat. I go to a little place across from Shaftesbury Avenue."

She left the offices with Deri looking interestedly at the traffic negotiating the Cambridge Circus roundabout.

"This way," she exclaimed, taking hold of his arm. The restaurant in which they found themselves dismayed him. He could tell that it would be expensive. Eira had no difficulty in following his thoughts. They were obvious from his dull expression. She said:

"Let us have no false modesty about this. It comes out of expenses."

The waiter who knew her approached with a "Good morning, Miss Shearme."

"What do you recommend, Gustav?"

He indicated the *plats de jour* and one or two alternatives.

"Have you any particular preference?" she asked Deri. He shook his head, unable to compete with their gastronomic erudition. "We'll accept Gustav's advice, then, about the main dish. I think I'll have melon to start. Would you like the same?"

The young man nodded, not caring either way.

Eira felt sorry for him. "Listen, Deri Rhys. These lunches are all part of business entertainment. I don't do more than sign the bill. Does that help to appease your masculine pride?"

"I couldn't take you out to such a meal."

"You will be able to, when you make big money."

"Damn it, I'm not used—"

She reached across the table and put her hand pleadingly on his. "I know you think me a career woman of the worst type, running up unnecessary costs because I like to swank. But that isn't the case. I would as soon eat at Lyons any day—" and she did her best to sound as if she meant it. "This place happens to be convenient. One runs into people that matter."

"You're a managing female, aren't you?" he spoke mildly enough. To his surprise she laughed with genuine appreciation. "No one has ever called me that before, Deri Rhys! I can't think why I don't slap your face for being so presumptuous." Her mood had changed to gaiety and she signalled the wine waiter. "I generally have a lager with my meal. What about you?"

He chose a stout. When the waiter had gone, Deri lowered his voice.

"I thought it would be champagne or nothing in a place of this kind."

She felt his conspiratorial manner to be an advance towards greater tolerance. For the moment anyway he was not fighting her.

They did not discuss business matters over lunch. Deliberately she kept him to general topics. He was rather silent, a little too concerned, perhaps, with eating unfamiliar, excitingly cooked food.

"Go on, tell me you prefer steak and kidney pud!"

He grinned, admitting that his mother made it very well. "This—" he waved his hand at his plate, "is a nice change from Welsh lamb."

Eira chuckled. "I thought it might be. If you take my advice you'll have the *crepes suzette* afterwards."

"What in heaven are they?"

"Pancakes," she whispered, "only done in rather a special way."

They had coffee and he felt in his pocket for a packet of cigarettes. It was not a brand that Eira particularly liked, but she accepted one. He held a match to light it. She noted the extreme steadiness of his hand.

She relaxed against the back of the chair. "What are we going to do about you? I think the first thing is to let Basilio Andres hear your voice. I'll ring him when we go back to the office. He is one of the few maestro's who stick to the Italian method. I should think he ought to be able to fit you in sometime during the afternoon. We'll have to go by what he says. I mean—as regards the amount of training you'll need. Then you will have to have somewhere to live. I suppose you can stay on at the Y.M.C.A. for a few days? I had better send young Gillian out with you to see about a more permanent place."

"I can do that for myself."

"Yes—yes of course," she lowered her glance before the indignation of his. "Then you'll need money."

"I have enough with me."

Eira forced herself to look at him. "You must allow me to know best about that. You can't live in London for the same as you do at home. I am not making you a present of it, so you needn't start refusing. It will be purely a business arrangement. I'll talk to our accountant. Shearme's will make whatever seems a reasonable grant, to be paid back—with interest —out of your earnings."

He moved his shoulders in a bitter shrug, of unwilling agreement.

"You—don't leave me much choice."

"Deri," she used his Christian name and for the first time
54

there was a note of pleading in her voice. "It would be so much easier if you didn't fight me at every turn."

"Why are you doing all this—for me?" he demanded.

"Because I believe in your voice and, as you reminded me earlier, because I am a meddlesome woman, or was the word—managing?"

"Managing," with a deprecatory grin.

She looked at her small diamond studded watch, a present from her father shortly before he died. The waiter had brought the bill, which she duly signed, then Deri and she walked back in complete silence to the Jollity Theatre.

"Will you stay in the waiting room while I make one or two calls?"

He nodded.

She caught Basilio Andres and arranged a time to bring Deri along, then rang for the accountant only to be told he was not yet back from lunch.

"Blast the man!"

Remembering Deri, presumably reading the magazines provided, she took a ten pound note out of her own wallet and slipped it into an envelope. There were two other people in the waiting room when she went to call him.

"Mr. Rhys!"

He rose obediently and directly they were in her office she rattled off the arrangements.

"The accountant isn't back yet but this will do to be going on with. I'll have him draw up a proper paper in the morning."

"It's your money, isn't it, Miss Shearme?" handing back the envelope unopened.

"Was ever a man so like a porcupine? Are you sure you can manage till I've seen Mr. Birdsall?"

Deri inclined his head in a way which made her ashamed of her clumsiness.

At three o'clock she drove him to Signor Andres, who lived north of Hampstead. The maestro was an old man now, but still one of the finest teachers of *bel canto*. Eira did not make the mistake of remaining in whilst the young man's voice was tried. When twenty minutes perhaps had passed, he and the maestro re-joined her. It was the first time she had seen genuine excitement on Deri's face. The maestro said that fortunately Mr. Rhys had comparatively few vocal faults to remedy. Already the voice was naturally placed.

55

A dozen lessons could put him right for audition purposes, if that was all that was required.

"In these days a singer cannot afford the luxury of three to four years of study."

Eira said that Shearme's wanted to take a long term interest.

"In that case," the maestro interrupted, "let me have him for three months' intensive study. Afterwards—once, twice a week—as he can manage."

"Thank you, Maestro. And when do you want Mr. Rhys to start his lessons?"

"I can take him tomorrow morning at ten o'clock. Oh, and, young sir, your voice would be better served if you were to stop smoking."

In the hall Deri handed her what was left of the packet of cigarettes. Gravely she thanked him. They were to part outside the Y.M.C.A. Before going there, however, she stopped at a newsagents' to emerge with three different kinds of sweets.

"To help you over the first difficult hours."

He flushed, but not from anger. Completely bewildered he said that he had never met anyone quite like her. She laughed this off, assuring him there must be plenty.

"When you've finished with Signor Andres come in to sign that paper."

"If I win the pools this week it might not be necessary," but he was smiling as he said it.

"You do them too, then?" her tone was business-like again. Perhaps on purpose. She had yet to learn how to handle him. They could not spend their time in a state of armed neutrality —with occasional concessions. Neither did she want him to become bogged down by enforced gratitude. Somehow she must make Deri understand that discovering young tenors was all in the routine work of Shearme's Enterprizes, Ltd.

At the Y.M.C.A. they stopped. He alighted but still held open the door, obviously searching for the right words of thanks. She held up her hand.

"Please! This is just a business deal."

"Just a business deal," he repeated it after her dutifully enough but she had the oddest notion that neither of them believed what they had just averred.

56

8

DERI'S FIRST weeks in London were not without their loneliness. He was thrust into an entirely different way of life, which left him by turn unhappy and bewildered. He missed the clean air of the valley and the evening strolls with Rhiannon. Even more he felt the lack of companionship of the men with whom he had worked in the mine. He had a countryman's slight suspicion of all town dwellers. There were moments when Garreg Wen seemed far away and unreal, whilst at others, he had to admit, he thought of it scarcely at all.

Never a letter writer, he forced himself into composing what ended by being stilted lines to his mother. He told her little beyond the main facts of his days. He was well. He ate enough. He had changed his underclothes on Sunday, but shirts never lasted more than a day in London, where laundry was expensive. Soon, of course, he was making up parcels for home washing. Even more difficult were the letters to Rhiannon. He was sure she did not believe in the impression he tried to put over of hard work and little leisure. Deri was no good at expressing his deeper feelings and it must have needed sublime intuition and trust on her side to believe they still existed. He was only too aware that the dutiful, meaningless letters he sent—and the scarcely more fervent ones he received back from her—made their engagement appear unreal. He would think how little there remained to keep alive a love so right and natural to them in the valley.

Conscience troubled him with regard to Rhiannon. He dared not face the outright question as to whether his feelings for her were changed, much less the possibility that the close community life had thrown them together and created a need by no means as pressing for him now he had the wider interests London offered. He castigated himself for not experiencing that ache of loss he considered right in the circumstances.

'Of course I still love Rhiannon.' He would try to re-assure himself.

That he did not think of her quite so often he explained away as best he could:

'There is so much here I must do and learn about. At home, when I came up for the day, there was no need to study. I was free.'

In London he had an almost claustrophobic feeling that he was never quite free. Largely this was because of his sense of duty to Eira. He could not forget—even for an instant—that her concern was financially behind him. He had to succeed, if only to repay her confidence in his ability to become a professional singer. At times Deri drove himself too hard in his endeavours. He would lapse into one of those dark moods of the Celtic temperament—of which Eira knew nothing—and approach the panic of extreme despair.

'I'll never be a singer. I can't master all I should.'

He would bow his head in his hands and say aloud in Welsh, his mother tongue, "Oh, God, it is tired of it all that I am."

Deri forced himself to stint, unwilling to spend one penny more of the allowance Shearme's paid him than he could help. This tended to restrict the pleasures of his free hours. Instead of going out for the convivial pint, as he would at home, he would sit in his hostel, reading books he believed could educate him better and studying vocal scores.

His singing lessons with Basilio Andres were the highspots of this London period. He quickly became fond of the old man to the point of veneration. Andres had a ready sympathy with the young. He did not have to be told all the things which sorely troubled Deri Gwilym Rhys.

The maestro finished playing a *vocalise*, which ended their half hour lessons, at that time composed solely of exercises to strengthen the voice and make it more flexible. His thin, ageing face was thoughtful.

"My friend," he said in his never-quite English speech, though he had lived over here longer than in the Italy of his birth. "You strain too hard. You cannot study all the hours. As to singing, at the most I permit two. Go out, boy, and enjoy yourself. It will not hurt you. Even it can do good."

Andres did not need reminding of his pupil's sense of obligation to the Signorina Shearme.

58

"What is it you fear?" asked the maestro. "You have a good voice." Twinkling, he added: "Which will be still better when I am through with it! Always there is room for a tenor of outstanding quality."

"I know all that, Maestro," yet still frowning perplexedly.

The old man laid an affectionate arm across the younger one's shoulder. "What was it your great Shakespeare said? That it was necessary to believe in yourself, *si?* You do not believe *enough*."

"I can't help fearing the future, Maestro."

"There is no need, my young friend."

It was easier to believe, in the maestro's studio, subtly encouraged to do so by the old man. Much harder away from the building.

Though the Shearme stipend was paid regularly, Deri insisted upon handing the accountant painstakingly detailed accounts as to how it was spent which, incidentally, that gentleman put in a file unread. Deri was making such a visit when he ran into Gillian, returning from lunch. She thought he looked down in the mouth and on impulse invited him round to the flat where the four girls would be entertaining a few friends.

"It will only be a fork supper and nothing stronger than beer, but you will be most welcome."

He hestitated. "You are very kind to ask me."

"Don't be stuffy, Deri," she exclaimed and was rewarded by a smile.

"It wasn't that. I would like to come. Indeed I would. It's just that I don't know if I ought to spare the time. There is a concert I should go to instead."

"Couldn't you skip it for once?"

"You make refusal very hard, Miss Lechmere."

She gave him the address and said any time from six thirty would do.

"We haven't a piano but Liz's boy friend, Jim, plays the guitar."

Deri did not know when he had enjoyed an evening more. His shyness was soon dissipated by the friendliness of everyone and though he had never sung to a guitar accompaniment, he found it an agreeable experience.

"Welsh songs, Deri," they kept crying. Standing very erect, to stray cords on the guitar and with tears of remembrance of Wales in his eyes, he sang "David of the White Rock."

"That was beautiful," Gillian volunteered, as the applause died down.

But the party was not all serious singing. They danced, too.

"You will fall over my awkward feet," Deri exclaimed, partnering Gillian, who refused to be put off by this. She was a good dancer and his natural sense of rhythm helped them.

"Not bad at all, Deri."

He laughed, easy and happy to be with her. If it had not been for Rhiannon, he would not have minded kissing her good night, as several of the young men present did to their hostesses. Gillian looked at him, secretly amused by the way he fumbled his adieus.

Going into the kitchenette she ran the cold tap. All the glasses being dirty, she filled a cup with water. She liked Deri Rhys quite a lot. Of course there was no romantic nonsense about it. (She was quick to remind herself of the late Alec). All the same Deri was nice and she did concede his power to sing like an angel when it came to airs like "David of the White Rock."

'He seems to trust me somehow. I think he still regards me as a sort of buffer state between himself and Eira. He must find London a bit bewildering, poor lamb. I am glad I asked him tonight. I hope he'll come over again.'

Basilio Andres had found an impecunious piano student, willing to practice songs with Deri, but it meant hiring a studio, which did not work out cheaply. There was no piano at the small establishment for paying guests where he now stayed. He had gone to the Y.M.C.A. once or twice, but it was not really a place for vocal practice. If he commandeered the piano someone would be sure to hear, poke an enquiring head round the door and bellow "mi, mi, mi, m—ah".

He had not meant to mention this difficulty of his when he made his fortnightly report to Eira in person.

"There's a piano going begging at my flat you could use—" Seeing his almost prim expression of refusal she hurried past that suggestion and bethought her of the office upright on which numbers could be tried through by clients.

60

"Or there is the piano here. When we close the doors at five thirty the place is empty until the cleaners come in at six the following morning."

"You are doing enough for me already, Miss Shearme."

She brought her hand down on her desk with a gesture of weary exasperation. "Oh, Deri, Deri, what am I to do about you? You still snap the hand that I suppose you consider feeds you."

"I didn't mean it that way."

"All right, all right. Up to a point I can understand your not wanting to come to my place, though there is not a soul about in the day time. You've only been there once, anyway, and that was only because I press-ganged you into it."

She had been entertaining a couple of West End managers to cocktails and it had seemed an idea to ask Deri to sing. Not, Eira felt, that it had been much of a success. He had been tongue-tied and ill-at-ease to the point of gaucheness. He had not even sung particularly well on account of a head cold.

"There is no reason why you couldn't use the piano here that I can see."

"I suppose not," but he was the reverse of enthusiastic.

"Why are you so reluctant to do the smallest thing I suggest? Is it just *because* I am suggesting it? I had a simple way in which to solve your practice problem and what do you say?" She mimicked his voice exactly and delighted to see him redden. "I can't believe you are like this with everyone. I seem to recall you behave differently with Gillian. She tells me you even condescended to go to a party with her friends. And, strange as it may seem, enjoyed yourself."

"I did. It was kind of the girls to ask me."

"And you would be prepared to go again, wouldn't you? I just can't see where the difference lies."

"Miss Lechmere isn't my employer."

"Must you always think of me as that?"

"How else would you wish me to regard you?" he asked with a surprise so genuine that she averted her face lest he read the chagrin in hers.

"Oh, any way at all except as someone to shun, except when you can't avoid seeing me on business matters. Do you dislike me so much, Deri?"

"I like you very much indeed, Miss Shearme."

61

" 'The gentleman protests too much, methinks,' " and her mouth had a wry twist to it as she altered the Queen in *Hamlet's* line from 'the lady protests . . .'

"How have I offended you? It is the last thing I meant." His tone was so honest that it broke her composure. She laid her head across her desk, pillowed in her arms. From the shaking of her shoulders he could tell that she wept.

His initial horror at having caused this to happen made him unable to act with the compassion he felt. Then, after hesitation, he crossed over to her. The misery of her humiliation had smote him very deep. He touched her, tentatively, unsure how she might react.

"Miss Shearme—"

His sympathy was something she could not take just then.

"Go away, please."

"Miss Shearme — Eira—" Such was the measure of his panic that he addressed her by her Christian name for the very first time, pronouncing it with his broad Welsh vowels. Any other time she would have exalted to think he had brought himself thus far.

"I'm tired, so please, please go away." Her hand felt in her pocket for the handerkerchief that should have been there but somehow was not.

"I haven't a clean one to lend you."

"That's all right, Deri. In my handbag—thank you." She found one at last and blew her nose.

Deri was still standing anxiously beside her. "It is very clumsy that I am. I don't intend it."

He reminded her of an overgrown puppy unable to understand what he had done to offend his owner.

"And now—leave me—" As he still hesitated she said, with a touch of irritability, "Oh, can't you see I am all right?"

"Perhaps I could get you something. A glass of water?" He looked almost wildly about him, missing the carafe on the filing cabinet.

"For God's sake, Deri!"

He still felt something should be done for her. A kind of instinct brought him closer. He held open his arms. She allowed him to comfort her. She leaned against him, all emotions spent, aware only of a tremendous solace. The rough material of his coat against her skin. The aimless pats on her back by his strangely gentle yet entirely impersonal hands.

'He doesn't care a damn about me,' she thought, as if that were a discovery, though in fact she had known it from the first. In a way it had happened to her the moment he began to sing on the small stage at Ballykenny. Only then, of course, she had confused the feeling with musical appreciation. Almost she had acknowledged the truth that day in his home, "Cartref". She had realised it over these weeks in London, where he had seemed to avoid her, unless summoned.

'I love him so much,' Eira thought, entirely without satisfaction.

It was bad enough to have it happen for the first time at thirty-five, when any self-respecting woman had built up reserves all too difficult to demolish again. She was a sensible business executive with male friends in sufficiency and no lover. In a way there was a secret shame that she should have reached this age without experiencing such a desire. To be that rather joked about thing, a maiden lady.

Neither scruples nor opportunity had necessarily prevented her from having those experiences other women enjoyed. She tried to evade the issue, telling herself "romps in the hay" were all right for the young. At thirty-five one wanted other, more important things from a man, such as companionship.

If it had been true, it was true no longer.

'I am in love with a mere boy,' she reminded herself. 'I don't want intellectual talk with him. I don't even care if there isn't the companionship. What I do want most in the world is to have his arms about me. Not as they are now, when he is just feeling sorry for me—but holding me tight, tight—'

As if a kind of sympathy with this guided him, he did momentarily strengthen his hold of her. She sighed, beyond caring if he heard.

'I want him to make love to me—to call me all those silly things I suppose he calls Rhiannon—I want to hear him tell me that I matter to him. Oh, go on, admit it, Eira. You want him to whisper in your ear, pick you up and do his damnedest.'

At that juncture her sense of humour began to return. Try as she would she could not picture Deri using a Charles Boyer tone and inviting her to come to the Kazbah.

Unutterable weariness filled her being. She recalled the

63

bad nights she was having as Deri touched the top of her head shyly with his lips.

Presently she disengaged herself from his clasp. He let his arms fall to his sides and hang there.

"Sorry to have sobbed all over you, Deri." She forced herself to adopt a light tone. "It won't happen again. Truth is I've had some bad nights lately. You know how it is—" he nodded gravely, "add a few business troubles on top of it, and one reaches the point where it takes only the smallest thing to—to—upset one."

He nodded again. She wished he would speak, for a change.

"I'll have a spare set of outer office keys cut, Deri, then you can use that piano."

"You are too kind."

'At least he doesn't dare to refuse me outright,' she thought to herself, wondering if he ever would play that particular piano.

Eira held out both her hands in a frank, friendly gesture.

"I don't have to ask you not to tell anyone about—"

"Of course not."

He let her hands rest in his a second then, bowing, turned to leave her. She remained standing just as she was, more alone than at any moment she could remember.

9

COMPLIMENTARY TICKETS were often among the staff perquisites of Shearme's. A system had been evolved to promote fair distribution, so when Gillian had seats for a revival of a Lehar favourite, she wondered whether Deri would care to come. He was delighted. They met at the theatre and his face showed unmistakeable pleasure as he shook hands.

"Posh seats we have," he whispered, as they went down to the stalls, where he bought her chocolates. Whilst waiting for the overture Gillian asked how he was progressing with the maestro. Deri's enthusiasn for the Andres *bel canto* system of voice production was infectious.

"I feel all the difference when I sing."

"How about the practice?"

"Miss Shearme said I could use the office piano—" he hesitated. "I don't like to keep on with that."

"Whyever not?"

"I hate placing myself even more in her debt."

"Oh, I am sure Eira wouldn't think of it that way." Though Gillian made the protest she knew precisely what he meant. He did not chose to mention how on the second occasion he had had the courage to go to the office after hours, Eira had arrived. True she had left behind some important papers which she needed, but instead of going straight out again, she had been unable to resist listening to him falter through a chromatic scale. Then, full of charm without condescension, she had offered to play the song he had with him. He had to admit that she was a superb accompanist, but his sense of unease increased when she said —casually enough:

"I wish you'd come round to my place once in a while then I could play for you there."

But he knew he would not accept. Eira Shearme was a woman he felt—in his simplicity—unable to handle.

Nothing more was said about her at the theatre that evening because the orchestra had finished their tuning up and were under conductor's orders.

Deri insisted upon seeing Gillian home, though Cordelia Crescent was in the opposite direction from where he lived. Her protests that she was "a big girl now" and capable of taking care of herself met with that obstinate inflexibility she had learned to respect in him.

"Won't you come in for a noggin—or a cup of tea, if you prefer?"

He hesitated, thinking of his journey home. She assured him he would be all right for half an hour. The others were out or in bed and she moved quietly about the place. In no time at all, it seemed, she brought a daintily laid tray.

"I have enjoyed this evening, Gillian."

"So have I," with a betraying warmth in her voice.

He had that sense of peace he always felt with Gillian. He decided she was an extremely nice girl. They looked at one another half shyly and Gillian was aware of a quickening of her senses, as he rose to leave. He had meant just to shake hands politely instead of which, they landed in one another's arms. Her eyes closed, his lips hard on hers, Gillian had the strangest sense of release; as if all the agony of Alec's death were expunged and she were free to take up un-sorrowing life again.

Shaken by the emotional impact, Gillian gently released herself. She was breathing quickly, as if she had been racing. He went on looking down at her, puzzled, wondering, vainly unable to explain what had happened to them.

Gillian recovered her poise first. When she saw he was about to speak, she shook her head and put a hand on his lips. "Don't let's — spoil things by — seeking explanations, my dear."

"Rhiannon," the name was forced from him when Gillian had removed a cautionary hand.

"I know. For me there was Alec." She knew that now he was really of the past.

"We must have been mad."

She smiled wonderingly, wondering if instead they had not experienced a second of profound sanity. She had no idea whether Deri were more than passingly attracted to her. She did not go as far as to question the possibility of his love. Too readily, perhaps, she had accepted his engagement to Rhiannon. After all, Gillian reminded herself, the kiss could have been prompted by several factors—their happy evening together; a man's loneliness; because she herself might have been looking extra pretty.

He passed a hand over his forehead in bewilderment. She was moved by compassion for him.

"Deri dear, this isn't the end of the world."

"I—suppose not," but doubt coloured his voice.

"It needn't affect our friendship."

The word seemed to jar him to realization of his predicament. "I don't think I love Rhiannon any longer." The shame of it made him stare down at his feet, seeming to him large and awkward -looking.

"Oh, my dear."

"Gillian?" He gazed at her, despair in his glance.

Neither dared to touch the other, knowing instinctively it could only end with a further embrace. Muttering something incoherent, he bolted from the room. She heard the flat door closing.

66

She stood a long while as she was.

"I love Deri." The strangeness of it transfigured her face and she repeated in wonderment, "I love Deri Rhys."

After that evening Deri avoided her. She argued that was only to be expected. If he did feel the same as she did, it would entail a spiritual struggle with his conscience.

'Poor Deri,' Gillian thought, unaware how her own happiness was betraying her.

Eira came through to "the overseas" one afternoon to find Gillian momentarily alone, gazing dreamily into the blankness of the wall, the sheet in the typewriter obviously forgotten.

"What are you looking so starry eyed about, might I ask?" the question was a mildly amused one.

Gillian flushed up at once. "I? Oh, just having a breather," her voice trailed off unconvincingly.

The elder woman smiled, seating herself on the corner of the desk, cigarette in mouth.

"I have noticed that for the past week or so you have been going about with a much happier expression. Does it mean that at last you have begun to feel yourself over Alec's death?"

Gillian bent her head.

"One can't go on grieving for evermore, my dear, and I am glad you have so recovered your ability to enjoy life. Liking the job all right?"

"Yes, Eira."

"Quite settled down now, aren't you? Listen, child, what about coming round to my place this evening? We don't see much of each other in business hours." Noticing the hesitation she said, with a touch of asperity, "Of course if you have something better to do."

"No, Eira. It was just that my smalls need washing. I guess they can wait another night."

"Good. Half seven suit you?" She made a little gesture of self-annoyance. "Here am I forgetting what I came through for—think you could turn up the file about the Malta production of *Princess Paula* for me?"

Eira lived in a ground floor maisonette in one of the quiet Kensington squares to the gardens of which she had a key.

Surprisingly, perhaps, her home was modern. Before Gillian had seen it, she had expected if not massive Victorian furniture then Queen Anne or Georgian styles. Instead Eira had had almost a clean sweep of family things, retaining only a few treasured pieces and for the rest shopping to suit her particular personality. The result was successful in the extreme. The decorations were contemporary without being bizarre and the same was true of the hangings, whilst the furniture, though of twentieth-century compactness, did not exhibit any oddity of design. The general effect was one of light and charm.

Gillian liked especially the sitting room, with its white grand piano in one corner, paper which successfully deceived one into thinking it was light-wood panelling, built in china shelves and bookcases—all in the same design—a rich wall to wall carpeting and medium sized sofa and companion easy chairs. Double doors divided the room off from a minute dinette, though when alone it had to be admitted that Eira preferred to eat in her gay scarlet and white kitchen.

Gillian was a little uneasy lest she betray herself to Eira, but had no need to worry. Eira was in a happy, relaxed mood, very different from the woman with the hollow eyed look that she had exhibited intermittently of late. She wore slacks and a gay coloured silk blouse. When they were having coffee after their meal she mentioned that the Ballykenny people wanted to do another of the Shearme pieces.

"I don't know if they'll try to engage Deri Rhys again. Still less whether he would want to go."

"I am sure he will be guided by you," the girl sounded a little stilted.

"Heavens above, am I expected to make all his decisions for him? Only this afternoon he rang to ask if I had any objections to his going home for a couple of days. It is his mother's birthday. Can't you just see him lighting candles on the cake? I wonder if she'll wear her hat that day, too? I expect it's really an excuse to see Rhiannon. Must be three months since he came to London."

The chocolate she was eating seemed to choke Gillian. She tried not to think of Deri and Rhiannon together. Back in his familiar setting he might experience a revival of his tender feelings for the girl he intended to marry. Gillian had no proof—she reminded herself—that these feelings had undergone any change. Only the intuition loving Deri gave to her.

Eira was curious as to the reason for Gillian's sudden choking confusion. Surely the silly child could not be carrying the torch for Deri Rhys as well? The idea was startlingly novel and Eira did not much like it.

"Something wrong with the chocolate you are eating?" the tone of voice was level but the speaker's eyes were cold.

"No, it's lovely. I think a piece went the wrong way," and Gillian hastily gulped at her coffee.

Talk turned to Ireland and soon they were laughing over their experiences. The horses at Dunloe, a farm wagon so old and battered as to seem to scrape the ground as it moved, the colourful tinker's cart and the way in which he had plucked his dog up to be part of the picture.

"And the garage without any doors and how they stored the pews there as well."

"What price the gentleman of the Garda asking you to move your car in such a way as to suggest it was for the sake of not spoiling the car?"

"One of our bobbys would just have taken out his note-book and brought me to court for causing obstruction. Oh, there's indeed a lot to be said for the South Irish way of life. Heard any more of the Cork relations?"

"They want me to spend Christmas with them."

"Do you think of going? You could take a night flight to Shannon and probably it wouldn't be too difficult from there. Nicer than the boat at that time of year."

Whilst they were enjoying girlish reminiscences, Deri was sitting upright in the cabin of the long-distance lorry taking him to Wales. His friend gave him all the latest news about the valley and the abandoning of the mine at Garreg Wen.

"It is bad, man, very bad. People talk of leaving the valley to find other work. They do not believe the Prydwedd Road Mine can absorb enough men—*when* it opens."

· Deri felt stiff-limbed and oddly depressed. When he had packed his over-night grip he had felt full of excitement at seeing his home. Now he was not sure it was such a good idea to be going there.

"How are you liking it in London?"

"It is all right."

"Know many people?"

"A few."

Mistaking Deri's quietness for extreme fatigue, the lorry driver pulled in at a garish looking all-night café called "Mac's Cabin". There they had mugs of strong, sweet, tea, doorsteps of thickly buttered bread, frizzled rashers of bacon and two fried-eggs apiece. Pastry cakes with fringes of cocoanut completed the meal. There were the usual coarse jokes and conversation lavishly interspersed with swear words and obscenities. It was all familiar enough to Deri. In fact how they talked amongst themselves down in the mine.

Perhaps it was having been out of it for three months that made him conscious how much was foul-mouthed and unnecessary.

"Come on, lad," with a playful kick at Deri's backside, the driver went on ahead to climb up again into the cabin of the lorry. Before starting the engine he rolled a cigarette in his little do-it-yourself machine.

Deri felt a bit of a cissy for not smoking, too, though his companion had to understand how it had been voted "bad for the voice".

"How do you like the London girls, Deri *bach?* Bit more of what it takes than ours in the valley?" and he dug Deri hard in the ribs.

"I wouldn't know," the young man answered, not having intended to sound so annoyed.

Deri felt a sight when the lorry lumbered up towards the hill at the bottom of which lay Garreg Wen. Every bone in his body ached from the roughness of the journey. He was being unnecessarily stoic travelling this way to Wales. He *could* have gone by rail but that would have meant using his Shearme allowance. Pride did not allow this. So as Taffy had agreed to take him whenever they could fit in times, Deri had snatched at the chance.

He rubbed his bleary eyes.

"Your girl will turf you out of bed, if she sees you like that, Deri boy," was the jocular comment.

He was too tired to defend Rhiannon against the rough assertion. Besides they were at the crossroads, where the lorry must branch off for Merthyr Tydfil. No point would be served by quarrelling with Taffy when there was still the return journey to endure.

"Ten o'clock Sunday night, boy, and not a minute later." Deri waved and his friend spat over the side of the driving

70

cabin as he swung the huge vehicle dexterously left.

Mrs. Rhys seemed frailer to her son and her joy in having him with her again, for however short a time, compensated for all the physical discomforts of his drive. He did not see Rhiannon that morning, as she was serving down at the green-grocer and he decided to have an hour or two's sleep before dinner. For this Mrs. Rhys had cooked two of his favourite dishes.

"I am sure you don't have food like this in London, my son."

As always they conversed together in Welsh. He told her what he felt he could about his daily life and she listened with evident interest and only occasional disapproval.

"Deri, love." It was Rhiannon, who had called in for five minutes.

He could not deny that he was glad to see her and their first embrace was entirely spontaneous. He kissed her as a man would, after not seeing his girl for three whole months, yet nothing had been aroused in him other than the purely male reaction of contact with the opposite sex. And why, Deri asked himself guilty later, had he had to think of Gillian at that moment? Rhinannon had displayed no shyness. She was eager to welcome her lover. Yet as she pushed him, gigglingly, away, she was conscious of some lack.

It was not in Rhiannon to analyse things so having decided Deri would "warm up later", she ran off, promising to be round when she had finished her work and had her evening meal.

"Tomorrow is the great day, isn't it, Mrs. Rhys?"

"Yes, girl," and the old woman found herself wondering what Rhiannon would bring; a justifiable exercise of the imagination for one on the eve of eighty.

Deri was not alone with Rhiannon at all that first evening which he found a curious relief. Mr. Pugh and several others drifted in and naturally wanted Deri to sing. They started off with hymns and national tunes in which everyone joined, then Mr. Pugh banged the piano top impatiently. He wanted to hear Deri's voice after his lessons with "the great London professor of music".

It was Deri's evening. He sang with finesse and feeling instead of just letting his beautiful tone pour out as in the old, undisciplined days.

By the second song Mr. Pugh had tears of pleasure in his susceptible eyes.

Rhiannon kept on the fringe of things. Now and again she looked troubled as if there were much to disturb her in Deri's moments of unguarded expression. She thought him quieter and in a subtle way—different. He laughed less freely at the old jokes and was easiest when left—for however short a time—with his own sex. Then his gay laugh would resound, just as it used to do before he went to London.

She slipped off at 10 p.m.

"Don't come with me, dear, the others want you. We'll meet at chapel in the morning."

He looked at her blankly, swiftly collected himself and nodded. She did not like to ask whether or not he went to chapel in London but from his manner she had an idea he might not do so. Anyway he arrived at the great, gaunt, four-square building with "Bethesda" written up in solemn black letters, his mother with him. Out of curiosity he had been inside several London churches all of which had struck him as much more beautiful. Until then he had not questioned the architecture of Welsh chapels in their native settings. Now it did occur to him that simplicity should be possible without downright ugliness of design.

They had a light mid-day meal to allow room for the birth-day tea for which at least a dozen people sat around the table. Mrs. Rhys—still in her hat—was obviously moved by all the presents and good wishes she received. Nothing here to suggest the hard times through which Garreg Wen was passing. Then most people had put by in the good days since the war. These were the funds upon which they now drew, with customary generosity, telling themselves—and their neighbours—it was not every week one of their number was eighty.

"Come for a stroll, Rhiannon?" Deri asked, when the heat of the overcrowded room began to make him headachy. He argued that he owed it to her for them to have a little time together before Taffy picked him up again at the crossroads later that same evening.

She went with Deri up the valley. It was not the time of year when they could lie together in some field, indulging in love-play on the whole innocent in character, for Rhiannon was a good girl and she never allowed "liberties", even though Deri was to become her husband.

72

He held her hand now but largely from habit and because he did not want to hurt her feelings.

They approached a gateway, traditional to local lovers. The evening was a fine one, fresh-smelling and sweet, and from further up the mountain road came the bleating of Hugh Morgan's sheep.

Deri knew that he would be expected to make a little love to his fiancée. He wished this kind of steeling himself to do so was not necessary. She nestled against him, too simple to feign the provocative. She had a nicely rounded young body and in the ordinary way his hands would have taken pleasure in caressing her, always, of course, within the limits tacitly understood from the day a man asked a girl to marry him.

They kissed, but to neither was it exciting. She pressed closer, as if by a sheer physical contact of their two bodies she could rouse him, but his hands just held her. They made no attempt to touch her breasts—to explore just a little. After a second kiss she pushed him from her in anger.

"What is it with you, Deri Rhys? Are you no longer a man?"

He flushed. It was a moment when he would have given his soul for a cigarette. He touched his coat pocket then dropped his hand again in remembrance.

"Did *she* make you give it up?"

"Give—what up?" his speech was slow—slurred with embarrassment.

"Smoking."

"If you mean Miss Shearme—no. It was the maestro."

"I see."

"Rhiannon, you have no call to be jealous of Miss Shearme."

"No?"

"No." He smiled. That at least was true. "In fact, I don't even like her much."

"Then it is some other woman."

"Rhiannon, you don't have any right to think that."

"Deri Rhys, I haven't been your sweetheart all this time without knowing when you do and when you don't want to kiss me."

He was no good at guile. Another might have told the tale but Deri could not pretend. Neither could he insult her intelligence by saying he was tired. That was no excuse at all. Without much hope of convincing her, he said it could be that a certain shyness had come over him as a result of separation.

"Because you have a girl in London." Her wish to believe that amounted to obstinacy.

"Truly not, Rhiännon."

"I would rather you sought to tumble me over there in that field than to be like this." She began to cry from a mixture of mortification and anger.

"*Cariad*," he pleaded, his voice full of sweet regrets.

"I hate you, Deri Rhys," stamping her foot.

He caught at her two hands, pulled her roughly towards him, determined somehow to convince her that he had not changed. But even as her lips parted beneath his he knew it was useless. He could not revive something if not completely dead, then dying.

They walked back, no longer holding hands. Rhiannon snivelled once or twice and Deri felt a brute. They parted in stubborn silence.

"I'll write," he called after her, but she hurried on towards the row of terraced houses where she lived.

Deri swore, using a string of abuse as he had not done for months. But none of it made the least difference to the issue. Though it was sad to leave his mother, he felt an instant lightening of his heart as soon as he climbed up on the wheel of the lorry. They would be heading for London—where Gillian was.

10

NOTHING WAS as reliable a barometer of mood and physical health as the human voice. No sooner had Signor Andres heard Deri sing the sustained notes which opened every lesson than the maestro knew him to be troubled. A little tiredness, brought on by the long journeys from London to South Wales and back by road, was not sufficient to account for the change in timbre. So at the end of their half hour together Basilio asked whether Deri would join an old man in a cup of tea?

This was a rare and coveted invitation, fortuitous in as much as no pupil was expected for another hour.

The studio had a gallery running round it and once belonged to a sculptress of note. There was, too, a tiny back garden, great source of summer pleasure to the old maestro. An Italian peasant woman acted as his housekeeper. Calling her, he gave his instructions in that language, which both preferred. Her English was colloquial to the point of being totally without grammatical foundation. The maestro, a devotee of that American language-murderer "Hyman Kaplan" (of the "Leonard Q Ross" [or Leo Rosen] comic novels) boasted:

"Anything Hymie could say my Pia can say worse!"

Deri liked the delicious foreign cakes but found the blend of tea too pungent for his plebian tastes. Strong, yes, but scented? No! The maestro talked well and impersonally, lifting out items from his vast store of musical reminiscence which he felt the young Welshman would enjoy. From that, Signor Andres came round to factors affecting the voice in a general way.

"I do not pry into the private lives of my pupils. I only warn of the things that harm the voice. It could be the journey, but I think the cause is quite other. Emotional, *si?*"

"*Si*," Deri admitted readily enough.

"Perhaps you like to talk? Sometimes it does good."

The young man was very conscious of having had no one of his own sex with whom to do this since leaving Wales. In London there were acquaintances. Natural shyness on his part made closer contacts difficult. He could no more have talked of his troubles to Eira, however sane her advice might be. If Gillian had not been so personally involved he might conceivably have confided in her.

Once he began to talk, the words came with increasing facility. He expressed his perplexity as to why Rhiannon should stir him so little.

"When I kissed her it was—"

"As nothing?" suggested Basilio.

"Almost. Yet I was so sure she was the girl for me. I've known her most of my life. We—belong to the same community, our interests were similar until—"

"You came to London? But, my boy, what more natural? Here you find yourself in a great, big metropolis. Beside it,

75

your valley is so small," he indicated a microscopic measurement with his finely shaped hands. Hands which Deri secretly envied. "This little sweetheart, very fresh, very pretty, very good—"

"No, it isn't that." He sighed, as if with regret. "There is someone else. A friend of Miss Shearme's."

"*Si, si.*"

He explained how his nervousness of Eira had made him strangely at ease with Gillian.

"She is *simpatica*, eh?" and the maestro gave his dry little chuckle.

"I don't have to think what to say to her, wonder if I am behaving correctly," ruffling his dark curls. "Miss Shearme makes me feel—oh, I can't quite put it into words."

"You are afraid of the Signorina Eira."

"I suppose so."

"She is a very good and capable woman. Also kind."

Deri did not look enthusiastic and the maestro asked about Gillian, of whom he had heard but never met. He drew Deri on to describing the evening in the theatre and its not unnatural culminating embrace. Poor simple-hearted Deri had gone home, hoping to find nothing changed!

"Everything was, except Mam," came the rueful admission.

"Your fiancée. She was not understanding with you?"

Deri, so completely honest, said that he rather thought it to have been the other way about. They had parted in an unfriendly fashion and he seemed unable to write to her to make the first move towards renewed amnity.

"I can't pretend what I no longer feel, Maestro."

The old man said that to do that would be not merely foolish but wrong. At the same time he thought Rhiannon deserved some consideration as regards the future. Could not Deri write, suggesting that he was no longer as sure of his feelings as he had been and crave her patience with him in this process of sorting himself out? No girl sincerely in love could refuse Deri that much. The maestro then passed to the matter of Gillian whom, he correctly gathered, his pupil had been avoiding.

"Tell me how you can make sure if you love her or not if you do not see her?"

"I haven't liked to, Maestro. I feel I am under an obligation to Rhiannon."

76

Privately Signor Andres hoped that the little fiancée would be what he thought of as "man enough" to terminate the engagement or to allow it to be considered on a "standstill" footing, say for the next three months. As he saw it, the fewer ties Deri Rhys experienced at the present time the better. The young man had more than enough to occupy his days. Singing lessons, coaching in acting, fencing, and "repetition of songs" in other languages. With his Welsh vowels he should find Italian at any rate easy to pronounce.

"You want my real advice?" Basilio asked, his dark eyes suspiciously a-twinkle. "It is—to hell with the ladies! But if you *must* have their company, then ask the Signorina Gillian out with you."

Deri laughed, feeling considerably happier in his mind as he took his grateful leave of the maestro.

However it was Rhiannon who made the decisive move. She had the fierce Welsh pride and no wish to be cast in the role of incubus. Though she was not expressive in any literary sense, her meaning was brutally clear. She was no girl to be filed for future reference. She wanted appreciation "here and now". It being obvious to all but a simpleton that Deri's feelings had undergone a catastrophic change, she saw no point in keeping him to their engagement. Therefore she returned the ring—which they had gone all the way to Cardiff to choose.

Rhiannon indicated no visible side door by which he might re-enter her favour. It was clear that nothing short of complete contrition and a fresh declaration of love could make her re-view their future. She gave no hint of being broken-hearted. That would have been quite out of the Garreg Wen people's character. The women of mining villages, with a heritage of years of bitter adversity behind them, did not dramatise life. They accepted its reverses stoically: its pleasures with mild good-humoured surprise. Always prepared, of course, for something unpleasant to happen and spoil the moment nearest complete happiness.

Perhaps Rhiannon did not know all this about herself. Undoubtedly she did recognise that no purpose lay in sobbing for Deri to return to her. If he wanted to run after some dolled-up London girl, let him; she wanted no reluctant bridegroom.

Deri did not know quite how to take what to him was her totally unexpected letter. His first reaction was one of gladness.

77

He was free! More soberly he thought that it was a pity about the ring. Perhaps the shop would allow him on it? That the ring could be given by him to any person other than Rhiannon was unthinkable. Instinctively he knew—now thinking dangerously ahead—the stones would not be Gillian's choice.

He was unhappy—though not quite to the extent Rhiannon intended—remembering all their plans. His home, ready for her to move into: the years of knowing one another in that close clannish way of any small community. It was through no real fault of his that all this was lost to him.

Angered, he told himself that if Eira Shearme had not happened on that Ballykenny performance the probability was that still faced with the same mining crisis, he would have acted differently, sought man's work, in Wales, if possible. And if he had had to go over the border into England, Rhiannon would have been prepared to join him.

'Instead I dream a lot of silly dreams about being a great singer,' he shook his head, muttering: 'Damn that Shearme woman for messing up my engagement.'

Then his sense of fairness prevailed. He grinned and decided Eira could not truthfully be blamed for Rhiannon having decided to set him free.

'If I hadn't met Gillian I suppose I could have gone on loving Rhiannon and everything would still be all right between us.'

Darkly he recalled that Eira also was responsible for his meeting Gillian.

"Oh, hell," Deri muttered aloud, not at all sure how to answer Rhiannon's letter. Acknowledge it he must, if only because she had registered the ring.

In his lodgings he spent a whole, unproductive hour, starting but never finishing the letter. This attempt seemed too sentimental—that too cold. One was actually callous. Finally he made the thing very short and inarticulate.

> Dear Rhiannon,
> Sorry you feel that way. Nothing
> I can do about it except say I'm sorry it's
> all turned out so wrong.
> Yours, Deri.

No crosses at the bottom of the note. No "s-w-a-l-k" on

the envelope. He went out to the post then called in at the Green Man, where he drank two pints of mild and bitter. The usual pub pianist was at work and Deri could no more help drifting over and starting to hum than voluntarily stop breathing. Those in the public bar called for a song and Deri found himself launched upon "When Irish Eyes are Smiling" and "She is far from the Land", the pianist being an ex-patriate from Co. Kerry.

The barmaid, a homely good natured rather sluttish Londoner, called out:

"I could sit up all night listening to you, ducky."

Someone made a ribald comeback and she slapped the speaker's face amid merry laughter.

Deri felt a little excited and not entirely sober—for there were several rounds handed him before "Time, Gentlemen, please."

"Come again any evening," called the barmaid, adding what was perhaps the supreme compliment of her day—"Why, you're better than what we 'ear on the Telly."

Deri wondered what the maestro would have had to say about the standard of criticism! Walking rather over-cautiously up the road Deri wondered still more what Eira Shearme would think of his singing in a public house.

'I enjoyed doing it,' he acknowledged. It had taken him back to evenings after some football match when a whole crowd of them had piled into the nearest bar and sung with their glasses of beer in their hands. Hymn tunes, national airs, "Pops" but never "When Irish Eyes are Smiling".

He began to laugh to the empty street, slapping his thigh with delight.

'Me, a Taffy, singing an Irish tune in a London pub!'

Next day was his morning for calling in at Shearme's for his "stipend", as the accountant politely termed it, and to make a progress report to Eira. Deri wondered whether he would be fortunate enough to see Gillian without actually having to seek her out, arguing that probably she knew his schedule at the offices.

He took the money, signing for it in his round, over-careful hand and making the customary crack that he hoped it would not be for much longer. They buzzed through to Eira who kept him waiting—deliberately, he suspected—for nearly ten minutes. Then he went into the office, with its cold efficiency oddly unredeemed by purely feminine touches. He did notice flowers on her desk. She saw his glance, grew a little pink, admitting that it was her birthday, whereupon Deri stood very erect and sang "Happy Birthday to you" in Welsh, using her Christian name for the second time in his life.

"That was nice of you, Deri."

She looked quite moved and it occurred to him that he could go out and buy her a few chocolates, since flowers she already had. To have given a woman cigarettes would simply not have occurred to him.

She asked if he had enjoyed his visit to Wales—she had not seen him since—and hoped he had found his mother and fiancée well.

"Mam was fine, thank you, Miss Shearme."

"And — Rhiannon?"

He nodded with discomfort. Oh, well, he might as well say—now as later.

"It's all off."

"What is? You can't mean your engagement? Oh, I am sorry." She did her best to look sympathetic.

"Rhiannon found I wasn't so keen as I used to be. At least, that's the way she saw it. The ring came back yesterday—or the day before."

'Dear Deri,' Eira thought with private amusement. 'How man-like not to be sure which day!'

"I expect you're glad."

The half-belligerent tone took her rather by surprise. Why should she be glad about his broken engagement? What concern was it of hers?

"You must be thinking I will have less on my mind."

"Oh, that!" In her relief she smiled. "I am not sure too many ties are good at the start of any career. On the whole, Deri, I think perhaps this is fortunate for you. After all, a broken engagement need not be irrevocable. If, later on you found you felt—as you used—about Rhiannon, I am sure she would have you back."

"That shows how little you know her, Miss Shearme."

"I suspect her to be proud and stubborn, just as you are yourself, Deri. Besides, what woman likes to share her man with another?"

80

"What makes you think—" for a moment he seemed startled out of his urbanity.

"When a man ceases to be attentive to one girl, it is because another has taken his fancy."

"I think I am in love with Gillian," falling headlong into the trap Eira had set for the purpose.

She breathed in sharply. Well it was no more than she had suspected. "They" were "of an age". Gillian was "over Alec" because of caring for Deri.

Eira had known from the first that for herself there was no expectation of romance with this golden-voiced miner. He did not even think of her as a woman, only as an interfering element in his life; or perhaps a kind of business automaton.

She wondered how much of herself she had betrayed to him that time, in this self-same office, when she had broken down and cried before him.

'I hope he doesn't guess. It would be too humiliating.'

Eira looked up, her expression under complete control, her voice full only of casual interest, as she wished him luck with Gillian. He stared at Eira for what seemed to her a disconcertingly long moment but she was able to stare him out, undismayed.

He gave his sudden grin.

"Glad it's all right with you."

Gently recalling him to the reason for these regular interviews, she questioned him about the progress of studies. His report was given parrotwise. He could not rid himself of the sensation of being up before the headmaster—or rather, mistress.

Eira nodded or made an occasional note on the pad beside her. She said that she would ring up the maestro and see if he thought Deri ready to start being auditioned.

"If you are, we can *really* plan your career." Her enthusiasm and confidence in him softened him so that he came up to her and, touching her cheek lightly with his lips, said:

"Thank you for believing in me, Miss Shearme."

11

DERI DID not run into Gillian that day and decided it might be better to phone her at the flat. He was actually in the tube on his way home when he recalled his intention to give Eira chocolates. He could have left it unfulfilled but that seemed mean so he alighted at Oxford Circus, went above ground to find a good confectioners and descended once more. He had left it too late to take the box to the offices. Having wasted both time, and half the value of his original ticket, he decided to deliver the gift at Eira's maisonette. The gesture would please poor Miss Shearme even though she was, as he saw it, really paying for them herself.

Eira was going out that evening with friends and on the way to her bath when Deri rang the bell. Swearing with a fluency that would have astonished him, she grabbed hold of a zip-up house-coat and went to the door.

"Deri!" Her look was of glad surprise as shyly he held out the box of chocolates, still in the shop's bag.

"Happy birthday once again."

"My dear—you shouldn't have bothered."

The bath idea abandoned, she invited him in for a drink at the same time explaining that she would have to turn him out quite soon as she had to be at *Chez Henri* in under the hour.

"What do you like, Deri? Sherry? A gin and something? Scotch? Or I have Irish, if you prefer it. The customs were very lenient to me."

"Quite a cellar you have," choosing sherry though he would have prefered beer, which was not mentioned. "They did a good sherry in Eire, as I remember it."

"Perhaps the same as we used to take," naming a brand that meant nothing to one ignorant in the choice of wines. "Slanta!"

Mention of Ireland made her ask whether the Ballykenny society had approached him regarding their next production.

He shook his head, then said that if they should, what did she wish him to do?

"Of course it is up to you," deferring politely to him.

"Yes, but you know best."

She answered that in her opinion it might prove a mistake to identify himself further with amateur performances when he meant to make professional singing his career.

"I know you must have had a great time in Ballykenny—"

"That I did!" laughing at his own recollections. Then sobering, he said that he thought Eira right.

"You're past the help amateurs can provide, Deri, but it was experience."

As they talked he wondered that a woman, in a kind of half-dress—which was how he thought about the highly respectable house-coat—should arouse no masculine instincts in him. He was sure that had it been Gillian instead . . . As always, he knew himself to be uncharitable about Eira. She could not help having no sex-attraction for him.

Unselfconsciously she leaned forward to take a chocolate and the side of the house-coat slipped off her bare leg. Still Deri remained physically unperturbed.

Having finished his drink and refused what he called his "encore" he rose, his feet clumsily rucking up the gay kelim rug, which he stooped to straighten.

"Mam always complains about my outsize feet."

"I hate a man with small feet, though," smiling at him. "It was kind of you to come all the way here, Deri. If I hadn't been going out, we could have had a session at the piano. Oh, that reminds me. We have a new score in which there are a couple of songs I would like you to try—sometime," she was quick not to seek to pin him down to a specific appointment.

Deri had the natural singer's urge "to have a bash", as he termed it and they agreed upon half five the following day. He was outside a few minutes' early and, as he had hoped, caught Gillian emerging from her day's work. She blushed prettily at sight of him. He explained how he was to try numbers out with Eira.

"Oh, I see," Gillian's face seemed to sag under the disappointment.

"Look, when can we see one another?"

"I am going round the shops. Thursday is the late closing, you know. I want a new day dress."

"Could we meet later?"

This was agreed upon and singing, he hurried up to the Shearme office. Eira appeared offhand or at least preoccupied. She looked as if she had forgotten having asked him to come. Memory returned.

"Ah! Yes! The songs from *Hyacintha*. The score is on the piano. Would you like to glance through 'Spring Love' and 'Days of Dreaming' whilst I clear up a little job?"

Deri went through to the minia-piano, picked out the notes of the first named song to gain an idea of its range and tempo. He counted the time aloud to himself, secretly bothered by the theory and harmony of music about which he knew so little.

Eira joined in, exhaling so tiredly that he asked if she would rather leave it to another evening?

"No, Deri. To hear you sing will soothe me. Truth to tell I have been having a spot of bother with—" and she named a well-known management—"over this particular show. I want an option on the amateur rights. They are asking far too high a sum."

She played the first song through and he did his best to read the vocal line in the absence of the tonic sol fa he had found so helpful in Wales. Still his sight-reading without this guide had undergone improvement. A good ear, an inborn sense of musicianship and quick memory of a melody helped him. Having dispensed with one song, she turned to the other, electing to sing it to him in her odd but by no means unpleasing voice. Shutting the volume when they had finished this, too, she asked his opinion of the music. He discussed what had been tried out with intelligence. She felt pleased with him. He had the right ideas. She asked if he would care about going for a meal and saw the dawn of embarrassment. Hastily she exclaimed: "But I expect you're booked."

A few weeks back he would have blurted out that he was meeting Gillian. In his new-found discretion he left the remark unanswered.

"Do you want to stay on and practice, Deri?"

"No, I will come now." He held open the door for her with a politeness she had an idea was quite untaught. She locked up and preceded him down, emerging by the side door between the upper circle and gallery entrances to the Jollity Theatre. Eira gave a casual salute and went across to the bombed site where she sometimes kept her car during daytime.

Deri reached Piccadilly first but spied Gillian held up on an island by the Coventry Street traffic. She had a gaily coloured paper bag in her hand and he devined she had bought what she had gone to find. They went into the Corner House where he felt none of the self-consciousness which still made him tongue-tied in ultra smart restaurants. Moreover Lyons provided the type of food he liked. None of what he thought of as "mucked about foreign fare".

They talked on everyday subjects until their order had been taken. Leaning his arms on the table, he told Gillian that his engagement was terminated. She blushed up, not concealing her pleased confusion any too well. Smiling he laid his larger hand on hers.

"Do I look broken-hearted?"

"Well—no—not really," and she showed the dimples he already adored.

"Gillian, the other evening—wasn't just—I mean. Damn it! What a place to tell a girl you love her!"

"Do you, Deri?" She sounded deeply moved.

The most uncurious of men he now wondered how the late Alec had made his declaration to her. But Gillian herself could not help recalling that the proposal had taken place on a bench in St. James's Park; one evening after the office.

"It's all right, isn't it, Gillian?" Deri's voice broke in on her half-reverie.

She smiled, all the gladness she had never believed capable of feeling in her face. She was too full of emotion to do more than squeeze his hand. In any case the waitress was advancing with a tray containing their order. After the meal with which they had a glass of wine—in the circumstances a justifiable extravagance—they went into a nearby cinema, where they held hands in simple pleasure and did not mind being much too near to the screen.

Gillian's happy mood evaporated slightly when Deri had left her and she recalled that next day she was visiting Alec's people. They had been very kind, regarding her as if she were already an extra daughter of the house. She had kept up with them, glad to strain towards anything that had identified her with Alec. Now she wished the relationship with the Trefuss's were less cosy. She could not believe they would be anything but hurt to know she had fallen in love again.

85

Gillian was sure she could not hide the ebullience that was the outcome of everything being right between her and Deri.

To her the two loves were subtly different. What she had felt for poor Alec had been more of a boy and girl relationship. Deri was fully mature, perhaps on account of his tougher life. Gillian realized she had grown up since Alec's death. Consequently her love for Deri had deepened in character. It was not just a young, romantic attachment.

'I love him as a woman loves a man.'

The realization did not shock. Neither did it remind her of how slightly she had thought of the physical side of marriage in connection with Alec.

His parents gave her the usual welcome; thanked her for the small gifts she never omitted to bring. The evening prepared to settle into its usual pattern. Then Gillian experienced a sharp attack of conscience. She could not resign herself to wistful discussion of the dead. She tried not to see the photo of Alec, so prominent a feature of the old-fashioned sitting room. Alec, rather grim and resembling a tailor's advertisement, flanked on either side by bronze statues of Greek heroes wrestling with horses. She never before realized how she disliked the statues. The room, too, if it came to that: coldly oppressive with its aura of grief.

'It's like being in Cheddar Caves where the sun never enters.'

Mrs. Trefuss, Alec's mother, had an air of unrelenting grief, bravely hidden yet always apparent. This in itself was a reproach. His father looked like a man in whom the spark of life had been nearly extinguished. They talked in voices that sounded permanently subdued. Gillian felt such a hypocrite she could not let them go on believing her still part of their morbid sorrow.

"I have some news. I am not quite sure how you are both going to take it," and in hurried, uncalculated words she told them of Deri.

The confession—if such it were—was received in absolute silence. Mr. Trefuss, the first to recover, said:

"It was only to be expected, Gillian my dear, though perhaps not quite so soon. I'm sure Mother joins me in wishing you and this young man every happiness."

She looked at her should-have-been-mother-in-law, now wearing a kind, forgiving smile. Gillian's eyes filled with tears.

"I couldn't help it," she whispered.

"Of course not," Mrs. Trefuss held out her arms.

Tears over between the womenfolk, Mr. Trefuss ventured to remind his wife that supper was probably spoiling in the oven.

Gillian survived the rest of an evening made wretched for her by its social falsity. She knew Alec's parents regarded her as unfaithful to their son's memory. Therefore their present kindness of manner was that much harder to bear.

Was she thinking of marrying soon?

Gillian answered that that seemed highly improbable. Did she detect a lightening of their expressions?

"Come and see us again soon, dear," Mrs. Trefuss begged, as Gillian put on her outdoor things.

"Of course!"

Both knew in reality it would be a long while before she visited them again.

As Gillian walked to Bounds Green station she acknow-ledged that one of the last links with Alec had been snapped by herself. She would remember Trefuss anniversaries, and similar dates: there it would end. She was not sure whether to be sorry—or not. She liked Alec's family and they had done much for her in those first agonising days of loss.

'I wonder how Mrs. Rhys will take to the idea of me?' Gillian speculated.

Theirs did not promise to be a very communicative relation-ship, unless Gillian were prepared to learn Welsh. She reminded herself that it was unlikely that Deri's future would have much connection with Garreg Wen. He would go there, of course, to see his mother and friends. Rhiannon too, or would the girl have too much pride to see her ex-fiancé?

'I am not sure that I would wish it, were I in Rhiannon's place.'

Not that Gillian worried about her ultimate reception in Garreg Wen. She would not be going there probably for a considerable time to come. Meanwhile there was nothing to show for the fact that she had promised to marry Deri Rhys. The omission he hoped to make good at the earliest possible time. First he had to write home and ask his mother to send him the small booklet of savings certificates. She would disapprove, thinking he had cashed enough already. At the same time she could not deny him his own source of money.

The certificates came and he filled in the necessary form for them to be cashed. To buy Gillian a ring from the Shearme allowance was to him unthinkable.

He rang the offices, asking if Gillian could meet him in the luncheon hour, which she did. He kissed her as if it were the most natural thing to do in the middle of a busy London street.

"I want you to come and choose a ring, Gilly. I can't afford all I would like to, but when I make money again, I'll buy you a posher one."

"Nothing expensive is necessary, dear heart. I would be happy with one from Wooleys!"

"I can manage a bit better than that, *cariad*."

"What does *cariad* mean? I don't think I've ever heard the expression."

"Sweetheart in Welsh."

"It's—it's a lovely word."

"For a lovely girl!"

This gallantry was unexpected, but she was finding that he was by no means as inarticulate as she once had believed.

Unabashed, he told the jeweller what he could afford and the man produced a tray of rings within the price range. Gillian hesitated between two, liking both.

"Which do you advise?" consulting the jeweller. He suggested that the amethyst in the platinum setting was rather more unusual. The fit was perfect and he turned tactfully aside to write a bill whilst the young man put it on her finger, kissing her hand when he had done so.

Arm-in-arm they left the shop, mindful that there was no time left for a proper lunch.

"Would Miss Shearme object if you took a bit extra?"

"Because she wouldn't, and because she is my friend as well as my employer, I would rather not be late. We can pop in here for a Whimpy."

"What, me breathe onion all over the poor old maestro?"

"You can have them without onion."

"I guess he has garlic himself," grinning happily as they seated themselves on absurdly high chairs before a counter covered with scarlet plastic.

Hatless as always, Deri saw her back to Shearme's and kissed her more lingeringly in the deserted passageway of the side entrance.

"Goodbye, darling Deri. I do so love my ring."

The addition to her left hand did not escape comment. Everyone knew about Deri and those who had met him liked him. Mr. Birdsall, Roger, Liz and one or two from elsewhere in the office were making rather a noise of celebration when Eira came into the overseas section, surprised that everyone should be crowding round Gillian, thumping her back, laughing, and expressing evident pleasure.

"Let me in on this," Eira's voice was bright.

"Gilly's been becoming engaged," Liz exclaimed. "We're admiring the ring Deri has given her."

"Let me see." The elder woman looked at it, smiled her approval and kissed the girl sincerely on both cheeks. "I am so glad for you, my dear. Deri Rhys is a lucky man."

Eira made arrangements to take them both out to a dinner of celebration, which he would have found embarrassing had she not handed him the money first.

"I know how you would feel, Deri, seeing me pay. You loathed it that time I signed the bill, didn't you? And listen. Buy Gilly flowers or something with the change."

It was a very grand and expensive meal, with accompanying champagne which he secretly disliked but the women evidently did not.

"How much should I tip?" Deri whispered anxiously and Eira told him what percentage would be expected. He muttered something in Welsh.

"More than a man earns in an hour down a mine," having worked out a sum in his head.

Eira explained that even since the Catering Act waiters relied largely upon tips and head waiters often paid to be on the staff of certain big hotels and celebrated restaurants.

"Only enough left for a buttonhole," he murmured under his breath as Gillian went to fetch her coat. Eira wore a stole which she had laid on the back of her chair. She was grateful for this new sense of comradeship which had arisen between Deri and herself during the evening. She had made him use her Christian name, though sure he would revert to Miss Shearme in all official matters. Quite spontaneously he put an arm in one of theirs and the trio walked out to where Eira had parked her car.

"Can you drive, Deri?"

"Why, are you too tight to do it?" he joked.

"I just wondered."

"I have handled Taffy's lorry but you wouldn't call that advanced motoring."

"You have to double de-clutch? I haven't done that since my very first car," and Eira changed gear through the smoothness of syncro-mesh. Her car had a single wide seat in front which took them all comfortably. She dropped Gillian first, waiting patiently while Deri saw his new fiancée up to the flat.

"I haven't been too long, I hope?" grinning as he rejoined Eira.

"Being in love with Gilly suits you," was her only comment.

"It's a lucky bloke that I am," reverting to Welsh sentence building in his enthusiasm.

"Oh, I don't know that all the luck is on one side," Eira observed in a curious tone, which he failed altogether to notice.

She drove on in silence whilst Deri looked out of the window, thinking, she felt sure, of those last precious minutes with Gillian.

Eira bit her lip. "Cigarette, Deri. You'll find them in my bag on the seat beside you."

Without a thought he lighted it and passed it over to her. Mutely she thanked him. Before long they had reached his place. She pulled neatly into the kerb. As he thanked her for having given them such a grand evening he experienced a fleeting kind of tenderness towards Eira.

'I have misjudged her often enough. Let me do the right thing, just this once.'

Aloud he said, "Goodnight, Eira," and leaned forward to kiss her. He could not understand why so normal a gesture of "brotherly" gratitude should have made her voice tremble as she bade him goodnight in turn.

12

ONE SUNDAY, some weeks later, Eira was enjoying her usual, leisurely bath. The morning was chill and foggy, so she played her favourite "escapist game" for disagreeable winter days, recapturing the memory of some pleasant summer scene. She selected Clonea strand, a beautiful Co. Waterford beach with rock formations that reminded her of Borthygest in the Lleyn Peninsular of Wales.

Gillian had been reading; Eira lying back against one of those reddish rocks, watching an Irish family in the water. The smallest member, a boy of perhaps eighteen months, costumeless, played on the edge with his mother; a picture of innocence that could have offended no beholder. Yet the mother had walked him towards the rocky end, apparently so that his nakedness might not be unduly noticed. Eira, who had little preoccupation with bodies, as such, had found it strange and said as much to Gillian.

"Who in the world could *mind?*"

Gillian wondered if it might not have had something to do with the Roman Catholic views on modesty.

"Don't they say that nuns bath in a shift?"

Eira smiled, recalling the conversation and pondering, momentarily, upon the—to her—pointlessness of such a procedure. She and Gillian had both been impressed by what they had seen of Irish family life. The laughing groups on the sands; the shy, nicely-mannered children making their own games without the aid of expensive toys. The young mothers gossiping at their gates or right out in the roadway, heedless of such traffic as passed.

"One child by the hand, one in the pram and one on the way," had been Gillian's observation.

Eira wondered whether the reason for the apparent security of Irish family life might not have something to do with the fact that few married women went out to work. As she saw it, they filled the traditional place of wives.

Heating up the bathwater, she asked herself whether she could be viewing these Irishwomen's lives with a degree of envy.

'I can't honestly say I've ever missed being married,' she attacked the problem quite seriously. 'I like my present life. I have only myself to please in all things. And Shearme's is an interesting job.'

Just lately, though, she had acknowledged a degree of loneliness which had seemed emphasised by the sight of Gillian's regained happy expression.

'Dear God, do I grudge the child that?'

Eira's fondness for Gillian had not changed. Neither was she anything but grateful to see the sorrowing over Alec's death lifted. Such things had to be transitory and were no less sincere because it was so. Eira's inate self-honesty made her twist her mouth into a little grimace.

'Might as well admit that I grudge her nothing in the world—except Deri.'

Almost angrily, she felt with her toes for the bath plug. The happy, tranquil mood which Clonea had induced, was shattered.

Dressing in slacks and a sweater she let her reflections shift to her recent dinner with Basilio Andres. It had been agreed that they should meet, once Deri's initial period of training finished. The maestro had discussed the young man's progress over a delicious Italian meal, for he knew Eira liked continental food.

"Your protegé could not hold his own at an audition, Signorina Shearme."

She had sipped her chianti and asked whether the maestro considered that Deri was cut out for grand opera. The old man shook his fine head, saying that that would involve long study in Italy.

"Yes, of course, Maestro."

"Neither do I think his voice would stand up to the demands on it."

The categorical statement had surprised her, though Andres subsequently gave some of his reasons. He did not consider Deri's to be a voice of outstanding power and in grand opera, the "stamina" counted. The quality was charming but the actual range unexceptional. It was opera comique that would prove the young man's true sphere as a singer. The maestro did not think that all modern musicals called for outstanding vocalists but acknowledged such productions outnumbered those of light opera. The concert platform could be ruled out as a paying career in these times.

He had very strong views about radio and television, saying that to a certain extent they were products of skilled engineers who could amplify the human voice to a remarkable degree.

"A pip-squeak soprano tries to be a second Callas! Tricks! All tricks! Half the time the voice is not properly produced. Of course it does not carry in a big hall or theatre. *Ecco!* We endure *this*," and he had given a mischievous imitation of a "Pop" singer wedded to his mike.

He had gone on to say that Deri Rhys possessed true resonance. He knew how to use the voice God had been bountiful enough to give him.

Eira had Deri's first audition fixed on the following day for a new British musical to be called *Coffee Bar Romantics*. She supposed it would be about the usual touts, tarts and teddies. Not really what she would have chosen for Deri, but he was increasingly anxious to start earning money. If he did not find a job soon, she had an idea he might act misguidedly. Even go back to Wales. The audition was at ten o'clock. She knew better than to offer to accompany him, but asked him to phone her or call in at the offices when he had been heard.

He rang her, speaking in that over-loud way of the person not really very used to the telephone.

"How did it go?" she asked with carefully studied calm.

Laughing, he said the theatre had been full of "kids in jeans."

"My hair was too short and I wasn't dressed right."

"What about your singing?"

"What they wanted was crooners and dancers. The serenade from *Student Prince* proved all wrong."

"Did you feel nervous?"

"Not too bad. But I guessed it was hopeless when I saw the crowd that were there."

She promised to ring Brad Stern. He was a reputable agent with whom Shearme's had a degree of influence. Brad was anxious enough to be helpful and mentioned that Sadler's Wells wanted a baritone.

"Yes, but Deri Rhys is a tenor," Eira pointed out with impeccable patience.

The agent could give him a call for the new Oscar Hammerstein show coming over from the States, but that would not be for about six weeks.

"Put him on the list, Brad."

"Very well, dear," came the silky promise, likely to be forgotten unless she sent him a reminder.

Thanking him, she hung up, then pressed the bell for office girl Poppy, sending her out for the current number of *The Stage*. In it Eira read that Tod Corcoran was sending out a tour of *Chu Chin Chow*, but when she called his offices she was told that the idea had been dropped. The sole outcome of her telephoning was the promise of a hearing for Deri with one of the younger managers. He was casting a revue by "one or two enormously clever people". Ed. Gordon did not know that he wanted a tenor, but if the young man was all Miss Shearme said, an opening might be found.

Eira did not expect Deri to like the idea of her taking him to this private audition but to her relief he raised no objections, even agreeing that she should act as his accompanist. They had a strictly business-like rehearsal at the offices. Eira discarded *The Student Prince*, replacing it by the traditional air "She is Far From the Land", which she considered he sang to perfection and one of the lesser known operatic arias—"I shall again her face behold", in Italian, from Verdi's *The Masked Ball*.

They met outside the Palace Theatre and Eira took him on foot to the audition room up one of the side streets near Cambridge Circus. They mounted a lot of stairs, arriving breathless at Studio 3.

Ed. Gordon was a tall, over-dressed man not quite so young as he seemed at first glance. He had a beguiling but insincere smile and a voice which Eira described as "too U to be true". He was in tight-fitting whip-cord trousers, hacking style coat and a waistcoat of rich claret red with silver buttons. Suede shoes completed the ensemble.

"Hullo, Eira darling. How nice to see you." He kissed her lightly on both cheeks before turning a somewhat critical glance on Deri. "So this is the young tenor?" Ed. Gordon's expression showed slight amusement. No doubt he was criticising the cut of Deri's suit and classifying him as "oop from ta country".

Eira hid her inner anger by trying the piano which she was glad to find in tune.

"We'll have the aria first, Deri," she decided for him.

Deri was very sensitive to atmosphere and could tell the manager was not really interested in his voice. Deri sang less well than usual in consequence. The violence of Eira's final chord was a reminder of this fact.

Ed. Gordon smiled in over-friendly fashion, and stopped swinging his foot with impatience.

"Charming, my dear boy. Have you anything a little less—er—showy?"

"Are you sure you really want to hear a second song?"

Deri knew he was being guilty of rudeness. Eira's averted face expressed private pain. She had not bargained for such animosity between the two men.

"Of course I do." Ed. allowed a touch of reproach to colour his tone and had the satisfaction of seeing Deri flush.

Eira looked at him almost beseechingly and because he wished to please her for having taken the trouble to bring him for a hearing, however unproductive it might prove in the way of engagements, Deri sang—she told Gillian later—"like an angel".

Even the manager slightly revised his opinion of the young tenor who had given a first impression of boorishness. He certainly had the voice. Ed. Gordon did not miss the singers's effect upon Eira Shearme. If a woman Ed. had always considered to be hard-boiled and unemotional could be so affected, what about the rest of the sex? Could not this young tenor be guaranteed to "send" them too?

Ed. began to figure how an improbable type like Deri Rhys might be fitted into a modern sophisticated revue. Romany attire would suit him. Those crisp curls would go well with such a costume and he had a reasonable figure. 'I could ask Treddie to compose something on Victor Herbert lines.'

A little guarded, Ed. observed that it *might* be possible to find what he referred to as "a suitable niche" for Mr. Rhys. It depended, of course, on various things.

"If Mr. Rhys would leave us for a few minutes perhaps we could discuss the matter in private?"

"Do you mind, Deri?"

All smiles, the manager followed up by mentioning that there was a waiting room just across the landing.

Directly they were alone Ed. eyed his companion shrewdly, wondering how much money she would be willing to put up so that her boy-friend might make his debut. For, being the complete cynic, Ed. had decided that Eira was in love with the boy. Quite probably they were living together. 'Chacun à son gout,' he thought maliciously to himself.

Aloud he said: "Shall we come to business, my dear? I have been promised a theatre. Dilys Gregen will star. What a witty comedienne she is, to be sure! We are negotiating for Siddy Hawkins—if those damned I.T.V. people are willing to release him. The book and lyrics will be by the same team as *Sitting Pretty*."

Eira nodded. She had seen that successful revue and considered it both clever and appealing; a by no means inevitable combination.

"There is only one little snag."

"A shortage of backers?" she suggested.

He grinned appreciation of her quickness of up-take.

"I see you are with me so far, Eira."

"Rather what I expected, when you asked Deri to leave us."

"Shall we say a hundred? For a start?"

She gave him a steady, appraising look. It need not be such a bad risk. Ed. Gordon was clever—if anything rather too clever. At the same time she thought it right to point out that Shearme's did not back West End productions.

"Shall we say—a private speculation, then?"

"I don't know, Ed. Honestly, it isn't a thing I could decide —just like that."

The manager quite understood her hesitation. He thought he understood women and had little doubt that ultimately Eira Shearme would be besotted enough to put up the necessary money for her "fancy man".

"Suppose you give me a ring in a day or two?"

She nodded and having shaken hands, went to collect Deri. They walked down the stairs in silence. He could tell from her thoughtful expression that there had been no facile decision.

"Let me take you for a coffee or something, Eira."

"Very well, Deri." She was still frowning slightly as she went into a café where the eternal espresso machine was letting off steam. He ordered, glancing at "goey" cakes which she hastily declined. Plainer ones were produced only after apparent difficulty.

"Mr. Gordon wants me to put money into his revue," she announced, dropping a spoonful of demerara into her coffee cup. "I promised to think it over."

"I know what I should have answered."

She smiled. "Yes, Deri, but you see it isn't quite so simple as that. I have to consider the merits of his proposition. It isn't exactly an unusual condition to impose."

"No backing, no job," he observed succinctly.

"More or less."

"Do you imagine I could agree to such terms?"

"The revue is a fair enough risk financially. His last one had a good run. This is probably to be on the same lines."

"I can't let you do it," Deri spoke decisively.

She looked at the table, with its not very clean cloth and wondered why cheap cafés in England had to be so sordid. Slowly she answered:

"I understand how you feel, Deri. In a way I don't blame you. At the same time there are—ramifications to the theatre business which you have still to learn. One way of landing a job is by influence. That sometimes works better in the case of my sex. Knowing the right people is terribly important. I can give you certain introductions, that is all. Putting up capital is a fairly general open sesame. Let us face it, Deri. Ed. Gordon's revue wouldn't be a bad start for you. And it would be in London."

"Either I am offered a job on my merits, or I quit."

Her eyes expressed alarm. "No, Deri, not after all that has been done for you so far."

"I won't let you buy me a part," he objected.

She sighed. "I didn't expect you to approve the idea. I shouldn't have told you only you would have been bound to find out—if I did invest in the revue."

Her air of tired despondency made him reach across the table and lay his hand momentarily on hers.

"Don't think I don't appreciate all you and the maestro have done for me. I want to repay you—both. But this was a pretty sordid proposition for Mr. Gordon to have made. Or don't you see it as I do?"

"Yes, Deri. All the same I can't dismiss the idea—just like that. I could afford to put in a little money."

"No!" His protest was loud enough to cause several previously disinterested people to turn their heads.

She pleaded with him to speak softly.

"Sorry." After a pause he said that he considered Mr. Gordon "a nasty piece of work".

Eira glanced at her watch and mentioned she would have to go back to the office.

"You won't forget—the revue is off, as far as I'm concerned."

"If that is the way you want it to be." She held out her hand, refusing his offer to see her back to the Jollity Theatre. She had various things to settle before phoning Ed. Gordon to tell him that she was not prepared to invest in the revue.

She did not see Deri again that week . . .

On Friday evening he went with Gillian to her home, having had her assurance that her parents would be sure to take to him. Actually, of course, she wondered if they might not consider her a little callous, having recovered as quickly from what she had felt certain was a cracked, if not broken, heart.

Naturally the Lechmeres were curious about this new fiancé of their daughter's. Gillian's father had thought Alec a little young and callow, but her mother had accepted him as the son she had never had. A Welsh miner sounded a surprising successor.

However Gillian hid private qualms behind a façade of over-brightness.

"Mumsie! Pop! This is Deri."

He could understand that they were reserved in manner. He had heard enough about their devotion to Alec. Deri guessed the Lechmeres thought him something of an interloper and his first meal under their roof was an agony of embarrassment to him. Conversation kept running out and even Gillian could not maintain an air of all-time cheerfulness. The fact that the Lechmeres did not keep looking at him in no way altered his sense of being studied by them.

The rest of the evening was spent before the television set. There was no piano so they could not ask him to sing, which might have been his one chance of personal distinction.

98

"How am I doing, Gilly?" he whispered, just before they parted for the night.

"Splendidly."

"If only I could have sung I wouldn't seem such a nonentity."

"Never that, my darling," she assured him.

Deri smiled, his hands on her shoulders. "You'll not make a social lion out of me, *cariad*."

"All I want is for you to be yourself."

"I'm that all right," and he kissed her gently on the lips.

In the morning Mr. Lechmere suggested that the two men strolled over to the golf links together. The excursion was less unpleasant than Deri had expected and it ended, very properly in his opinion, in the public bar of the *Coach and Horses*.

Conversation had been easier because, as Deri explained later to Gillian, men could always find general topics to discuss whereas women kept returning to personalities.

Mr. Lechmere wanted to satisfy himself as to the sort of person Deri Rhys was. He had seemed unpretentious and genuine. Gillian's father was relieved that no early wedding seemed indicated.

"I couldn't possibly marry until I had something reasonable to offer your daughter," Deri spoke most emphatically.

In their absence Mrs. Lechmere had created opportunities for making Gillian talk about her fiancé. It was obvious that the girl was genuinely in love.

"What did you and Pop really expect Deri to be like?" Gillian asked, a little curious, whilst helping her mother with the beds.

"As your father and I had never met anyone from a mining village, I can't honestly say."

"I suppose you expected him to be common?"

Mrs. Lechmere looked disconcerted. Her daughter rattled on in defence of Deri, saying that he was quite as well educated as Alec had been, though by different schooling.

"I've seen Deri's home, remember. It wasn't at all how either of us imagined. Oh, Garreg Wen is a bit grim—as a village—but it has heavenly hills all round and grass has sown itself on the slag heaps. Besides, I don't suppose we'll ever live in Wales—not that I would mind. After all, Deri is going to become a great singer."

"Indeed I hope so, dear."

Gillian put her arms about her mother pleadingly. "You do like him, don't you?"

Mrs. Lechmere smiled as she kissed her daughter's cheek.

"I am sure your Deri is a very nice young man."

After Saturday's mid-day joint and fruit pie which, with growing confidence, Deri compared favourably with his mother's cooking, they went to the local picture house and had tea out in the town. During the evening two or three friends came round to coffee. Again Deri felt himself an object of close scrutiny. He noticed how they all avoided mentioning Alec.

Deri was quite glad when bed-time arrived.

He wondered if the family went to church on Sunday. Gillian he knew rarely bothered to do so in London and he had fallen into slack ways since leaving home. It was Mrs. Lechmere who suggested a- general attendance of Divine Service.

"Our vicar is rather high church. I don't know if you have objections to that, Deri?"

He said that he had been brought up a chapel goer but that was no reason why he could not attend a slightly different type of church.

"I mean, if Gillian had been a Catholic I would have to become used to the idea, wouldn't I?" and naively he looked to them for confirmation.

Deri at least contributed to the volume of the congregation's singing. The vicar, who had an ear for music and was all too familiar with the limitations of his parishioners, had been quick to notice a new voice. He waited to talk to various people and broke off one such conversation a little abruptly in order to approach the Lechmere group.

"Ah, my dear Gillian, we don't often see you in these parts, these days," shaking her warmly by the hand.

"May I introduce my fiancé, Mr. Deri Rhys?"

The vicar was not taken by surprise having already heard the news from her mother.

"The young man with the ringing tenor voice!" and the vicar beamed. "Perhaps next time you are here you might be press-ganged into singing a solo?"

Deri answered that he would be delighted.

Although Sunday luncheon was cold Mrs. Lechmere was

anxious to put on the vegetables and made the first move.

When the meal was mutually cleared away Deri begged to be allowed to give a hand with the washing up.

"I always used to help Mam."

Mrs. Lechmere demurred then agreed to let the young people carry out the chore between them. They did so with much gay laughter. Then, as the elders liked to rest, went for a walk on their own. Deri said he felt as he used as a kid when he had been let out of school.

"I realise it is all a bit of strain for you," Gillian acknowledged. "It has been for me, too. I've hardly been home since Alec died and everyone probably considers me a heartless baggage."

"Rubbish! The vicar didn't seem at all taken aback by your fresh engagement."

"Mumsie is sure to have discussed us with him. She does quite a bit for the church one way and another. I suppose one has to, living in the place, or take a firm stand—like the owner of Challacombe Cottage—" pointing to a hill on their left, "and never go at all. By the way, darling, you made a real conquest of the vicar. He won't be happy until he has you standing up there in front of the choir singing—"

" 'Oh for the Wings of a Dove'?" suggested Deri, smiling. Then his face sobered. "I would rather have made a hit with your folk."

"I am sure you have, darling: Mumsie and I had quite a chat about you yesterday morning."

"Did she expect me to eat peas with a knife?"

"Of course not!" But Gillian looked guilty as she said it. He laughed. What did such things really matter?

"Your dad wasn't at all unfriendly when we were out, at the same time I can't help feeling—on trial."

"It will be easier next visit," was her cheerful-toned prophecy.

13

THE MAESTRO gave his usual end of term studio concert at which Deri was to sing before an invited audience. With some embarrassment he asked Andres whether evening dress would be necessary. Guessing the young man—and other pupils—might not have one, Andres made the affair lounge suit and cocktail dress: a post war departure unthinkable in earlier times. Deri grinned his relief, adding that he supposed some time he would have to purchase a dress suit.

"Meanwhile," suggested the maestro, with a twinkle, "there is always that admirable firm that hires such apparel."

Both Gillian and Eira were present. Though Andres was always saying there were no longer great voices to be trained, on the showing of his students there were at least some very passable make-shifts. As an outcome of the evening Deri was given an engagement to sing at a social luncheon for members of an organisation similar to the Rotarians. Unfortunately there was no question of a fee, only travelling expenses and a gift of cigarettes, which he despatched to Mr. Pugh for distribution amongst the miners.

"Real posh they are," Deri scribbled on the box.

The maestro warned him about accepting too many such luncheons. True they gave him the chance to be heard but were likely as not to lead to further unpaid work. Any audition to the B.B.C. would be dependent upon at least one previous bona fide professional engagement. This came about through the—for Deri—fortuitous illness of a tenor taking third part share of a programme of operatic music at the Institute for Modern Culture in South Kensington. Andres tried him in several of the arias they had studied together before making a firm choice.

"This time I am afraid it means full fig, my friend."

A little nervously Deri took himself off to the hiring firm and had to admit that the result was good. The fee left very little over, but what it did he spent upon a present for Eira.

"No one deserves it more," he said gently, handing her a small box as they left the Institute together. Gillian had been unable to come as she had gone home to attend the wedding of an old school friend.

Eira was a little curious as she undid the wrappings in the lighted interior of the car. What would the boy have chosen, she wondered? Some impossible brand of scent? A piece of garish jewellery? She felt immediate contrition. Taste, apparently, was not necessarily a matter of education or environment but an inherent or instinctive quality. Some possessed this, and others did not. No training could make one acquire it. Deri had chosen well. A Georgian snuff box, from a second hand dealer even, perhaps, in the Portobello Road. Had Gillian made the suggestion? Eira was inclined to believe not. Deri would have considered it a personal matter.

"It's delightful," she spoke with genuine appreciation.

"I thought it would sort of go with your place."

"It was a sweet thought." She turned, lightly touching his cheek with her lips, ruefully removing, thereafter, the trace of her lipstick. "I ought to take you to task for spending part—if not all—of your fee on myself. Surely Gillian—or your mother—"

"No." He was quite emphatic, implying there would be time enough for them later.

Eira switched off the car light and proceeded to pull out the choke. She told him he had looked splendid in his dress clothes and that she thought he would need to buy himself such a suit.

"A dinner jacket should suffice."

"Wouldn't that cost a lot?"

She banished the dubious note by a quick exclamation.

"Heavens, man, it is part of your professional requirements."

"If you say so, Eira."

She drew carefully out from the kerb and into the main thoroughfare. She asked whether he felt like a drink, and hearing that he did, stopped outside *The Bunch of Grapes*.

"Do you know this is the first time I've been into a pub with a woman?"

Eira supposed it would not have been done in Garreg Wen and that presumably he and Gillian frequented coffee bars.

103

"Happy days, Deri."

"Happy days."

She watched, with a never tiring fascination, the male ability to down huge glasses of beer. The sight of so much liquid put her off; half a pint was her absolute limit. They sat on high stools at a fairly modern bar. *The Bunch of Grapes* was doing its best to attract the newer-type of drinker without altogether frightening away the regular patrons who preferred mahogany, plush drapes, and sticky glass topped tables.

Deri produced "a present from Ireland" lighter which he still carried, though he no longer smoked. Laughing he said that he had been afraid to use it on the *S.S. St. Andrew*, waiting to do so until he was safely through the customs on the other side. Eira smiled. She had seen plenty of those little cheap lighters, some with shamrock on, and rather ruthlessly classified them as "tourist trash", along with Birmingham brassware and china ornaments with the coats of arms of seaside towns upon them.

"I don't seem to have been very successful for you up to now, Deri. I think perhaps you should put yourself fully in the hands of an agent. He might do more. I will have a further word with Brad Stern."

The latter saw Deri, took his particulars down in a bulky book and, after cogitation, asked if his client had any objection to appearing in a "Workers' Playtime" programme.

"I'd sing in the street, if the fee happened to be right," was the assurance.

Brad produced the engagement, which was at a Bubble Car and Scooter factory in the Midlands. Deri was given first class travel, but chose to use second class and pocket the balance. He had never gone first in his life and saw no reason to begin. A works' car picked him up at the station and drove out to the industrial perimeter of the town, turning in at the gates of a huge "E" shaped building. There was a courtyard in front, with grass beds a-riot with flowers in the normal season and a huge dolphin fountain forming a roundabout in the centre. An extremely cubist group of men toiling flanked each side of the entrance steps on the central block. He was led past a billiard room and a "wet" canteen, through the "floor" of the massive factory itself, where the clang and roar of machinery made Deri wince. They climbed more stairs and crossed over to the central part of the "E" where the canteen was situated.

Deri was taken to the partitioned-off end of the room which served for the artists' use.

Introductions were perfunctory. Two Lancashire comedians, a soubrette who also did a whistling act and a saxophonist.

The accompanist, a world-weary little man, thumbed through Deri's music—carried in the leather case Gillian had given him as an engagement present—tossed aside what he considered unsuitable, leaving two hackneyed musical comedy pieces and an encore ballad.

"They like to join in the chorus here."

"O.K.," Deri answered, agreeable to anything.

He was not quite prepared for the clamour which, despite the announcer's extortions, accompanied the preceding turns. Shifting feet, scarcely subdued talk, giggles and coughs. As Deri mounted the platform he was aware that four hundred bored, even hostile faces were turned upon him.

"Another flippin' vocal this week," a fitter was heard to remark in the front row to be frowned at by the charge hand beside him who suggested that "the poor s——" be given a chance. Whistles greeted the opening bars.

"Come on, ducks," encouraged a woman in one of the canteen staff caps.

Deri had never known such acute nervousness as at that moment. Nor realized the thoughtless cruelty of what—in a less democratic era—would be termed his own class. White overalls with the works' insignia stretched for row after row right back to the half visible end of the canteen, where a couple of youths played darts. Bang in the centre of the front row were two expressionless men in lounge suits—presumably from the managerial side.

Taking a deep, steadying breath, he began to sing. Gradually the rustlings died down somewhat and he felt he had at least their half attention. Applause, a little luke-warm, was whipped up by the announcer-compére, who nodded to the pianist to strike up the next number. In a gesture of defiance, Deri took the song off the piano "desk".

"I'll sing something different," he whispered as, without any pre-thought, he faced a more interested audience. Interested simply because they could see the look of annoyance on the accompanist's face.

"You don't want any more of that stuff, do you?" Deri asked them.

Cries of "No!"

"I would much rather give you something from my own land. *Molawd Cymru*—'Praise of Wales'—which we used to sing going down into the mine. If I might just have a chord—"

The rest was drowned by applause which only stopped on the promised chord. Standing absolutely still, Deri sang to them from his heart. The reception was so great that he had to follow on with 'Song of the Flood' (*Cywdd y Dilw*). Still they did not want him to stop. The announcer looked anxious; the accompanist helpless.

Deri smiled at his audience, now loving him as he had not been loved since he had sung to his own people in Garreg Wen.

"I appeal to all those of you who also come from Wales to join me in *Hen Wlad Fy Nhadan?*"

Soon the splendid sound of "Land of My Fathers" was heard, as the whole of the works shuffled to their feet to stand at attention.

The announcer, recovering his aplomb, spoke hastily into the microphone. "After that grand national anthem anything must feel a bit of an anti-climax, but we still have one more turn. Flip Right and his sax."

Chairs grated back, talk resumed and a hot, perspiring young man with startling red hair wooed them back from the world of beauty to that lesser artistic one of rock, boogie, and cha-cha.

Two or three people slipped out at the back and the darts match—suspended only whilst Deri sang in Welsh—crashed back into being.

Deri was putting his music soberly back in his case, wondering what had made him do this impulsive, revolutionary thing. He did not in the least regret his conduct. Someone tapped him on the shoulder and greeted him in his native tongue. His hands were wrung by a dark, hollow-eyed man in whose cheeks the bright colour of happiness blazed.

"Oh, it was good to hear those songs again, *bach*. I am from the Rhondda Valley myself."

They were still talking when the accompanist came back, reproachful of eye, pursed up lip.

"You certainly pulled a swift one on us, Mr. Rhys."

"I am sorry. No, damn it, I am not in the least sorry!"

"It was wonderful man. You don't know what it meant to the Welsh boys here."

"Are there many?"

"About a hundred."

"Then it was worth while."

"I'll say it was. Now can we give you a drink?"

Others were waiting with equal excitement to carry him off with them for what remained of the luncheon break.

"Extraordinary fellows the Welsh," one of the suited gentlemen in the front row was heard to remark, as he walked towards the exit.

"I couldn't agree more, Mr. Ffaulks," Rather hesitantly his companion added: "But you must admit it went down very well."

"Quite so. Now about those brake linings—" Conversation was put resolutely back upon works' topics and the playtime concert forgotten for another week.

Back in London that same evening, Deri phoned Gillian and told her of his rebellious conduct. He sounded excited, almost a little drunk with it all.

"If you could have seen the face of that chap at the piano!"

"It was rather naughty of you, darling, but I am glad they all enjoyed it."

"My first cheque, Gilly. Think of it."

She supposed that in Ballykenny and at the Institute of Modern Culture he had been paid in cash. She agreed to lunch with him the next day when he would be coming into Shearme's to pay his first commission on the loan. Eira did not send for him—as he had half expected she might. Truth to tell she was closetted with an important client at the time. Deri was surprised that he should be disappointed.

Gillian was outside the Jollity as arranged and while they ate heard all about the concert.

"I wrote a long letter to Mam last night."

"I expect she will be pleased. Then won't she have listened-in to you for herself?"

"I never thought to let her know!" he banged his head with his bunched fist. "There is a scatter-brain I am!"

This was a new, rather puzzling Deri and Gillian wondered —uneasily—if it could be the one Rhiannon had known better than she did.

Eira had news of the factory concert when Brad Stern rang her to say that young Rhys had behaved very unconventionally, but that everyone had loved his singing. Eira, who had begun to think him changed to a conformist, was secretly elated that he should have shown such spontaneous judgment of his audience by identifying himself with them in such a way.

"All the Taffys are clamouring for a return date for him," Brad added, jokingly.

"I wouldn't like Deri Rhys's individuality to be ironed out," she said slowly. "Don't you agree that it would be rather a pity?"

Brad began to talk of further work. Did she suppose he would go to an audition for provincial panto?

"Deri as 'Puss in Boots' or something? I can't quite see him in that line, can you? Still, send him an admission card. We can't afford to turn down anything reasonable at this early stage in his career."

The manager thought enough of Deri's voice to put in what he called "a solo spot" during the ball scene of *Cinderella*, which was what was to be produced. Opening week in Brighton, then up to North West England. The money was good and rehearsals shortly would be starting. Since Deri was only engaged to sing one "Pop" number he would not be needed until the final stages were reached. The contract signed, he decided to run down to Garreg Wen and see his mother, whom he was conscious of having neglected. This time he went by train, telling himself it was quicker.

He rather hoped he would not have to see much of Rhiannon. She knew of his engagement to Gillian. He had felt impelled to make that fact clear to her. He had no idea what his mother would be thinking about it. She had set her mind on a valley girl for him. The Garreg Wen Halt stationmaster greeted him with reservation, being a relative of Rhiannon.

"Are you staying long, Deri *bach?*"

"A day or two only."

The walk to "Cartref" seemed longer than usual, and he found himself wishing he had persuaded Gillian to accompany him, which she had been shy of doing.

His mother, still in her hat, greeted him in stoic silence. Neither did she talk over the meal she had so lovingly prepared

108

for his welcome. But she listened to all he had to tell her, alternating between pride and alarm for him.

"And this English girl you wish to marry. Why has she not come with you?"

"Gillian felt it was better not."

Mrs. Rhys bridled. Was she then ashamed of his people? Were they not good enough for her in the valley?

"It isn't that way at all, Mam. You have seen Gillian. You should know."

"I forget her," the old lady murmured, not quite speaking the truth.

"Really Gillian was scared of meeting Rhiannon again. How is it with her?" He found himself having to think for the right Welsh words now that he was no longer speaking it from day to day.

"She does not discuss you with me."

"Will she expect me to see her, Mam?"

Mrs. Rhys shrugged, unwilling to commit herself.

The faithful Mr. Pugh and one or two others were quick to call round to hear of Deri's London adventures. Soon the old piano was being played, the music previously dug out of its plush-covered stool and piled on top. They clamoured for their old favourite, "The Foggy Foggy Dew", which Deri always sang with a touch of humour, because there was something about that song that appealed particularly to him.

He saw Rhiannon next morning in chapel. She nodded her head gravely to him then looked pointedly down at her hymn book. He felt his face redden up to his ears. The urge came to speak to her, if only to reassure himself she had no hard feelings. So he hung back after the service, signing to the midwife—a close neighbour—to walk back to Glendower Road with his mother.

Rhiannon came out at last. She seemed to him thinner in the face and more subdued in manner. He called to her softly by name. She started, as if she had not known he was there.

"Rhiannon, you can't send me back without a word."

She raised her eyes to his, her expression grave but not— he was relieved to find—tearful. "What is there for us to talk about any longer? Your singing?"

"Oh that—" he made an angry little gesture. "I must know, Rhiannon, if you have forgiven me."

The slightest of smiles touched her lips. It came to him

that her mouth was sensual compared to that of Gillian.

"I thought it was I who broke off our engagement," the girl observed in the same unruffled fashion.

"Yes, but I was the one to fix up with another sweetheart. Oh, Rhiannon, please say you aren't still angry with me?"

"Angry? No, Deri. Perhaps it was never meant to be between us. Sooner or later your singing would have taken you away from me. You don't belong here any more either."

He looked down at his shoes, knowing the full truth of what she said. How loving a place and its people was not in itself enough for him. He had gone away from Garreg Wen only to stand, unsure, at the crossroads between the old and the new life. As yet—he belonged not wholly to either place and the thought saddened him.

"I hope you are happy," Rhiannon was saying in that unbearably brave little voice of hers. A voice as clear and true as its owner.

In that moment he almost could have forgotten London, Gillian, the career upon which he had finally started for one forgiving look from Rhiannon. He stretched out his hand in a hopeless gesture which she preferred not to see.

"Goodbye, Deri." Still outwardly cheerful she turned and walked away from him so that he should not witness the tears that filled her eyes.

Swearing with an all-but-forgotten coarseness he made his way down the hill, wishing it were an English and not a Welsh Sunday so that he could lose his identity in the companionship of some public house. Instead he was forced to walk soberly back to his mother: the cold Sunday joint and tart of bottled fruits which she would have slipped into the oven immediately after the service.

14

DERI WAS oddly depressed as he came on to the platform of Paddington Station in a cheerless fog which made him turn up his coat collar against the weather. He hated hurting people and it seemed to him he had hurt Rhiannon. He did not know quite what he had expected from her. In a foolish sort of way he had supposed that she would have been just the same as formerly towards him. He saw now his stupidity; that he understood less than ever about women. Why should he be glad that she was not going with Goronwy Evans, Dai Price or one of the other lads? There could be no blame attached to her if she had been doing so. It might have made him feel less guilty.

He swore expertly and disappeared into the entrance to the tube.

His digs, when he reached them, seemed as cold and unwelcoming as the day.

"So you're back," was all the lady of the house said to him.

"Yes, I'm back," he answered, hesitating, as if he meant to catch the next train bound for Wales.

"Phone message for you from a foreign gentleman."

"Thank you." He picked up the written slip and found that Basilio Andres had cancelled the next lesson, being laid up with influenza.

"Poor old chap," Deri exclaimed, wondering if there was anything he could do for the maestro. To have ordered something from a store would not have occurred to Deri. So, stopping only for a wash and to toss the few things from his case into his chest of drawers, he set off again, buying a bunch of luscious black grapes from the fruiterer's nearest the Andres residence. Pia, the faithful, opened to him and clucked in pleased surprise. She called out in Italian to the invalid and a weak voice answered from the gallery bedroom above them.

"Tell Deri please to go. I can't have him catching this devilish germ of mine."

"Speedy recovery, Maestro," the visitor shouted back, to be drowned by a fit of coughing from the sick man.

"He sounds bad, Pia." Deri was all concern.

"It is not good with him, Signor Rhys. But—God willing—" and she crossed herself automatically. "He be well soon."

After a few minutes' conversation with her, Deri made his return journey, conscious of increasing tiredness. He knew Gillian would still be working, but could phone her to see if she were free later in the day. Roger-the-Dodger took

111

,the call and made some flippant remark that Deri could not quite hear as Roger's pudgy hand was clamped over the speaking piece of the receiver. Presently Gillian answered in what Deri regarded as her office voice. She seemed to have expected him on the following day and happened to be going to a theatre with Eira that evening.

"Enjoy yourself, *cariad*," he said, trying to be cheerful of tone. They made a luncheon date for next Monday, when Gillian told him that the show had been very enjoyable. Had he had a nice time in Garreg Wen?

"Not particularly," he admitted. Yes, his mother was well. After thought he added that he had an idea she was wearing a new hat. Gillian only just prevented herself from asking if Mrs. Rhys ever took it off her head. Maybe the old lady had what used to be optimistically spoken of as a "transformation".

Garreg Wen was not the same, Deri went on to remark. He could not quite see where it had changed, just that it had.

"Sure it isn't you, darling?"

He gave a quick smile, nodding. Gillian was longing to ask about Rhiannon and wondered if he would mention her, which he did, looking very puzzled indeed. Gillian began to have the uneasy feeling that he still might be the least bit in love with Rhiannon.

'Perhaps after all she is the right girl for him and I am not. Probably Rhiannon understands his nature far better than I ever shall, since they're both Welsh.'

Gillian realized that Welsh or Irish, both temperaments were foreign to the English. As if guessing something of what was passing through her mind—she had never been good at hiding her feelings—he reached out his big hand and let it close over hers.

"I don't love anyone else but you, Gilly. It's just that— I suppose I don't like having let Rhiannon down either."

Gillian could have reminded him that it was Rhiannon who had released Deri and not the other way around. They talked more cheerfully about different matters, including his rehearsals for *Cinderella* which would soon be starting. Gillian was sorry to hear about the maestro's indisposition. Deri said:

"I am keeping in touch with his studio."

"You're very fond of Signor Andres, aren't you?"

The question was weightily considered. "Next to Mr. Pugh, I like the maestro better than any man I know."

Basilio Andres recovered slowly but the illness had taken much out of him and made the giving of singing lessons an irksome task through which only his strong will carried him. Deri was frankly shocked when he saw his teacher. The Italian's dark eyes were sunk back into their sockets.. His olive skin was sallow and he still had a tiresome cough.

"Would you rather I didn't remain for a lesson, Maestro?"

"No! I must stop being sorry for myself," and the slender hands played a few chords on the piano as if searching for notes.

Later the young man lifted a sheet of music from his case.

"This is the song they have given me for the pantomime," handing over his professional copy of a number with the succinct title of "Sugar".

The maestro made an uncomplimentary comment in Italian, sighed, then played the opening bars. Both men were relieved when the end was reached.

"I do not think that will overtax your vocal powers, my young friend! If only Schubert or Mozart could live again today there might be hope for the world of music."

Deri's previous knowledge of rehearsing had been confined to the amiable gatherings of the local amateur operatic society and the short period during which he had been fitted into the cast at Ballykenny. At Garreg Wen everyone knew everyone else and Mr. Pugh had taken them lovingly over the scores. It had not greatly mattered much if a member were late. Also it was an ordinary sight when half the men put on their pit safety helmets and left the hall for night duty.

In Ballykenny the set-up had been very similar. Even if he had not known the people when he arrived, it was impossible to remain long in Irish company without becoming absorbed into their welcoming hospitality. And perhaps the best part of those rehearsals had been the subsequent adjournments to O'Reilly's Bar!

Professional rehearsals he found quite different. The call was for a stated time which was intended to be kept. Apart from being a stranger, he was not even "a theatrical". The cast regarded him a little suspectly, aware that he was a complete novice. The man taking the part of "Buttons" was

113

the first to bother to speak to Deri. This early middle-aged actor, caught in France when it was overrun and kept there under surveillance as a civil prisoner, was marvellously funny on stage and serious enough off it. He gave Deri a friendly smile and asked if he were the bloke landed with that damn-awful song in the ballroom scene? Indeed Freddie went out of his way to introduce the young singer to others in the company, at the same time saying to him:

"You mustn't mind if you seem a bit out of it at first. We've been rehearsing for several weeks and quite a few of us meet up in panto most years. But I can tell you a new face is a real pleasure—ain't it, ducky?" giving "Cinderella" a playful slap on her seat as she passed them.

Deri, shy of girls, was surprised that they showed they thought him attractive. That he might be, never troubled him. Interrogated, he would have admitted that making love to Rhiannon within certain prescribed limits understood between them. That these same limits were unsuitable technique for Gillian he had accepted in advance, because she was "different" to himself. He would not have wished to displease with the rougher, bucolic ways to which he previously adhered. There had to be a keeping in check which, because he loved her, was not always easy.

Deri had no idea, of course, that fundamentally Rhiannon and Gillian were by no means as different to one another as he believed. That Gillian did, in fact, consider him rather slow. Certainly Alec's caresses had been of a far more advanced kind. Therefore she was half amused by what she took to be proof of Deri's shyness. Once or twice she had had qualms that she ever would be able to ignite his passion. Then a hasty retreat on his part, a certain trembling of the voice, would reassure her.

Some of the *Cinderella* cast found Deri so unforthcoming as to be inexplicable. They knew him to be engaged but that need not have rendered him incapable of outside appreciating. One of the dancers, "a hot little number" according to "Buttons", determined to test Deri's reactions. As she said to her friends, it was not normal for any man just to be polite and pleasant to females. "One of these days I'll find out for myself!"

It took until the opening week in Brighton to make this opportunity. Sitting beside him during breaks for food, accidentally tripping so that he must catch her for safety—all these measures proved useless. So she decided that the walk from the theatre to the back street hotel demanded an escort. She let it be known that one of the teddy boys had followed and annoyed her.

"I'll see you back, Jen," Deri offered, instantly gallant.

Of course when they reached the hotel she thanked him, standing closer than he found good for his morale.

"You're very sweet," she whispered, pressing her body against him, her chin tilted upwards and her eyes greedy for him in the half-darkness.

Deri was, after all, human. He caught hold of her roughly and kissed her hard on the mouth.

"That was nice," she told him, "but you're a bit of an amateur in that, too, aren't you?"

"What do you mean?" suddenly angry.

"You may know how to sing, darling, but you don't know the first thing about kissing a woman."

He emerged from the lesson with several prize illusions about the sex shattered. He did not know what to say to her so stood, looking very doubtful. Jen laughed, put a hand to his cheek, and gave it a playful pat.

"Young, aren't you, boy? Goodnight. Sweet dreams!" She blew a kiss and disappeared into the shaded entrance of her hotel. He remained to mop his forehead, then a grin broke over his face as he wondered what on earth Gillian would think if he tried out the new technique with her.

"She'd give me back my ring and she'd be damned right!"

He decided that henceforward Jen was to be handled with extreme care. He would see that he was never left to be her sole escort. Once having "tried him out", as it were, she lost immediate interest, and turned her greedy eyes upon one of the dancing boys. Deri was not required to walk to the hotel with her again.

Gillian, who still intended to visit her Cork relatives at Christmas instead of going home to what she described as "a dull as dishwater celebration", could only come down to Brighton on an evening train and return by the last one up after the theatre. She had almost no time with Deri, who in any case seemed to be surrounded by other people. She gathered briefly that he was quite liking the pantomime

115

experience and that he was now on the friendliest terms with the company.

"I thought 'Cinderella' rather a pretty lass."

"If you're trying to make out anything, you'll be quite wrong. Her husband plays the double bass in the orchestra." Rather virtuously—Gillian thought—Deri announced that most of the girls had regular boy friends.

"No fun, darling?"

"Not much," laughing as he saw her up to Brighton's crest-of-the-hill station.

Eira came down mid-week. Deri did not know in advance, but thought he recognised her car outside one of the hotels. He was trying to make up his mind about this when she came out of the entrance.

They shook hands and Eira said she felt like stretching her legs after a better-than-usual timing of the run from town.

"Must be the 'Clearways' that are such a help. Well, Deri, how are you liking it? And are you still in what the maestro calls 'good voice'?"

Doing a Whittington when they reached the Portslade end, Eira suggested a cup of tea together. She knew that he was likely to have something before the performance and her own hotel dinner was on the early side, according to local agreement which permitted hotel and boarding house residents to eat in comfort before any of the cinemas, ice rinks or theatrical performances began.

"I like panto least of any form of entertainment," Eira confessed, refusing a pastry.

"Then you are being exceptionally noble to want to come."

"Even as a kid I was disenchanted because—dare I confess? —I never believed in fairies, only in people."

He wondered why that admission should have made her look so sad.

"I don't care much for panto either," Deri told her. "The first I saw was in Cardiff, when I was frightened by the robbers. It must have been *Babes in the Wood.* Did I tell you I had a greetings telegram from the maestro for the first night? Oh, and of course yours. And the one from Gillian."

"None from home?"

"I don't think they would think of such a thing."

His expression told her that in Garreg Wen the telegraph

service would be confined to grim tidings of death or perhaps, on occasion, of marriage and birth.

"Wires mean a lot to one's prestige in the theatre, don't they? I hope yours are pinned up in the dressing room."

"There isn't too much space. You see I share with the Ugly Sisters."

This made her laugh, as he had intended it should. They parted company for the time being and she said she would be round after the final curtain.

She listened, as always, with deep pleasure to his singing, deploring the actual song, of course, but liking him in white wig, silk coat and knee breeches. The audience encored him, for which the conductor was nightly prepared. Also a reprise of Deri's solo had been worked into the finale. During the grand entrance of the company at the end he gained a high share of the general clapping.

As Eira rose from her circle seat in a theatre not so very dissimilar from that in Ballykenny, she thought again of the way in which Deri had chanced into her life. She had watched his constant development both as a singer and as a personality. With a wry smile she acknowledged that it was the man rather than the voice which now mattered to her, but it *had* been the voice—just at first.

'Curious I should love him.' It was consolation of a sort that he was no longer so ready to quarrel with her. In his way he might even be becoming fond of her. 'Always with reservations,' she reminded herself, shutting the case which held her opera glasses.

She was no longer actively jealous of Gillian. Even less of that little Welsh former sweetheart of his, Rhiannon.

Eira asked nothing of Deri for herself. She admitted the absolute impossibility of his coming to regard her in any other way except as a friend.

'And by God I've worked for that, too.'

15

EIRA SPENT the sort of Christmas an unmarried woman, without close relatives, usually did. That is to say she had hospitality on both days from long standing friends. An uncomplicated and yet not very satisfactory way of enjoying the holiday in an all-adult world where everyone felt—as she was beginning to do—that the work and expense of Yuletide festivity had become a social duty instead of a personal inclination. They ate more than at any time of the year and drank with proportionate unwisdom, feeling faintly stupid as they pulled crackers and sat about in paper caps.

She tried not to recall, too nostalgically, those home Christmasses of her childhood and adolescence, with a ceiling high decorated tree in the corner of the sitting room and exciting packages waiting to be opened. The parties she had attended and, later on, the rather foolish flutters beneath the mistletoe where hearty young men had kissed her. And those war years, where Christmas had achieved especial poignance and regained—for its Duration—something of the religious significance.

Her paper hat askew, a cigarette drooping at the corner of her mouth, she tried not to think of the past; even reviewing it, as she was, in the over-replete solemnity of after teatime on Boxing Day. She felt that perhaps of all her Christmases the most vivid remained the war ones, where a group of people on alien combat duty, had created their own fun out of very little. The enjoyment had been all the more sincere for being coupled with the relief of not hearing "action stations".

There was no denying that the present childless Christmas had an emptiness which, at any other date in the calendar, she would not have chosen to dwell upon. It was ridiculous to sit, making half-attentive conversation with her friends whilst one half of her mind was occupied with Deri. How he was enjoying his Christmas in theatrical digs.

The answer, as she might expect, was "not very much".

Not only was he lonely, but intensely homesick for Wales. There was a quality about the perfectly simple fun and feastings of a Garreg Wen Yuletide that he missed acutely during this, his first absence. All the women of the valley would have had weeks of preparatory cooking before they stooped, uncomplainingly, over kitchen range or gas cooker, basting the birds, and rising to assure themselves that the great fruit-black puddings had not boiled dry.

He recalled his mother, in her very best hat, drawing the carving knife, sharpened to a stiletto's narrowness down the years, across the bursting breast of one of Farmer Evans's best turkeys. A while after his father's death Deri had ventured to ask if he should take over the carving? Mrs. Rhys had said, with her curious brand of dry humour:

"You're not old enough, boy."

The previous year Rhiannon had been there and his big foot had sought hers under the table so that she blushed all rosy. People had come in and gone again. Endless cups of tea had been made and successions of sandwiches cut. Then he had walked home with his girl in the frost-laden crispness, his arm about her waist. In the darkness they had stood close together and kissed.

Deri sighed, running a hand through his curls, trying not to blame the landlady for the indifferent meal she had served and the air of bother she had made it seem. Oh, the company had done its best. Drinks in the dressing rooms. A good deal of indiscriminate public kissing and exchanging of presents. But everyone was glad that Bank holiday meant two performances at the Hippodrome.

"It's the kiddies' laughing faces I always love to see," Deri's friend "Buttons" remarked in the wings, before going on to inveigle the audience into singing a silly song which even a moron could not help learning with the aid of a sheet upon which the few, repetitive lines of the lyric was displayed.

Standing by for entrance, Deri wondered how Gillian was enjoying herself over in Eire. He had had a letter, duly stamped with the face of Mr. Guinness, saying she had found her first experience of air travel uneventful. (They had exchanged presents before she left). He would have liked it if Gillian could have rung him, but perhaps that was difficult. To his surprise, Eira did, between the two houses.

"Not too miserable, I hope?" she asked, her voice clear and business like. He was in the cramped quarters of the stage doorkeeper's office and the latter's heavy breathing made an odd accompaniment to the telephone conversation. Yes, Eira was with friends.

"It was nice of you to phone me," he said, with something rather emotional in his voice.

Eira laughed and it would have touched him to know that she was keeping back the tears.

"That your girl friend?" asked the interested doorkeeper.

Deri hesitated then, grinning, answered that he could call it his female-boss.

"Christmas isn't much cop when you're getting on in years," was the dour observation and Deri immediately began to feel decrepit.

"Damn the man," he muttered to himself, climbing the stairs to his dressing room. Once there he let his glance linger on the photograph of a South Wales bus, which a crowd from Garreg Wen had hired in order to see his panto. They had come up on a day's excursion the previous week; his mother, Mr. Pugh—everyone who mattered but not Rhiannon. He had asked after her, rather self-consciously, and been told only that she was quite well.

"Breaking her heart over you, Deri *bach*," Mr. Pugh had hinted, but whether in levity or seriousness it was impossible to tell.

This quick visit—they had travelled back straight after the show—had somehow made Christmas the more cheerless to him when it came. Especially as they had brought little gifts.

Definitely Gillian was the one who had much the best time. Though she was no regular churchgoer it had seemed perfectly natural to accompany her Cork relatives to Midnight Mass. She had found it beautiful and inspiring. On Christmas Day there had been plenty of children about the house and Gillian had been kept constantly busy, either helping in the kitchen or playing games. In Irish fashion they sat up till some impossible hour and it occurred to her that she had had quite a lot to drink without any ill effects. They had slept a bit late on Boxing Day and after lightish lunch, exchanged various visits in the vicinity, walking from house to house, well-wrapped against the weather. She was conscious of the sheer weight of charm around her and of having laughed immoderately at native wit.

That they could joke about themselves so readily never ceased to surprise her.

"We have to," she was told, "to sense a seriousness beneath the bantering tone.

They were all very interested in her engagement and the fact that she had met Deri originally upon Irish soil.

"You'll be after bringing him with you next time, I hope."

"If he isn't working."

That work could be a bar when it came to enjoyment elsewhere was dismissed with an airy shrug. She had to laugh yet again at this attitude of mind.

Certainly she was sorry to leave from Shannon; especially as the flight was direct to London instead of the Midlands, where Deri was appearing.

As scheduled the pantomime ended on the last Saturday of January. By no means all of the company had further engagements. One or two were off "to Rep", the Gingham Girls, Speciality Dancers, bound again for the ever-dwindling field of variety. A few people hoped for advertising "Spots" on I.T.V. or work in films. Neither prospect seemed to provide stability of employment.

"Buttons" took Deri across to *The Golden Fleece* for a final beer together. Perched on a high bar stool, the comedian spoke of the future with his accustomed seriousness.

"It wasn't so bad before the war, when there were still a number of concert parties functioning. (Those that exist today hardly require counting on both hands). Then one started rehearsals in good time for the Easter opening, which didn't leave so many weeks 'out' in the meantime. But now—" he sucked in his cheeks reflectively.

"Have you nothing in view either, Freddie?"

"Oh, West End managers are falling over themselves to engage me? Didn't you know? Actually I am going to inflict myself on my old mother. She lives in an alms house in Winchester. That surprises you? I'll do odd jobs for the old folk whilst I am there. Painting. Fixing door catches. Handiman Herbert, that's me. I'll read the jolly old *Stage* each week and waste valuable money on postage to agents and managers. If I am lucky, I might find someone on the radio who wants a 'feed'. Otherwise there is always demonstrating. 'Can I interest you in our new carpet cleaner, madam? It removes simply everything, including the piles.' " He went on for several minutes in the same brand of middle-low humour. Then his alert, sensitive face relaxed. "The next milestone is the Ideal Home Exhibition. The money's good, Deri boy, the hours peculiar and the products we have to push are more peculiar still. Do you know an actress—I won't tell you her name, but you probably wouldn't have heard of her anyway—who used to tour with Sir Frank Benson was grateful for a job in one of the cloakrooms at Olympia last year?"

"There are times when I become frightened about the future."

Freddie smiled. "You're luckier than I am, laddie. You have a voice, whilst I—well, let's face it. There are enough comedians and to spare. No one wants soft-shoe dancing these days and my style isn't all that original. Still, damn it, I do think up my own gags."

Knowing that this man had made people laugh over his nimble antics and comic expressions, Deri was genuinely astounded that work should be so hard for his friend to find.

"The summer does offer alternatives," the latter continued. "The land, if you're soil minded. Flogging deck chair tickets in London parks or down beside the sea. That is, if you don't want a job at one of the holiday camps. Mind you, even that is likely to be behind the bar rather than the footlights. If panto shouldn't materialise, one can usually put in a couple of weeks or so at the post office, sorting Her Majesty's mails."

"I would never have thought of that," Deri admitted.

"Ah, where you come from, dear boy, I suppose it's just a case of Gwenny-the-post putting the letters in order before 'humping' them round the valley on her bike. Or does she walk up and down the blue hills of Wales?"

"She walks up and rides down," laughing a little. "Another beer?"

" 'I don't mind if I do'," in perfect imitation of 'Colonel Chin Strap'.

The girl behind the bar called Freddie "a fair scream". The two men left a few minutes later, as the darts' board was occupied and neither cared for shove-halfpenny.

"Well, this is the parting of the ways," and Freddie held out his hand. "I hope we meet up again sometime in the same show."

"So do I," Deri answered and meant it.

He travelled down to London next day, delighted that Gillian should be at the station barrier, her face eager with searching. He waved as he swung along the platform whistling just as he used to do coming off duty from the mine. They went into the refreshment room, more because it was a place where they could talk than that they wanted a coffee. Gillian listened eagerly to all he had to tell her.

"You've let me do all the talking, *cariad*," his tone was reproachful. "I haven't heard a word about your holiday."

This subject lasted them until the waitress had slapped a damp rubber square on their table, obviously expecting them to move, since they had not collected a second trayload.

"By the way, Eira wants to see you. She suggested tomorrow evening at her place. No, I am not going to be there, darling. She wants to talk business."

He presented himself after telephone confirmation and Eira noted that tidiness that went with the wearing of a better tailored suit. His ties, too, had become quieter as a result of discreet guidance. He never minded being told about things; on the contrary, he was almost over-anxious to learn. He had flowers for her with him. She found this thought of his touching.

"Nice to see you again," he exclaimed and she really believed he meant this.

"Come along in, Deri. There is nothing elaborate, I am afraid. Help yourself to a drink. I just have to put last minute touches to a sauce that I couldn't make until you were actually here."

In a man's fashion he wondered why women always had to rush to the kitchen directly guests arrived. Mam was just the same, bless her.

Eira joined him momentarily for a sherry. It was the brand she had liked in Southern Ireland and Gillian had brought back with her.

"We won't talk business until we've eaten, Deri. You may help carrying things, if you like."

"You know I do." Warmed by the sherry he gave her arm a friendly squeeze.

The meal was elegantly served, which fact he still only half appreciated as being the result of a good deal of trouble on Eira's part. He ate with an unsophisticated relish she

123

was pleased to see. Nothing, she thought, was more dismal than left-overs for consumption next day. He spoke cheerfully of his landlady's indifferent cooking. At best it had bulk to recommend it.

"Perhaps you have put on a little weight," looking at him judiciously.

He laughed; the merry open laugh which so pleased her.

Eira decided that the pantomime had done him tremendous good. He had lost the last traces of awkwardness and assimilated most of the theatrical terms, though not always used by him in their right context. She had bought him in Caerphilly cheese—personally she found it insipid—and Danish blue for herself. He insisted on helping to dry the dishes, while they waited for coffee to percolate. She had cleared most of the cooking paraphernalia in advance.

Watching her put away, he spoke of "Buttons". Not only did Eira know Freddie by name but she had seen him on the stage. In fact before the war he had toured for a while in one of the Shearme musicals. She said:

"The trouble with Freddie is he was never really *London*. He is all right in the provinces. Makes a good dame, when he isn't doing the 'Buttons' type of part. But don't you agree that his effects are largely achieved by pulling comic faces?"

Deri had not been educated up to first hand theatrical criticism but now that she had drown his attention to the point, he agreed. Freddie was largely as she had said when it came to being the professional funny-fellow.

"He is a nice person," Deri spoke with simple dignity.

Eira made no direct reply. Instead she remarked, "Now we must talk about your next step on the ladder of fame—"

"Shouldn't it be 'the ladder of love', or weren't you meaning the song?"

If not scintillating wit, at least the remark showed a lighter touch in conversation. Deri was improving in that direction as well as several others.

"I thought your foot was pretty firmly on *that* ladder already," she answered, smiling.

He came forward to light her cigarette.

"Don't you ever long for a smoke, Deri?" she sounded curious.

"Sometimes," carefully blowing out the match. "Do you

124

know the maestro once made me stand in front of a lighted candle and let out my breath evenly enough not to make it flicker? I suppose you haven't heard how he is?"

"Oddly enough I ran into him at Chappells last week. He didn't look at all well to me."

Deri frowned. "I am afraid that illness took more out of him than he knows. I wonder, couldn't he go south at this time of year?"

"Maybe he can't afford it though for a singing teacher I imagine he does pretty well."

"I must let him know I am back in town."

She nodded, turning the conversation adroitly back to his career. She was afraid that he had missed the call for the new Oscar Hammerstein musical through being away at the time. Shearme's were not having any fresh shows "on the road" for several months.

"When we do cast again, I am sure I can fix you up all right."

"What you say goes, I reckon."

She thought: 'three months ago he would have meant that sarcastically'.

The point that troubled her was whether or not a hall should be taken for him and recital given. Another artist— probably an instrumentalist—might be found to participate.

"Ask the maestro what he thinks, will you?"

Before the matter was decided one way or another the tenor in *Princess Paula* was taken ill with sudden appendicitis. The understudy had gone on but the management wanted a substitute sent immediately. Excited, she rang Deri's place, found him out but finally located him at the maestro's.

"Listen, Deri, do you remember anything of your old part of 'Ivan Nicholai'? If not, can you study it in the train to Lincolnshire? I've said I'm sending a first rate tenor, so you won't let me down, will you? It may only be for ten days or so until the regular man has recovered. Are you still there? I've checked the trains. You have time to go home and pack, if you take a taxi. Charge it up as expenses. Do you hear?" Repeating the station and the departure schedule, she wished him luck. "Ring me when you've made your first appearance and let me know how they like you."

Excitedly he received the old maestro's subsequent congratulations.

"My old part! Isn't that luck!"

"What I believe is called a piece of cake, *si?*" Andres watched the young man bundle music into his case. The maestro's face was still drawn and he had to remember not to let his shoulders sag.

"*Arrivederci*, my young friend."

"Not *arrivedera?* That means ' 'till I see you again', doesn't it, Maestro?"

For some reason Signor Andres did not answer.

16

DERI SAT in the corner of a second class compartment mouthing over his script. Whilst it began to come back, he was aware that in the main he was having to learn afresh. The music was more easily remembered, also he had sung the solos during the intermediate months. It was simply a case of picking-up again his various places of entry elsewhere in the score. His concentration flagged a little and he found himself wishing that he saw more of Gillian than he did. Between them, they had a habit of one being busy when the other happened to be free. He could not help thinking how excellent it had been in Garreg Wen with Rhiannon almost always at his pleasure in their hours of freedom.

He wondered how much notice to take of Mr. Pugh's latest letter which had stated that she had begun to go out quite regularly with Goronwy Evans, who had been taken on at the Prydwedd Road Mine, which was just beginning to be re-worked after years of neglect.

Deri knew Goronwy to be a nice, decent lad—somewhat younger than himself. It was good that Rhiannon was not bidding fair to remain unwed simply because she no longer had Deri's love. He hoped, indeed, that she was beginning to find similar feelings towards Goronwy. And yet—could it be that Deri felt the tiniest tinge of jealousy?

'That is absurd, man,' he reminded himself sharply. 'You

don't love the girl any longer. Would you padlock her against seeking a successor?'

No, of course not! Still it did seem to him that perhaps after all Rhiannon had not cared as deeply for him as he had been led by her to believe. Could it be that all women were, as the Duke in *Rigoletto* maintained, fickle of heart?

'Not Gillian,' he told himself firmly only to recall the fact that she was supposed to have been cherishing a permanently extinguished torch for Alec, her late bridegroom-to-have-been. Yet she had fallen into Deri's arms with what appeared to him genuine cries of gladness.

He shook his head, wondering gloomily if men were the true and faithful sex.

" 'So, you would send me away from you, Princess—' "

He turned a page in the script with a feeling of sleepiness which slowly caught up on him. In another moment he had succumbed . . .

Having changed at Nottingham, he arrived eventually at his destination, unmet, and having a taxi straight to the Grand, hoping to find someone from the company there. The stage manager was about and after looking at Deri vaguely, recalled that he must be "the London tenor".

Things were—the stage manager explained—somewhat in a state of flux. The understudy would be going on for the evening performance and since it was late afternoon, would Mr. Rhys like to have a meal and then report back at the theatre?

"The best thing would be for you to sit in front tonight and see the production. A general call had been posted for ten o'clock tomorrow morning. If you are all right after rehearsal, I assume you take-over tomorrow evening. By the way, where are you staying?"

"I have no idea," and he explained, "I simply hopped into a taxi and here I am."

The other's expression suggested that whilst it should have been someone's duty to see to accommodation, Deri must not expect feather-bedding conditions on tour.

"Better try the *Gainsborough Arms* in Spittal Street. Just round the block—" he was proud of having been to the States in the cause of the theatre and liked to use an occasional American term, to emphasise a personal familiarity with that sizeable continent.

Deri thanked the tubby, bald headed little man, picked up his old-fashioned grip and made for the hotel, a commercial one, gloomy on the outside but of a moderate, beery cheer within the revolving doors. He was given a small room on the first floor and told he could have high-tea right away.

'Shades of Ballykenny,' he thought, saying he would be down directly he had had a wash.

The meal over, he went back to the Grand, was introduced to such members of the cast as were not occupied in their dressing rooms and taken to one side by the musical director, who put him through a quick catechism. The producer had not yet come into the theatre. Deri met him during the first interval, when he appeared, like a genii from a trap door, to stand with beckoning finger in the entrance of the stage box into which the abashed young tenor had been shown.

"Rhys? Are you word perfect?"

"Pretty well."

"Can you ad. lib where you are not?"

"I guess I might." He tried to sound accustomed to a thing he had never—in practice—done.

"Think you are picking up the positions?"

"They seem the same as we had at Ballykenny."

"Oh, yes. I suppose they would have used our production—in the main." The speaker, a tall, cadaverous man, did not want Deri to run off with the idea that this was a carbon-copy performance of Shearme's marked book for the piece. "See the rest of the show and be at the call in the morning. *Adios, amigo.*"

(The producer had had a holiday in Spain that year).

The rehearsal was stiff, but everyone was helpful and Deri did not feel he would make too bad an impression. The leading lady suggested that they went through their scenes together after a luncheon break.

"You'll do, Deri boy," she announced, at the end of this session.

"I am awfully grateful for all your help—Miss—"

"Call me Pam. We're a friendly crowd, as you'll find."

Everyone set out to help him over any small, awkward moments in the evening's performance and from the first he had a tremendous reception for his singing.

"Barry isn't going to like this one bit, poor darling," Pam informed him, laughing. "Shouldn't wonder if it gave him a relapse. No! on second thoughts, it will speed his recovery."

"Is—er—this Barry person in a local hospital?"

"They took him to the Greyfriars Memorial one."

This told Deri precisely nothing since he had seen only the station at which he arrived, the theatre and the streets immediately between that and his hotel.

Next day was the mid-week matinee, played to a half empty house. He learned that two of the company had been along to see their sick comrade who, it appeared, might not be out of hospital quite so soon as he had hoped.

"Adhesions or something, darling," one of the girls told Deri with a stage person's vagueness of matters not directly connected with the theatre.

He had written a quick letter to Eira, who had replied, on Shearme notepaper, evidently dictating in the office. She was glad he had fitted in so well and had a good reception. She knew he would be sorry to hear that Signor Andres had again "taken to his bed".

> 'There was a short paragraph in the morning paper.
> I rang the house and it seems he is rather seriously
> ill again.'

From his hotel, Deri himself put through a call to London to find the maestro's housekeeper voluble but largely incoherent. The Signor was allowed no visitors. All very quiet—she pronounced it "quite"—But she would tell him Deri had enquired after his health. She was sure the Signor would be pleased.

Deri's mood was saddened by thoughts of his loved singing teacher but he did his best not to show the fact in his work.

'I'll sing in such a way as he would be proud of me,' Deri vowed. The almost ecstatic volume of applause seemed its own answer.

"What's up, ducky?" Pam asked. She had attached herself to him in a friendly, uncomplicated fashion in which he was relieved to find no elements of danger. She was a serious-minded girl, not much interested in men and perhaps, for that reason, a little cold in her singing. 'Competent' was the term that most readily occurred to managers engaging her. Just because she was so reliable and free from quirks of temperament she found herself more regularly in work than some of her sister artists: many with greater gifts than her relatively modest ones.

Deri explained about his old singing master's illness. Pam gave an appreciative whistle. To have studied with Basilio Andres was not the luck of everyone.

"How ever did you manage the fees?" her question had a directness robbing it of possible offence.

"Shearme's backed my period of training."

"Aren't you lucky! All I ever had was the local L.R.A.M. in Puddledock-on-the-Ouse followed by a term or two at the Tripe Shop."

"The Tripe Shop?"

Laughing, she named one of the London centres where singing was taught. He looked a little shocked.

"They call it that because most of us only could afford twenty minute lessons and the professors had three pupils regularly to the hour."

"Your voice has done pretty well on it, Pam."

"You needn't be nice about my singing, ducky. I know my limitations. No good above B flat. Can't do a proper shake to save my life. Still, I suppose I do just about know how to punch over the average number."

"Without the support of a mike at that," and he laughed in his turn. Finished work, they walked up to the dressing rooms together. Hers was opposite to his and as he had carelessly left the door open when he changed for the last act, she followed him in, to glance at Gillian's photo, which was propped amongst his make-ups.

"That the girl-friend? . . . Nice . . . lucky, aren't you?"

"Naturally I think so," and his eyes softened as he looked at Gillian's face.

"You're attractive to women, you know. Or—didn't you know?"

"I don't think I've ever thought about it," he confessed.

"It will be a great standby in your work, but it may cause you a spot of trouble, too. Ever heard of Carl Brisson?"

"Just about." He recalled that Eira had mentioned the late dimpled Dane in the same regretful tones of loss she expressed over Jack Buchanan.

"Brisson was in a show once—*The Apache*, I think it was. Oh, before my time, thank God, but I've heard them talking.

130

The women went mad about him. Mobbed him outside the theatre and generally made life difficult."

"Sounds as bad a treatment the teenagers give these Pop people like Elvis the—"

"These weren't just teenagers, though," she smiled. "How would you like to climb across the roof of the Grand, with a crowd of dames howling for you in the street?"

Having said this, she gave his shoulder a good natured pat and retreated to her own dressing room.

When he came into the *Gainsborough Arms* the porter-cum-everything told him there had been a phone call and that the party would ring again just after 11 p.m. in the hope of catching Deri. There came a tinkle.

"That'll be it, I expect, sir."

Unfortunately the hall landing kiosk door was broken. In the hours when the bar functioned, private conversation had become difficult.

The porter picked up the extension on the reception desk, flicked a lever on the small switchboard and indicated that Deri was to take his call upstairs.

"Hullo?" he did not know why he should have sounded nervous. Perhaps he was tired. Or it may have been that he had the same feeling about long distance telephoning as Garreg Wen people did in the matter of telegrams.

"Eira here. Listen, my dear, I am afraid I have bad news for you—"

"Not—the maestro?"

Back in her London flat, her body bare (from bathing) beneath her housecoat, she suffered for him as she broke the facts of Basilio Andres's death. Pia had let her know earlier in the evening, but the morning papers had already indicated that he was "sinking rapidly".

"I never saw today's paper," Deri was saying, as if that were vitally important.

"There it is, my dear. I know how much you—venerated the old man."

"I loved him." There was no sense of sentimental shame in such an admission. Many, many pupils had felt precisely the same.

"I don't suppose there will be any hope of your being able to attend his funeral."

"Oh, God. The funeral!"

She heard Deri's voice break. 'Poor boy,' she thought. For he was that still, in so many things.

"There is sure to be a memorial service. Perhaps later on? Anyway, the—other—is bound to be within the next few days. Golders Green, I suppose," her voice dropped as she remembered the services she had attended there, including that for her own father. "You don't know how long you will be with the company?"

He told her that Barry was still in hospital and in view of things, it was unlikely he would be allowed to appear for at least another two weeks. There was talk of a short convalescent period. The producer thought Deri would probably do the next two dates: Hull and Blackpool.

"Would you like me to go to the funeral in your place, Deri?" Even hating them, as she did, she readily made the offer and it did not seem in the least unnatural that this should come from her instead of from Gillian.

"I would be most grateful."

"Shall I see about flowers, too?" She knew Deri would want them sent. "Any special kind you would like?"

Panicking, he said he would leave the choice to her. She would know so much better what was suitable.

"But I would like you to say on—on—the card that goes with them—how grateful I am for all he has taught me."

"I'll do that for you, my dear."

The pips went for the second time but he did not appear to have noticed.

"I can't believe that the maestro has gone."

"No. It must be hard for you. I wish I had known him better myself. He was a very great teacher."

"*The* greatest," Deri said gently, then, feeling unable to speak any more replaced the receiver without having said goodbye. But he knew that Eira would understand, as indeed she did, lighting a cigarette and sighing to herself as she did so.

Deri stood quite a time in the phone kiosk, not moving, just staring into space. With a last effort, he made himself, vacate it and went along to his bedroom. Still rather dazed he undressed, washed and did his teeth, to kneel then—as he had since childhood—for his prayers. When at last he pulled the bedclothes across his body he was aware of coldness and experienced a half formed wish that he had taken a bath before retiring.

132

'Poor old maestro,' he whispered, and tears collected in his eyes to slide down his cheeks. He made no attempt to prevent this upsurge of Welsh emotion.

Deri had not, in fact, cried since he had been a little fellow, standing with his Mam at the pit head and seeing the blanketted body of his dead father brought up from Prydwedd Road Mine after the 1946 explosion. A year or two before its closure until the re-opening during the present period.

17

THE FUNERAL of Basilio Andres was not at any of the London Crematoria but at the Roman Catholic church of Holy Mary, which was nearest his residence. A point Eira realised she should have anticipated. She did not consider it necessary to go on to the cemetery for the interment, which followed the Requiem Mass. She had no opportunity to do more than bow to the one or two people she recognised. The maestro had had many friends as well as pupils. Yet she was quite surprised when, a day or two later, his housekeeper, Pia, rang to say that Signor Andres had certain wishes regarding Deri Rhys.

"My master think much of young man to sing. He wish leave him memento."

"I am sure Mr. Rhys would be most grateful to have some small thing after the maestro. I know Mr. Rhys was very fond of his teacher."

"Sì, sì."

The woman babbled on in her quaint English and Eira gathered that Deri was to select what he liked from amongst the fine collection of operatic and other scores.

"I will write and tell Mr. Rhys, asking him to phone when he is back in London," Eira promised, rather glad once her voluble caller had said goodbye.

Deri had another week to fulfil after Blackpool, as his principal would not be back until Bristol had been played. Being so close then to South Wales, Deri decided to spend one night home to ensure for himself that all was well with his mother. Apart from a tiresome cold, she seemed much as usual. But it was evident the loneliness was beginning to tell upon her. Now that extra men—redundant elsewhere—were coming in to the district with the re-opening of the Prydwedd Road Mine, he suggested that she should take a lodger.

"It will be a little extra money, Mam."

Her face hardened, for she saw in this a retrograde step. Yet she knew he was perfectly right. Now that they were making a singer out of her son it was no good thinking he would be wanting his old room kept empty. He could not as yet send her much money. There was that Miss Shearme to be re-paid.

"I could ask for someone," Mrs. Rhys admitted, without enthusiasm and he bent to kiss her, happier in the thought that she would have someone to look after again. That was what she had been used to all her life. Up to her marriage, it had been brothers: then her husband and son. And now, no one, unless she took in another miner, as many who had a room already did.

"How is Rhiannon, Mam? Not married yet to Goronwy?"

"The banns are being called in chapel quite soon."

Evidently this time Rhiannon did not intend to wait. He wished her only well and if he should meet her and Goronwy in the short time he was there, he would say as much.

Mr. Pugh came round and sat hunched uncomfortably on the piano stool, as he always did. What he had to tell about the mine was not good. He felt many of the old workings to be in a dangerous condition.

"In fact there is not enough coal to be worth the worry of bringing to the surface. They should never have closed the Garreg Wen one, boy."

"We wanted the mines nationalised," Deri pointed out, "and now we have to put up with the changes. In London no one seems to burn coal. All is electricity or oil." He glanced across at the brightly burning "nuts" in his mother's grate. Better stuff by far, he hazarded, than found its way to some of the coal merchants.

"They are all too busy in London, I suppose?"

Deri nodded. As always he was interested in hearing the local gossip, though he was himself removed from its immediacy.

134

"I hear Rhiannon is having the banns put up shortly."

"Yes."

Mr. Pugh was not very communicative on the subject.

"It is—all right? I mean—" Deri blushed, because he was not quite sure what he *did* mean.

"You know Rhiannon."

Mr. Pugh was perfectly right to sound reproving. The idea that there should be expediency about the marriage was absurd.

"I didn't mean anything more than that I hoped it wasn't on the rebound."

"No, Deri *bach*. I think she is genuinely fond of the lad."

And in that cussed way of a young man Deri was not sure whether to be glad or sorry. He did not see Rhiannon or her betrothed, but whether they kept out of his way, he could not tell. Having impressed upon Mr. Pugh that he was to see that Mam found a decent lodger—and as soon as possible— he caught the next train back to London.

Eira had gone to Paris to see a French musical for which Shearme's had been offered the English rights. On impulse she had taken Gillian with her. After all, Paris was a very lonely place for a woman without travelling company. They flew over and stayed at one of the smaller hotels to which Eira had been recommended. She did not profess to know Paris more than moderately, though she had been several times. It was Gillian's first time and she was all starry-eyed. Eira smiled a little ruefully, then decided she was being sour and showed Gillian just as much as could be managed during the short time they were there. The latter's French, being indifferent, did not allow her to understand much more than what was rudimentary. Apart from an occasional line or two or dialogue, and enjoyment of that peculiar sad-gay music that was so characteristic, too, of London's *Irma la Douce*, Gillian did not consider herself able to pass any judgement upon the show Eira had come specially to see. But the audience laughed a lot and several songs lingered in the mind. After, they had left the theatre and wandered into one of the many cafés.

"Like it?" Eira, who had obviously understood a great deal more of the entertainment, asked, stirring her hot chocolate, while Gillian was having a *café mélange*.

"Very much. Are you going to take it on?"

"I have a conference about terms with Monsieur Duprez in the morning. Do you think you could find your own way about for an hour or so, Gilly. We could meet up at *Les Deux Matelots* for an *aperatif* about noon. If you should be there first, order." Smiling she added that she did not advise a Pernod at Gillian's more tender age. "It's quite potent, believe me, and I would probably find you telling the story of your love-life to *le garçon*."

Gillian quite enjoyed window-shopping in Rue de la Paix and walking along the Champs Elysées, under the warm, appraising stares of passing Frenchmen. The first day she had found this mildly embarrassing.

"In Italy they pinch your bottom," Eira had told her, laughing.

Gillian felt quite brave, even bold, as she sat in *Les Deux Matelots*, waiting for Eira, who was less than five minutes' late.

"Oh, how these Frenchmen talk!" she ordered a *fin* for herself. It transpired that a satisfactory agreement had been reached and *Madelon* was now added to the list of Shearme Enterprizes. "I don't very much want to go back to London yet, do you, Gilly? Ah! I see that you do! I was forgetting that your Deri is due in from Bristol. The show's run hasn't been too bad for him, as it was only in the way of a stop gap. I did wonder if they would keep him on—but I suppose both Barry and the understudy have contracts that it would be difficult to break."

Shearme's only dealt with the leasing of a particular show to a specific management; not the drawing up of contracts for the cast, though under Equity rules, these probably did not differ greatly, one from another.

"I am very pleased with the way Deri has done," she said gently, a 'disc bleu Gaullois' alight at the corner of her mouth. "Did I tell you that the maestro wanted him to have some vocal scores?"

Deri went to the studio to choose these, sad at its emptiness of personality now that the things were piled ready to be sold. It seemed that the maestro had had no near relatives surviving and his instructions had been that the faithful Pia should keep what she wished and dispose of the rest. It was understood that she wanted to return to Italy, where she had a married daughter living. The studio had been a leasehold property and was now destined to be pulled down in a re-development scheme.

Deri packed such scores as would be of use to him in the small case he had brought and accepted, too, a photograph of Signor Andres, which the heartbroken Pia pressed upon him. He had not seen Gillian since she came back from Paris but was meeting her that evening. There was much they would have to tell one another.

As Gillian greeted him she thought he was looking tired, even a little discouraged. She could not quite understand why he should have taken the maestro's death as deeply, but supposed it to be a sentimental side of a singer's make-up which she, as a more or less unmusical person, could not appreciate.

"It was good of Eira to go to the funeral on my behalf," he remarked.

Gillian looked frankly surprised. For some reason this had not been mentioned. She knew Eira disliked funerals in any case.

"Did she go?"

"Yes." He glanced at Gillian's parting lips. "Why, was it wrong?"

"I would have gone for you."

"I don't think either of us thought of that. Eira rang me in Lincolnshire to say the poor old chap was gone and as she knew I couldn't leave for London, said she would stand-in for me at the service. Surely it is nothing to make a thing about, *cariad*."

Gillian's face cleared. She knew she was being femininely unreasonable. Not that she was jealous of Eira where Deri was concerned. Gillian rather airily concluded that people of Eira's age did not have love affairs. Anyway Eira had never seemed the type. All the same, as Deri's fiancée, Gillian thought that if anyone had to represent him at a funeral it should be herself.

"Darling!" Deri's soft voice protested with her.

"Sorry, I was just being stupid."

"You were a little," he agreed, smiling at her. They were at the flat she shared and though one of the girls had popped in to pass the time of day, they were now alone. "Chaperoned-by-remote-control," as Gillian once termed it.

He asked about the Paris trip, evidently amused at the idea

of her and Eira frequenting the alleged-wicked metropolis on their own.

"I hope none of the Frogs made passes at you, darling."

"And I didn't have my bottom pinched once."

"Were you expecting to, then?" He looked a little shocked at this idea.

She burst out laughing, remembering in time that Eira had said that was Italy, not France.

"I don't know, really I don't," and he scratched at his head.

Gillian left her chair and popped a kiss on his cheek, saying she was going to make tea. He heard her talking to Liz— he thought it sounded like. When she came back he had the radio on softly and was listening, in his spellbound fashion, to a recording of Gigli.

"Oh, if I had a voice like his," Deri whispered.

Gillian had to admit that her fiancé was still wonderfully unspoiled. Eating a thick slice of the not-too-good cake she had bought, he talked of his home visit and how glad he would be when he heard his mother actually had a lodger in his old room.

"It isn't good for her to sit alone and brood. I am sure she does not eat enough by herself."

"What woman does, darling."

"Mam looked much too thin."

Gillian tried to recall Mrs. Rhys but as usual found it difficult to think of anything much except that she was wearing a hat in her own home. Gillian did have a vague impression of a birdlike face and spare frame.

"Did you see Rhiannon?" the tone sharpened a little at mention of her old rival.

He shook his head, his mouth too full of cake to answer. When he had washed it down with a long draught of tea, he mentioned about the banns, seeing instant satisfaction set in on Gillian's face. It occurred to him that she really was jealous of Rhiannon.

He was about to tell Gillian how absurd she was being when an imp made him play up a little, as he enlarged upon Goronwy's good fortune.

"I believe you still hanker after Rhiannon for yourself."

"It could be—" then, seeing her aghast expression, he relented. "Do you really believe that, darling?"

138

"Well, she is from your precious valley and she is Welsh. I am neither."

Deri moved from their only large armchair and knelt beside her, resting his arms on the elbow of her seat, as he regarded her with big, serious eyes.

"You know, Garreg Wen and everything there—except Mam, of course—belongs to another world."

Gillian's eyes filled with tears, so moved was she by his simple declaration.

"I couldn't go back," Deri went on gently; "whatever happens, I can only continue forward. With you—at my side."

18

EIRA WAS arranging for a London production of *Madelon*, which the Shearme Enterprises had so recently acquired from Paris. It was possible that there might have to be a short provincial tour owing to those long-standing successes which limited the number of West End theatres that might fall vacant. The situation, as someone said, was equivalent to airliners having to keep flying round the air ports until permission could be granted for them to land.

As sponsor of the production she considered that she should have a reasonable say in the casting. Certain names were necessary and few shows could hope to succeed with no star whatsoever. She was in entire agreement as to the choice of the leading lady, a part demanding frivolity with some real acting and the ability to create a specific style of café chantant singing. Several comedians came up for discussion and here again Eira was prepared for easy agreement. Beside the more minor characters, that left the bass-baritone "heavy lead"—and 'Marcel'.

She sprang her little trap at the casting conference by saying that she had someone in mind.

"Yes, Miss Shearme?" attention was polite and she had an amused feeling that they were humouring her.

"It's a young man who has already had touring experience—"

"But not London?"

"Not London," she agreed, smiling with great amiability. They were up in the green room of the Jollity Theatre at the time and the air was thick with the smoke of their several cigarettes.

"Deri Rhys has a quite remarkable tenor," Eira went on, smoothly confident in manner. "In fact we thought enough of his voice to provide a short period of tuition under the late Basilio Andres." (She could see this made its mark). "He is Welsh and therefore could pass for a Frenchman."

"Can he act?" the producer's tone was—from experience— dubious.

Eira smiled with assumed sweetness. "Isn't that something for our producer to find out, gentlemen? I saw the Paris 'Marcel', who sang scarcely at all but had tremendous charm. Deri Rhys can sing like an angel. Charm? I don't know— appeal to an audience, very definitely. At least you will agree to have him along for audition?"

There could be no dissent upon that.

Eira thought the whole thing sufficiently important to drive round to his place of residence that same evening, a thing she had never previously done. She found it—passable: fair to middling for the money. For herself, she would have considered such a place depressing, still realized that her minimum standards of comfort probably were a good deal higher than his. He had been away quite a bit, and she supposed the digs good as any of their type. It would have to serve until such time as he and Gillian gave active consideration to marriage. Then possibly they might come to some agreement with the girls who at present shared the flat with her, taking over from them for their two selves. Eira was not anxious to see Deri finally committed to Gillian for in some strange fashion just as long as he remained free Eira felt she had at least a small claim upon his friendship. More than that she had long since ceased to expect.

Deri was plainly perturbed by her unannounced arrival. Primly he explained that lodgers were not allowed to entertain members of the opposite sex. She dismissed this as absurd— at six o'clock in the evening. Besides, her visit was purely a business one. Still, if he thought it less compromising, he could leave the sitting room door ajar. After hesitation, he closed it.

"Listen, my dear, this may be your first London engagement," she told him, having briefly sketched-in the details. She had no worries about his singing. The songs were not difficult. "You and Gillian did see *Irma la Douce*, didn't you?"

"You gave us the tickets," and he smiled. "Very shocking it was," lapsing into Welsh syntax.

"Don't be stuffy," she chided. "It is purely a matter of how the thing is handled."

"Oh, I agree it was in perfect taste. Still to make a musical about a prostitute—"

"Wasn't *The Dubarry* that—more or less?" Eira argued, seeing his shrug. "*Madelon* isn't another *Irma*, if that is what you fear. It has quite a respectable story. What I meant was, it was the same type of music as Marguerite Monnot's."

He nodded, waiting, with a St. Bernard-like patience for her to continue. She explained that what she was a little troubled about was how he would manage the dialogue. It was quite unlike the steady, prosaic sort of stuff that he had done up till that time.

"I would like you to let me coach you a little, Deri, before the audition. After all, I saw the Paris production and though I suppose the English one is bound to differ greatly from it, at least I have a first hand idea of the lines on which 'Marcel' should be played."

"I am entirely in your hands."

She smiled, glad he had been so amenable. She did not want the arrangement discussed—even with Gillian. A stipulation he personally considered unduly cautious on her side, but had no option save to obey.

"I don't want it known outside this room that you've been coached," she went on. "I want you to give the impression of—having arrived at the right ideas yourself."

"I can only do my best, Eira."

"Good enough." She made arrangements for him to come to her place the following evening. A moment only he hesitated. It was obvious that he had been going out with Gillian.

"Say you have a cold," Eira instructed with sudden curtness.

He came exactly at the time she had said and found a simple meal ready for him. She would not allow his help with

141

washing-up, she was anxious they should go straight to work. For the best part of two hours she led him relentlessly over the lines, upbraiding him for stiffness.

"Quicker, Deri. Much quicker."

At one point she flung the libretto down with a cry of vexation, reminding him that he was supposed to be in love with the girl.

"Good God, man, is that how you talk of love to Gillian?"

Blushing furiously, he said he did not really know. Eira had him kneeling beside her, hoping that in trying to act he might achieve something approaching what she wanted.

"You love me madly," she prompted, working now with her mind, oblivious even to his nearness of which at any other time she must have been so intensely aware. "You are doing your damnedest to make me sleep with you—"

"Eira!" he moved away, abashed.

Her impatience with him grew. Could he not leave personalities out of it?

"I know I am probably the last person in the world you would want to sleep with, Deri, but you're not Deri now. You're 'Marcel', the *Blageur* and I am the not-so-cold-really Comtesse."

Under her tuition he began at last to put meaning into the lines. Her excitement increased. If only he could lose the last of his self-consciousness—

" 'You are divine, enchanting, perfectly adorable and'—" suddenly he broke off, embarrassed all over again. "I can't do it, Eira. It doesn't sound like me."

She sank back, closing her eyes a moment as the energy drained out of her.

"It's all right, Deri. I've been too demanding for the first run through. Go and put the kettle on. I've cut sandwiches."

He came back presently with a tray which, she noticed, with affection, he had taken pains to make look nice. She was composed again, the inevitable cigarette between her lips. They drank their tea almost in silence, She could see he was more tired even than she. Three—no, four days—was all she had.

He looked at his cheap watch—Eira longed to give him a nicer one—but guessed he would be offended, since he had bought it himself, probably in Cardiff.

"I ought to be going."

"Yes, Deri. The same time tomorrow."

The next night it was better. He worked with a dogged, impersonal determination as again she took him over each intonation and inflection. She had made only hot soup for his arrival and for later a bigger plate of sandwiches together with cake.

"Let me put a spot of Jamesons into your tea," she suggested, pleased with his greater acting progress.

"You still have some Irish whisky?" he sounded amazed.

"Sure I have!" with laughing mimicry.

He sipped, nodding approval. "I've only had tea with rum in it before. Isn't that what they call Irish coffee?"

"I think that is cream and sugar actually in coffee, plus a mighty whack of whisky. A 'jigger' of it, is what they say on the tea towel I bought in Dublin."

They worked again the following evening, simply at the lines, though the occasions when she pulled him up were correspondingly fewer than during the previous session.

"You see, Deri, you can do it."

"With you to make me," he agreed, smiling, his hand on her arm. "Sometimes I wonder why you take all this trouble, Eira."

"Call it—belief in you," she answered, twisting away from him in sudden fear he might read the truth in her eyes. Nothing, she reminded herself, would be more humiliating than to have Deri pity her love.

The final evening together began with a certain tension. Truth to tell he had had trouble with Gillian, demanding to know the reason for his evasiveness.

"I shall begin to think you're with another woman," she had said and only just in time he had prevented himself from answering "only with Eira". At any rate they had quarrelled and Eira guessing as much, promised to release him from his silence directly Monday's audition was safely past.

"Will you be there?" he asked, suddenly anxious that she should be. In a sense he was a child, needing the comfort of his nanny.

"Better not, my dear. I might make you nervous."

"I rather think you would give me a feeling of confidence."

"In that case—perhaps," smiling non-committally.

She had made him walk through rough positions. He held

143

the script in his hand but did not consult it every second, as on the first evening. He had made an effort to learn some of his part. This he found a great help. They came to the love scene and Eira surprised him with her acting ability. She broke off a minute to laugh.

"Bless you, my dear, I have been in and out of theatres ever since I was a nipper. Though I have never actually played a part, I have seen enough actresses in my time to know at least a little how it should be done. 'Ah, Marcel, what a fortunate coincidence,' " her voice changed to that of the woman anxious to bring the young man to her pretty feet.

As she had intended Deri forgot this was Eira. He began to let himself go, she had hoped he might, and took her in his arms quite convincingly.

" 'You are divine, enchanting and, any—' "

"Kiss me," she prompted, her voice a caress and he found himself holding her closer still as their mouths met. Eira closed her eyes, aware that it was, of course, only make believe, but the sole time Deri had put any meaning into his kiss. Perhaps he did not notice her response, or he may have put it down to sheer acting. When he released her he was unprepared for her wet lashes.

"Eira! Have I offended you? I forget everything except the part."

Not trusting herself to speak for a moment, she nodded, then, directly she could find her voice again, told him she was pleased with his handling of the scene. But she felt his eyes, curiously speculative, still on her face.

He went to the audition on the Monday, having on her advice, spent the Sunday walking out in the country with Gillian and not thinking about his part. There were several other applicants to be heard. This Eira had not been able to prevent. He looked round for her but did not see her, so concluded she had not come. He was told to try one of the songs first and handed the M.S. sheets to the unusually jovial looking accompanist. (The English version of the score was not yet back from the printers).

Deri faced the little group of influential men with that feeling of gloom inseparable from all auditions. He did not know, of course, that Eira had slipped in at the back of the

144

Phoenix Theatre—where the trial was being held—and was almost literally praying for him to sing his best.

The pianist played the final chord with a flourish.

Someone out in the gloomy auditorium spoke.

"Thank you, Mr. Rhys. We are taking dialogue a little later. Next, please."

A tall Scot with a small but quite pleasing voice was followed by one of those soft-throated Irish songbirds in the Count McCormack tradition and two or three rather indifferent people, probably choristers of an opera company and as such, admirable, no doubt. But as soloists they stood little chance of being engaged. Deri thought the Irish tenor probably had a lot to recommend him but did not much fear any of the others.

They began all over again with the dialogue, taking the entrants in reverse order. As Deri's turn came he had every reason to be grateful for Eira's tuition. He could almost feel her still beside him, prompting, indicating, correcting. He did not know that he was over that part of his ordeal far better than the rest.

An elderly man sitting in the second row of the stalls now rose, his hand held up for silence.

"That is all. Thank you for coming along, gentlemen. We will be writing you."

The Scot cleared his throat noisily as he snapped the lock of his music case.

"And that," said the Irishman jauntily, "would seem to be bloody well that. Any one feel like a drink?"

Auditions were apt to engender an air of mutual distrust which led applicants to slip out of the theatre with never a backward glance. However, Deri, essentially a convivial being, accepted the Irishman's invitation.

"That is the first time anyone has at these affairs, so it is. New to the game?"

"Fairly."

They adjourned to the nearest public house and Deri began to feel that welcome ease he still experienced only when in male company. A relaxed air he had not yet acquired in mixed society, much less alone with a woman—even Gillian. Instinctively this was reverting to life as he had lived it in Garreg Wen. Those Saturday nights at *The Gwent Arms*, only there they had sung. Here a loud-speaker was pouring out the stomach-aching sentiments of a slurring Pop singer. No wonder, thought Deri, the poor old maestro had called the British an unmusical nation.

By the second beer he and the Irishman were discussing Ballykenny which the latter knew though, as he humorously said, he himself hailed from "the Black North."

They parted on such good and slightly befuddled terms that each wished the other success with 'Marcel'. Not until the cooler air of the walk to Leicester Square tube station had begun to take its effect, did Deri find himself questioning the logic of this.

'If I play the part, he can't.' Then, with delightful inconsequence, Deri thought how pleasantly the one might understudy the other. A passing policeman glanced at him, then decided that the young man was only slightly unsteady.

"A single to —" blankly Deri tapped his forehead, unable momentarily to think of the right station. Beaming fatuously he said "a six-penny", his enunciation over careful. That would give him time to remember where it was he wished to alight.

That evening he had two phone calls, the first from Gillian, who wanted to know how he had done at the audition.

"No idea, darling, but I met a very nice Irishman," from which it will be gathered that the effect of the drinks had not entirely worn off, even then.

Eira came through a few minutes later, saying that the selection people had been uncommittal. She had not been able to "feel" how things stood with regard to his chances.

"Though I would think you have relatively little to fear. There wasn't another voice worth mentioning, except the Irish chap and with the best will in the world I can't see him as a Frenchman."

"I didn't even know you were at the Phoenix, Eira."

"It was not part of my plan that you should," was her reply. She complimented him on the dialogue. He had, she said, remembered most of the things she had taught him. Then having noticed something about his manner added, "You sound happy."

"Had a few drinks with Paddy O'Reilly. We're buddies." She laughed in mild reproval. "Really, Deri!"

"No one else wanted to go with the poor b——" just in time he remembered the word was not one used in the best society though it was normal conversational coin in Garreg Wen.

"You are still half blotto. I suggest an early night."

Though Deri was never to know precisely how much he was engaged on his own merit and how much as a result of Eira's string-pulling, the great thing was that he was asked to rehearse 'Marcel'—"on approval."

"What exactly does that mean?" he demanded of Eira, when reporting to the Shearme offices with his contract.

"That they reserve the right to chuck you out, my sweet, if you don't put up a good enough show." She gave his cheek a pat of encouragement. "Just sign on the dotted line, sir."

He wrote his rather careful signature. She always noticed that he handled a pen in the manner of one unused to writing.

"I am sorry about the Irish fellow," Deri was saying, a little pucker on his forehead.

"He is probably singing 'Kathleen Mavoureen' to enraptured audiences at the Met. in Edgware Road." The old music hall she mentioned was, at the time, London's only home of Irish variety.

Deri grinned, folding the contract and slipping it into his pocket, enquiring of her, as he did so:

"Do I have to thank you for the job, Eira?"

She shook her head then, half sharply, asked if he were not going through to the overseas department to tell Gillian his good news.

19

THE FOUR weeks of rehearsal for a London production, whether or not with preliminary try-out in the provinces, proved harder than anything Deri so far had encountered in his brief experience of the professional theatre. There was an almost brain-washing technique of repetition of line after line of dialogue, bar after bar of song and of step following step in the dance routines. Rest periods and times for meal breaks were of the briefest. The producer—he liked to follow the modern trend and be called Director—lacked the one quality which might have injected a feeling of good cheer into work, however hard. He had no sense of humour. He had, too, almost myopic vision as regard to what he wanted. No one could be less open to suggestions by the cast.

"I just don't feel it that way, Mr. Wingtangle," one of the small part men grumbled.

"I can't help that. It is how I want the scene played," a fair example, Deri always thought, of implacability.

Those of the company who were content to do precisely as they were told and bring no individuality to their work, came off best. That went for the soulless, efficient chorus, who could throw off a high kick or a top note with equal aplomb.

Ferdie Wingtangle had no place in his theatre for temperament. Sarcastically he would remark that only the first six letters applied. The leading lady was a little given to displays of this kind, some a genuine outcome of over-tension. Once she even fainted on the stage. Still that did not move the director to do more than signal to the two nearest girls to go to her assistance.

But—the leading lady had a husband, who, though unconnected with the theatre—subsequently saw Wingtangle in private. The ultimatum was that unless greater consideration were shown, a new lead would be required.

"She is under contract," was the reminder.

"My wife's health is more important than any lousy contract."

"We open in Wolverhampton on the seventh," was all the director said in reply to the overt threat by a mere husband.

Deri felt himself floundering. He was fast approaching uncertainty as to what he could do well. Most of his sketchy stage training seemed to be wrong. He walked, stood and sat in ways that displeased their stern disciplinarian.

"Didn't your drama school teach you on which knee to go down on a stage?"

Useless to reply that he had never had that sort of training. On the whole Wingtangle did not go contrary to the broad lines of Eira's tuition in the dialogue. With only one or two changes, that passed. When he sought to interfere about the style of singing—Deri—backed by the musical director—would not give way.

148

"I am sorry, but I can't take the passage that way. It amounts to crooning."

"And what is so wrong about crooning?"

"Only that I happen to be a straight singer."

"That's right, F.W.," cut in the musical director. "We don't want him to turn on all the vocal vices of a 'Pop' artist. Slurring, falsetto—and—"

"All right, all right. Carry on your way, Mr. Rhys."

A victory won not without loss of friendliness on both sides.

Even Deri's sunny disposition became affected. He began to look drawn and tired. On the rare occasions he could spare time for Gillian, he talked exclusively of *Madelon*.

"You are becoming as bad as the rest of 'em, darling," she chided gently.

"There are times when I could slam the bloody pass door of the theatre and go back for good to Garreg Wen."

"That would be pure defeatism."

"I suppose so." With glowering brows he added that in any case he owed it to Eira to stay the course. It had become apparent to him that Eira had had the most say in his being engaged for the part of 'Marcel'.

"Do you know, Gilly, some times I wonder if her confidence in me isn't misplaced."

Gillian soothed and cossetted sending him back—or so she hoped—revivified for the next day's rehearsal.

Eira herself was exceptionally busy and preoccupied, otherwise she would have wondered more about his progress. Coming through to the overseas department—temporarily deserted by all save Gillian—Eira completed her errand and then, pausing, asked after Deri. Gillian told her that he was finding the *Madelon* rehearsals a great strain.

Eira nodded. "Ferdie Wingtangle, I suppose? He is a fiend to work for but one of our relatively few *avant garde* producers of musicals. He nearly kills his companies, yet the results somehow justify the means."

"I hear nothing but theatre all the time."

Eira's mouth slipped into a wry smile of sympathy. "My poor Gillian! How boring can it become?"

"Oh, I know Deri is not himself. Eira, do you think he will be all right?" the question sounded painfully anxious.

"Of course. Don't you believe in him?"

"Not—as you do," she confessed, her hands folding and unfolding a piece of scrap paper lying on the office table.

"And you love him." Eira's voice was very soft.

"Yes, I love him," answered Gillian, in a strangely depressed way.

There was no longer any sense of glory in the words and for this, Eira felt a secret romantic's regret. She wondered if the couple were not finding the period of engagement difficult for reasons which, perhaps in their mutual "niceness", they did not altogether appreciate.

'I can't very well tell Gillian that it might help Deri if they were to sleep together.'

Eira was sure he was not the type of man to seek sordid consolations elsewhere. He loved and respected Gillian. He was not helped by being out of his natural element. In Garreg Wen the pace of life had been deliberate. In London it was accelerated. He was working with his brain and his voice instead, Eira supposed, with his hands and trained senses. He lived in dreary digs and Gillian, on her side, spent an almost nun-like existence amongst her girl friends at the flat.

Eira decided it was all very difficult. She did not even know where to begin to advise Gillian. Taking the easy way instead, Eira said she expected things would improve once *Madelon* was before the public.

Largely at Eira's instigation, Gillian took two or three days off from Shearme's in order to accompany the company to Wolverhampton. She found travelling with a theatrical group a novel experience. Some played cards, some slept, knitted or merely reminisced. Everyone was very nice to her in that warm way of actors and actresses.

"Like to hear me in my part?" Deri suggested, when, sandwiches and fruit eaten in the compartment, the remaining four people were reading paper backs. "We needn't disturb the others. Besides, *cariad*, it will be good training for the future."

Suddenly Gillian had a vision of many journeys, many parts to be heard and smiled.

"I may as well be blooded now as later."

"If you just whisper the cues—"

The murmur of their voices persisted for the next half hour or so.

150

Then one of the solo dancers, sharing the reserved compartment with them, yawned daintily.

"Why don't you give us a spot of music, Deri boy?"

"Do you think I should?" remembering other train journeys across Wales where the sound of men's voices in harmony had persisted most of the way.

"*Not* the dear show! Anything but that. I am sure Miss Lechmere will agree?"

"Oh, Gillian, please. Miss Lechmere sounds so formal and I hope we are all friends."

The other four concurred and Deri began to relax in his corner seat, singing whatever they wanted. Passing down the corridor the musical director slid aside the partition and said, pleasantly:

"We seem to be on the wrong train. This must be the Welsh express!" With a mock salute, he closed the compartment door again.

Gillian had accommodation at the hotel where Deri was staying and they took their meals, as far as possible, together. Breakfast on Monday was rushed, there being a band call for ten o'clock but he had time to stop a minute, his hand on her shoulder and to whisper:

"One day this is how it is always going to be."

At his request she was not coming to the rehearsal, so amused herself—as best she could—until he returned for a late luncheon. During the afternoon they went for a walk together then, after a cup of tea, he took a packet of sandwiches with him to the theatre. Gillian thought that *Madelon* went down well, having lost, perhaps a little of its Gallic flavour in transit. Wingtangle's discipline paid its dividend and the audience applauded a slick, pleasing evening's entertainment, Deri made quite a gratifying personal success, stopping the show with his slow-tempo, haunting little waltz with the off-beat lyric, "Mocking Madonna".

But to Gillian, who knew him so well, he was not on top vocal form. His nervousness occasionally came through his performance. At the curtain fall she found herself invited round to an informal dressing room party at which even Ferdie Wingtangle was seen to smile.

"Nevertheless I want you all round at the theatre at 11 tomorrow morning."

Groans greeted the announcement. However he promised

not to keep them long. It was only the first act and finale that needed pulling together.

There had been no opportunity for Deri to see the evening paper, which a sleepy night porter produced for him on the return to the hotel.

"Anything special?" the question was light, casual.

"Two or three chaps trapped in some Welsh mine. You'll see it in the stop press, sir, if you're interested."

"If I'm interested!"

The porter was taken back by the peculiar violence of the remark, then he was not to know of Deri's origin and up-bringing. Anxiously the young man turned to the report. It was brief enough, stating merely that owing to what was believed to have been a fall of rock in the S. Wales pit at Prydwedd Road—"a site where only recently mining operations have been resumed—" several men had been trapped. The full extent of the disaster was not yet known. However at present there was every hope that some, if not all, might be brought out alive.

> "Meanwhile miners from various parts of the country have left for the Rhondda Valley area."

Sudden whiteness of his face made Gillian clutch anxiously at his arm. Was he all right?

"I'll have to go," he said, as if it were obvious.

"Go—go where?"

"Read—" thrusting the paper at her. Turning again to the sleepy porter, he asked: "Have you an A.B.C. handy?"

"Yes, sir," producing same with commendable speed.

Deri thumbed over the "w's" until he came to Wolver-hampton's down trains. There was nothing until morning. First he must make for London. So much seemed certain, then pick up a red dragon class train from Paddington. He might have to make for one or other of the Welsh junctions and proceed from there by branch line. As far as he could see he could make his first connection within half an hour or so of arrival in London.

He gave instructions about the time he wanted to be called and when a taxi was to be ordered to take him to the station. Meanwhile Gillian, roused from her own tiredness after what had been an emotionally exhausting evening, regarded Deri 'questioningly, the paper still in her hand. Surely he was not contemplating going to the scene of the distaster?

"What else? God, you don't understand! My own dad was killed in that mine. I started down it, myself. I know it, like the back of my hand. I must help bring up the boys."

"Are you mad, Deri? Don't you understand you have your duty, here?"

He looked at her almost pityingly, not expecting that he would have to *explain*. Never had he sounded more sincere, more Welsh. It was almost as if he found himself talking in a foreign language to her. He reminded her that whatever he might have become since he left Garreg Wen, he remained first of all a skilled miner, experienced in rescue work. With pride he told how fellow miners were already congregating in other parts of Britain. No national call had to be sent out for such emergencies. The boys just came, without any prompting, from the N.C.B. or anybody else.

She saw then that nothing in the entire world could move him from his resolution.

"I can't explain better, love."

"Eira!" Gillian remembered suddenly. For a moment he looked disconcerted, though still undeflected from his purpose.

"I am afraid I have to let her down in this instance. Don't look so stricken, *cariad*. I may be away only a short time. Once we have reached the boys—"

"You seem very sure that you will." Gillian had not realized that her own anxiety was making her sound bitter. In some horrible way Alec and Deri were merging in her mind.

It was as though an element of physical danger had brought the dead into line with the living. As yet she did not dare think of Deri in terms of mortality, only that the possibility that he might be maimed or injured—beyond that she dared not consider. This had brought him closer to Alec. The one had been taken away from her. The other—

"No!" She pressed her hand to her mouth to stifle the near-hysterical sound. To give way now could do no good and it would only make things harder for Deri. But he did not even notice her reactions. He had but a single purpose before which all else was unimportant. Still he did realise that he still had certain obligations in Wolverhampton, so rang Ferdie Wingtangle at his hotel. Deri told him briefly that he was leaving the cast for what he hoped was only a

153

few days and therefore the understudy must take over from him.

"Sorry, if it's putting you on the spot rather."

"You must be out of your mind, Rhys!"

"I used to be a miner, that's why," Deri ended the conversation, as if the fact were an explanation of his present conduct.

"Suppose they won't have you back?" Gillian asked.

He shrugged. The risk was one very small and unimportant beside that to which he was already committed. She made a decision.

"I am coming with you, Deri."

And on that resolution she stood firm. They reached London. There was time for no more than a hot cup of tea in the station buffet before he needed to take the underground from Euston Road to Paddington. There were several trains he might catch, depending upon the route. Kissing her a little solemnly, he exclaimed:

"Don't look so stricken, *cariad*."

When he had gone, she still stood, undecided what next to do. It was too early for Eira to have reached the office. On impulse, Gillian made for a phone box. She explained as briefly as she could what had happened. There was a long silence from the other end as if Eira were trying to assess the situation. She said she had read of the trapped men but had not connected it with the Garreg Wen area. Dismally Gillian observed that even had the fall of rock occurred in one of the Durham mines, Deri was just as likely to be on his way to report on rescue team duty.

"He never seemed to stop to think about the way he was letting you—and—and the show down, Eira."

"I rather think that *Madelon* has become a relatively unimportant issue."

They both knew that there was a competent understudy. The name of Deri Rhys meant little or nothing to an audience. If there was any consolation for Eira, it lay in the fact that Wolverhampton was only the first week of the prior tour. There was still time for Deri to appear in London, though she guessed there might be a bit of a battle over this with the management. Not that Shearme's Enterprizes would be shy of using publicity probably unique in the theatrical history.

All these factors skipped into her mind and out of it again.

In a sense they were but reflexes of her business training.

'Tenor deserts show to help trapped comrades—'

Oh, yes, it would be a good press release . . .

"Are you still there, Eira?" the girl's voice was anxious. 'Had the child thought I had fainted or something equally foolish?' the older woman wondered.

"I'm still here. I was just considering the situation."

Almost briskly Eira said that no good could be done by their remaining in London. Gillian had her own night things?

"Take a taxi straight to my place. By the time I've made two or three unavoidable phone calls and thrown a few garments into a bag, we'll be ready to leave by car for Garreg Wen."

20

EIRA DROVE at the greatest possible speed that lay within England's fantastic traffic conditions and the margin of personal safety. There were moments when Gillian caught herself praying only to realise that after all Eira was not taking undue chances. She kept within her particular lane of traffic, overtaking only when she could see sufficiently far ahead.

Looking back afterwards on what—at the time had seemed a nightmare journey—Gillian conceded Eira's to have been a superlative driving performance.

Beaconsfield in under fifty minutes was fair timing but the progress through the two Wycombes lost them far more than they had gained.

"We have leisure in which to take in every detail of each building on either side of the road," Eira remarked with frustration. She had talked but little, devoting the whole of her attention to the road, except when indicating that she wanted a fresh cigarette.

Just beyond Witney she agreed to stop for a drink, according to motorists' custom, at the first public house on the left side of the road. She ordered a stout for herself and Gillian chose a pale ale.

"Have you any cheese and biscuits?" Eira asked the barman, who had 'cheese biscuits'—not quite the same thing but better than nothing.

Eira leaned against the counter, already showing that tired-tension of driving against the clock. It was obvious, of course, that Deri might not reach Wales greatly ahead of them.

"What a mad caper this is, Gillian," putting on her leather gauntlets.

She did not speak again for the best part of an hour, when they made their second stop at the Birdlip side of Gloucester. Here they had a hot meal in one of the interminably dull little cafes that had no ideas beyond Welsh rarebit, baked beans and various alternatives "on toast" with chips and tinned peas as the only vegetables. The two women ate, without enjoyment, merely because they were hungry.

"I wonder if Deri will ever stop thinking like a miner?" Eira spoke in a sad voice and Gillian could tell that her friend was seeing the fruitless waste of months of work and of belief in his ability to become a singer far above the dull average talents. Eira had found him a part, not perhaps ideal for him but better than most, and without even an apology he had walked out before the second performance. Could she expect any management, even one bound up with the Shearme Enterprizes, to re-consider him? As she saw it, when he did go back—*if* he went back—he would be told he could stay out of the theatre.

"It's all so—so—" words evidently failed her and Gillian could only bow her head in agreement. How could she expect Eira to forgive Deri?

"Surely there are enough men capable of the rescue work without *him?*"

"I don't know, Eira. But I do know that nothing in the whole world could have prevented him from going."

"Oh, I realize that, my dear child."

"He did admit that he was letting you down, Eira."

"You surprise me," her smile was twisted, as if she were in pain.

Then, because she could not sit idle any longer, she drained the last of her coffee and indicated that forthwith they should resume their journey.

As Gillian re-settled herself in the passenger's seat she could not help thinking it was like, yet curiously unlike the many miles they had travelled together during the Irish holiday. She knew nothing about driving, save how to stop the car in emergency. Looking at Eira's grim determined countenance, still as a carven statue, Gillian wondered if it would have helped had she been capable of taking over the wheel.

They came on through Monmouth and Abergavenny, keeping just south of the Black Mountains, pulling up in Merthyr Tydfil for another cup of tea. Eira bought a local paper there in the hopes that it might have news. It said only that four local miners were trapped in the Prydwedd Road workings, far below ground, by a fall of rock. Rescue was in progress but it was likely to be many hours before they could hope to be reached.

"For us—another twenty to thirty odd miles," Eira observed, slamming the driver's side door and pulling out from the kerbside.

They approached the road which led to the Gwent Arms. Here Eira stopped as, whatever the outcome, they could not start back for London without at least one night in the vicinity. The man who owned the place had an outstanding memory for faces and recognised her at once. She explained that there were two of them, as before, and he nodded.

"I can let you have numbers 7 and 9 on the first floor."

She thanked him then asked what the latest news was about the mine. He said that some of the volunteer rescue men from other districts were already on the scene. He understood further men were coming from as far north as Durham.

"Deri Rhys. Do you know whether he will have arrived?"

"Is he coming, miss? The boys will be glad to know that. But I thought he had left to become a great singer?"

Eira gave what was growing to be her slow, sad smile. "That was the idea. Still I suppose this takes precedence."

"Oh, it would, miss."

The extraordinary lack of doubt in the man's tones gave the two Londoners an odd feeling of apartheid. They could not begin to grasp the psychology of a mining community. How men could rush to the scene, oblivious of the probable danger, with but one selfless thought in all their minds. To "bring up the boys" to safety.

"It makes one feel very humble, Gillian," Eira observed, as they went up the stairs to their rooms.

They had washed and tidied themselves and began to feel better. When Eira tapped on Gillian's door to ask if she were ready, it was to express the wish that they could have a nice stiff drink. Only it was not then within licensing hours.

It was a very short run down into Garreg Wen, which bore a curiously deserted appearance. Eira had no idea where the Prydwedd Road Mine was. Luckily there was one old, old man moving slowly and painfully along ahead of them. When he turned in response to her call, she saw that his face was scarred from burns.

"Could you direct us to the mine where the men are trapped?" Eira's courage over Welsh pronunciations had temporarily deserted her. In his gentle, soft, countryman's voice he gave clear directions, to add:

"But what would two young ladies like you want with Prydwedd Road, I wonder?"

"I—that is we—know one of the rescue men."

"Oh. Ah." He smiled, his faded blue eyes regarding Gillian's face the longer time.

"Is there any news?"

"That I could not say, m'm."

Eira looked at him with open curiosity. Had he had anything to do with mining?

"Most everyone does in these parts, m'm. I was a foreman in my day."

"Just how serious is the present situation?"

The old man lifted one rheumatic shoulder slightly. "It is always serious, m'm. You can only wait and pray." With great courtesy he raised his worn cap and went on ahead of them. From the interior mirror Eira saw that he had turned into the stone grey building of the Ebenezer chapel.

They drove on until they came to a small new-looking hamlet rising to a steep hill, slag-heap crowned. There seemed a lot of parked vehicles ahead and Eira stopped her car on their extreme limit, proceeding with Gillian the rest of the way on foot.

The scene was not how either of them had imagined it would be. No shawled women, patiently awaiting the worst news. There was an air of almost cheerful efficiency. Heavy vehicles with unfamiliar lifting gear, South Welsh ambulances and a fire engine were standing by. There was also a mobile canteen, "Gwent Mines Welfare". Serving in it were Mrs. Rhys (in hat) and Rhiannon. Some men with blackened faces, wearing safety helmets, boiler suits and heavy industrial boots, were standing around, drinking steaming mugs of soup or tea. They looked curiously at the two strangers, but moved aside for them.

"Rhiannon! Do you remember me? Eira Shearme. This is Gillian Lechmere, Deri's fiancée."

Rhiannon completed the pouring out of another well-sugared tea and passed this across to a little whippet of a man, who spoke with her in Welsh. Only then did she feel free to reply to Eira, of whom the girl asked:

"Why have you both come?"

"We knew Deri was on his way—if he hasn't already arrived."

"I see." She turned to one of the soup-drinkers and they spoke together quickly. "Deri is already here."

"Then perhaps—?"

"Apparently he went straight down the mine," she gave a strangely calm smile. "Waited only for some clothes and a helmet. I did not see him."

"How long do you suppose —?"

"Who can say, Miss Shearme?" Rhiannon looked now at Gillian with keenly interested eyes, as if taking in every detail of the girl who had supplanted her. Gillian felt herself colouring up and growing pale again. Inadequate, embarrassed, she stammered:

"It is dreadful not knowing what is happening."

"You grow used to it." Mrs. Rhys spoke in her hesitant English.

"It must be awful for you, Mrs. Rhys, I mean, you will have thought Deri was away from it all." Rather desperately Gillian addressed Rhiannon direct. "Does she understand?"

"I will translate for you." Rhiannon's glance mocked a little and she spoke to Deri's mother in their own tongue.

"Are you waiting for news of him, too?" Eira asked.

"Deri? A little, but my Goronwy is one of the six who are trapped." The girl spoke with simple dignity.

Six? The paper had said four, but neither Londoner questioned the discrepancy.

"There was a further fall two hours' back," Rhiannon

159

explained. "Goronwy had gone down with the first team."

More miners were queing for hot drinks and feeling an awful sense of uselessness, Eira and Gillian moved aside. They went and sat a while in the car, Eira interminably smoking. They did not speak to one another; just sat on in troubled silence as darkness gathered.

"I wonder if we couldn't help them in the canteen?" Gillian suggested, all of sudden.

Eira seemed grateful for any ideas that might halt their inactivity. They found that Mrs. Rhys had been replaced by another woman but that Rhiannon was still there, now cutting sandwiches. She looked up at them, shaking her head without stopping work. Both thought how deadly tired the girl looked. Their offer to help was refused with a politeness tinged with irritation.

"Look, Miss Shearme," Rhiannon explained, handing a doorstep of cheese between bread to an ambulance attendant. "It may be many hours yet. (They have to tunnel to them.) Go back to your hotel. I will promise to phone, if there is any news. You are at the Gwent Arms?"

Eira nodded and thanking the girl, walked in silence back to the car. They drove straight through Garreg Wen, the way they had come in before dusk. On arrival at the Arms, Eira put the car away in the parking lot behind the building. Both were conscious of hunger added to tiredness. The London papers were on the old-fashioned hall table and Eira threw the correct money into the ashtray left for the purpose. There was half a column put out by the Shearme publicity department. It related Deri's dash from "Stardom to rescue work". As she read it, Eira felt a little ashamed, wondering what Rhiannon and those other bravely cheerful women at the Prydwedd Road Mine would think. Eira knew that in comparison it was all a little cheap.

The manager asked solicitously whether they had had a meal. On learning that they had not, he said that he would see what he could find even though it was long after the normal dining time for hotel patrons. He brought them soup, cold meat and salad, apologising that there was no sweet other than ice cream.

Eira thanked him, finding that the double whisky she had ordered began to put a bit of feeling back into her cold body. Gillian was having a gin and lime, which Eira privately

160

thought an insipid drink. She had two telephone calls to make; one to Wolverhampton, the other to London. The first was a personal one to Ferdie Wingtangle, who fortunately was still in the theatre. She explained that she was speaking from Wales and would keep them informed, as best she could. Ferdie gave his hotel phone for such times as he was not likely to be about in the theatre. He said that the understudy had made a good job of the part of 'Marcel'.

"Talk about the show having to go on, Miss Shearme—"

"There was nothing I could do to stop young Rhys rushing off," she pointed out, thinking it unnecessary to add that in fact she had been among the last to know of his intentions.

"We're managing nicely without him." Wingtangle sounded very annoyed over the whole business; as he well might be.

"Carry on as you are for the present," were her parting instructions. She rang off feeling that he was very far from feeling cordial towards her. The London call was to Mr. Birdsall, of Gillian's overseas department, one of the most reliable Shearme employees, trusted to see that business was carried smoothly on in Eira's temporary absence. She left her phone number and promised to call the office on the following day. As far as she could see neither she nor Gillian would be starting back for London during the next twenty-four hours. Mr. Birdsall wanted to know how the young lady was "bearing up under the strain". Eira said that she quite honestly did not think that Gillian realized that there was actual danger to Deri's person.

She found Gillian sitting dismally in the lounge, too tired to move and slipping an arm round her, led her towards the staircase.

Neither slept much but by the time they came down to breakfast they were at least physically rested. The one waiter said there had been no further news from the mine. Neither was there until much later in the day. Then it was learned that Deri's team had reached the second fall of rock. Rhiannon was replaced in the mobile canteen and was standing at the pit head when, to a cheer, the first stretcher was brought to the surface. It was Goronwy's companion, with head bandaged and mining helmet consequently placed on his chest. He gave a tired grin as he was lifted into the waiting ambulance. A few minutes later two other miners came,

Goronwy between them, dragging his left leg with each pained step. Rhiannon gave a sudden cry and went over to him.

Eira and Gillian turned aside, aware of their closeness to tears.

The ambulance doors slammed and they saw that Rhiannon had gone with it.

"Where do they take them?" asked Eira, of one of the lorrymen.

"St. Donat's Cottage Hospital."

This, she learned, was five miles distant.

Eira and Gillian were still at the site by dusk, having had nothing to eat, save what the welfare canteen provided. They would not accept money and Eira could only see to it that she sent a cheque of appreciation to their organisation.

By seven p.m. there was a general stir as it became known that the four originally trapped men had been reached. The next news was that one of them was dead and a second severely injured. More than that was not at present known. Again the same procedure as before, only this time four stretchers were carried up within a short sequence of time and taken away in the second ambulance. The first was back and standing-by for the rescue party itself.

Neither Gillian nor Eira recognised Deri in his safety helmet, his face grey black and bleeding. His boiler suit was stained and torn and his left arm held in an improvised sling. The ambulance doors had already closed behind him and two others before the women learned who one was. Mrs. Rhys tapped Gillian on the arm, pointed at the disappearing backlight of the white vehicle and nodded.

"Deri?" they cried in unison.

She indicated her left arm and nodded again.

There was nothing to do but go back yet again to the car.

"We had better have a meal now, Gillian, and phone the hospital from the Gwent Arms."

This they did and heard that Deri was being kept in but would be allowed no visitors that night.

"We must wait until morning, Gilly my dear. At least he is safe."

"Yes, he is safe," and Gillian began to cry softly at first, then with great shuddering sobs.

162

Eira held her close, wondering why it was that she herself, who felt—she was sure—so much more deeply about Deri remained dry-eyed.

"It's all very well for you, Eira," Gillian said, a little later, sitting on the edge of her bed, mopping at her eyes. "You aren't in love with him and I am."

Eira made a strange sound which drew Gillian's attention. The girl turned to her, seeing for the first time all that Eira would normally have died rather than reveal to her.

"You—too!" the words sounded half incredulous.

Eira gave a strangely, wistful little smile. "It just happened."

"Does Deri know?"

"Why should he? I didn't even intend that you should." The tone implied that as far as Eira was concerned love was an entirely private business.

"Oh Eira dear, I am so sorry for you."

Gillian's generous, concerned outburst was received with coldness.

"If there is one thing I abominate, .it is people feeling sorry for me." She paused, then went on to say that loving Deri did not necessarily mean the end of everything. The weakness—and it was typical Eira should see it as such—doubtless would pass.

Patting Gillian's still-damp cheek affectionately, Eira left the girl to herself.

21

St. Donat's Hospital was relatively small and built in the grey slabs of stone so reminiscent of Dolgelly. Eira parked to the right of the entrance gates. As she and Gillian crossed to the block where they were told the mining casualties had all been taken they saw Rhiannon emerge. Though she carried herself with her usual air of pride, her eyes showed that recently she had been crying. Gillian's anxiety was given a sudden jolt.

"Deri?" she exclaimed, before she could stop herself.

Rhiannon stared at her, momentarily without recognition then, turning her head so that in turn she saw Eira, gave a little start.

"I am sorry. I didn't see who it was."

"That is quite to be understood, Rhiannon. I am sure the three of us must be equally anxious. But you haven't told us if you are upset because of Deri."

"Deri?" she repeated, almost stupidly, then shook her head. "I haven't seen Deri."

"Then it is your —"

"Goronwy. Yes." The tears came back to the girl's eyes. "It is very bad with him."

"Oh, how I feel for you," Gillian was hardly aware of the strong emotional colour in her tone.

Rhiannon's gaze swung from Eira, then back, in puzzlement.

"Gillian was engaged before ever she met Deri. And Alec was killed in a motor-scooter accident shortly before they were to have been married."

The Welsh girl looked away, embarrassed.

"I hope it isn't really serious with your Goronwy?" Eira's voice was full of kind concern.

"He may have to lose his leg. It is worse than was thought at first."

"Didn't he *walk* to the ambulance?"

She gave a momentary smile. "Goronwy is very obstinate. He hates all fussing." The girl hesitated, never quite sure where social occasions demanded handshakes. "You will forgive me? I have to go."

"Of course, my dear. I hope the news will be better for you," and Eira took the strong, work-hardened hand in hers and, more shyly, Gillian did the same. They watched Rhiannon hurry through the gates and a few minutes later a South Wales bus had picked her up at the corner.

"How little we realize of their lives. They make my world of the theatre seem unbelievably small," and Eira sounded depressed as she spoke.

The sister on duty said that two visiting at a time could not be permitted.

"Then you go in, Gillian, he would far rather see you, I know."

"Perhaps if Mr. Rhys is not too tired you could pop your head round the door when the other lady comes out?"

Eira nodded. Deprived of opportunity to smoke, she paced the cold stone corridor, looking in at the kitchen where a plump and very young nurse was washing up a feeding cup. Carbolic, distant traces of anaesthetic; squeaking trolley wheels and the swoosh of heavy doors closing—was any hospital very different from another as regards its smells and sounds?

Gillian came out in five minutes' time, looking cheerful enough and signed to Eira to slip into the ward.

"He is in the second bed down on the left," she whispered.

Eira entered, passing an un-noticing staff nurse carrying a tray covered by a clean towel. This she took to the top bed which was screened-off. Deri, his arm in a sling and some strips of plaster on his face, was half propped up by pillows. His face was an unhealthy grey colour.

"So you came, too, Eira? To give me the sack?"

"The show seems a long way off, doesn't it? Well, how are you?"

"Could be a lot worse. Tired. Blasted tired, in fact."

"Of course. I won't stay, Deri."

He smiled with a certain grim amusement. "The faithful Eira!"

Was there an implied sneer?

A little hurt, she went quickly from the ward. Gillian thanked Sister, to whom she had been talking in the meantime, and they left the hospital with permission to return at visiting hour that evening. Gillian said that from what she could gather Deri was suffering from extreme exhaustion. Apart from quite minor injuries, he was physically in good shape. Eira could see that he was unlikely to be back in *Madelon* at least while it was playing Wolverhampton and only hoped that she would be able to circumvent the calling of another singer permanently to replace Deri in the cast. She knew they would not carry on over the week with an understudy. Indeed they already might have contracted a fresh 'Marcel'.

During the day she phoned Ferdie Wingtangle and her own London office, where she was able to clear up two or three small queries which had arisen during her absence. The afternoon was spent lying on their beds at the Gwent Arms. Eira wondered whether or not to call upon Deri's mother, offering a lift to the hospital. It seemed a—gesture.

So when the two of them set out again after an earlier meal,

165

Eira made for "Cartref". A young man opened to her. He explained that Mrs. Rhys had already gone by the bus.

"I only lodge here, you know," he told them.

Was there any message the ladies would like him to give? Eira said that the chances were they would see Mrs. Rhys in person, as they were also on their way to St. Donat's Hospital.

"Our not knowing Welsh makes communication a little difficult," explained Eira.

"Oh, ah, it would. Indeed, yes." He seemed at a loose end and would have been inclined to prop up the door and converse indefinitely, if they had not made a move.

This time Gillian generously said that Eira should see Deri first. However a staff nurse told them that his mother was there. Presently Mrs. Rhys emerged, a small empty basket on her arm. She did not seem surprised to see them and bowed gravely at both, before passing on without comment. After a short wait, Eira was told she might see Mr. Rhys.

Deri looked a bit more rested. On his locker were several newspapers.

"Are you responsible for this foul publicity?" he demanded in his earlier truculent manner.

Eira knew prevarication would be useless. She said that Shearme's had been bound to make a brief statement to the press.

"After all, you *did* walk out, Deri, however worthy your object in so-doing."

"Have you read it yourself?"

"There hasn't been much time."

"Mam brought the papers with some other things."

Eira saw it would be wrong to under-estimate Mrs. Rhys.

Eira scanned them with a quick professional eye. They played up the angle of the brave young tenor, risking his life for his friends. One of the dailies had evidently done some research and included the facts of Deri's father's death as a result of an accident in the same mine.

> " 'Yet Mr. Rhys never had a moment's doubt where his duty lay.' "

The evening edition had been out after contact with the Wolverhampton company.

" 'We are thrilled to have such a brave young man in our midst,' one of the cast told your reporter."

"They make me want to spew," Deri commented in a hard voice.

She re-folded the papers, put them back on the locker and, after reflection, answered, "No comment."

"Is there no decency left?" he demanded angrily.

There was no defence, which she could offer and at the same time expect him to understand. Neither did there seem any point in reminding him that he had consulted no one about going to Wales, much less waited for permission to leave.

"We won't enter into the reasons for what you did, Deri. I—I accept them. And, however—inconvenient to myself and to the many others involved, applaud your conduct. But that did not make it obligatory on our part to see that there was no press puff. All the department did was to put out a simple statement of fact. The—embroideries, I fear, were only to be expected. I am not prepared to take the blame for that side of the business. Believe me I had nothing to do with concocting that glowing column about you in the *South Wales Argus*. I have no doubt that whatever the local Garreg Wen paper is called —"

"*Y day*," he pronounced it "ee dith".

"— will similarly feature your action. Why do you mind so much?" The question was frankly curious.

He said that he was but one of a team of men, sharing the same risks and no single one should be given greater credit than any other.

"Look at that poor devil Goronwy, now. Likely to lose a leg, so Mam tells me. And I have only a few scratches and this arm, which will heal in a matter of days."

"I am sorry you should feel so bitter about this business, Deri."

"I damn well wish I had never done as you suggested and come to London—"

His raised voice drew the attention of Staff, who hurried to the bedside, taking hold of his wrist as she noted the flush on his face. She told Eira:

"You will please to go now."

And Eira obeyed with an air of quiet defeat. The waiting Gillian was allowed to do no more than step just inside

167

the ward and wave to Deri, round whom screens were being placed.

"I have failed dismally," Eira admitted, for once crashing her gears and wincing at the sound she made. "Deri hates me for uprooting him in the first place and for trying to make him the vocal artist he may never become now—thanks to this wretched affair."

"He will calm down, Eira, I feel sure. In a way I think it rather natural that he should resent being made into copy."

"From the way he spoke anyone would think I had drafted the paragraphs!"

"You aren't in the least to blame. If you've failed, then so have I."

"In what way?"

"For not realising how totally different he is to either of us. Eira, don't you see what he—and the others need in their life is a woman like Rhiannon. I wouldn't have had a quarter of her courage if they had just told me darling Deri was to have a leg amputated. I would have been afraid. Begun to wonder if my love were big enough to bear with a mutilated lover. Rhiannon has no doubts of that sort."

"She is a very brave lass," the other agreed. Then, feeling her way a little, said that loving Deri required a different sort of bravery. "Being able to make allowances for his many shortcomings and still knowing, in your heart, what a completely worthwhile person he is."

Eira changed down for the hill up to Garreg Wen, as the evening shadows lengthened and the mountains beside the valley seemed to close in upon them.

Next day Eira decided that she must go to London, but not the whole of the way by car. This she left in a garage at the main line junction. She promised to be back, if possible, by the following evening.

Meanwhile Gillian shared the visiting hours with Mrs. Rhys, who, through the mouthpiece of her more fluent-in-English lodger, offered Gillian accommodation in the house. Gillian was very tempted to accept, feeling that it might make for a more understanding relationship between the two women, but she had Morgan Hughes—as the young man was called—explain that she could not desert Miss Shearme, whose absence was of a most temporary nature.

168

"She loves my boy also?" Mrs. Rhys suggested, having taken in so much more than either of them suspected.

"She is very fond of Deri, yes," Gillian thought the slight amendment politic.

When Gillian walked into the ward on the morning Eira had left, Deri asked whether the latter were very displeased over his behaviour.

"I don't know what made me go at her the way I did yesterday evening. But I was so hopping mad —"

"— that you had to take the micky out of someone?"

He nodded with a shamefaced air. "I can see her point, of course."

"Well, you did let the show down rather badly, didn't you, darling? After all, Eira has gone to a lot of trouble over your career."

"Yes, damn her," but the expletive was mildly spoken.

"She believes in you just as much as ever she did. I am sure of that, Deri. Even if you should have spoiled your chances over *Madelon*, I don't doubt something else will turn up before too long."

"I am not sure I shall be going back to town."

Gillian looked so startled by this announcement that he was forced to smile.

"It could be that my right place is still here—in South Wales."

"Oh, Deri! It isn't possible!"

"I could find a job in the mine. They would take me on gladly enough after all that's happened."

"But, Deri, think of the waste! Many men can learn how to hack coal out of the earth, but so very few have your gifts as singer."

"They're not all that big," he reminded her, adding that so far as making big money went, he would have to let himself be turned into a microphone-hugging Pop singer. Once established, he would record and have his discs jockeyed to fame.

"If you've even stopped believing in yourself," her eyes filled.

He looked at her with a trace of disgust. Was he thinking how Rhiannon probably had gone dry-eyed into see Goronwy and only cried a little in the hospital corridor outside the surgical ward? (Deri was in men's medical).

"It is an aimless sort of life," Deri seemed to be thinking aloud rather than addressing Gillian direct. "I was happy in Garreg Wen."

"With Rhiannon! But she doesn't belong to you any more."

"True enough. And I suppose you would be too grand for life in a mining village?"

One part of Gillian's mind prompted agreement. To tell him that a woman in love had no other happiness than in the place where her man was. But another more sensible, less romantic side of her brain reminded her how she would hate a life bordered by these high hills and plunging valleys—however beautiful in themselves. That it would be spiritual death to shop in a single small street and, if she wanted nice clothes, have to undergo a tedious bus ride either to Swansea or Cardiff. She could not expect him to understand she had nothing at all in common with the Welsh women, however much she might admire their staunchness and grit. And it would be amongst the women that most of her days would have to be spent, since the men would be down the mine.

Because she had hated the narrowness of small town life existence—and Garreg Wen was not even that—she had left her parents' home in the first instance. She had grown accustomed only to London. Could she therefore settle permanently after it in a tiny place? She doubted this capacity very much.

All that apart, Deri himself was no longer quite the same man as the one Eira had uprooted five months before to become a singer. He might *think* that he was, now that he was back amongst his own people.

Interrupting this thought-train of hers, he said:

"I notice you haven't answered me, Gilly."

"Because I just don't know how to do so."

He smiled with sudden grief. "No, I don't think I can see you settling in Garreg Wen."

She was quick to defend herself against the implication of unreason.

"I am not made the same way as Rhiannon and the other local girls, Deri. I can't help it, I suppose . . . Mind you, I don't ask for luxury. Only not to be—buried alive."

He gave a strange laugh. "As I nearly was the other day! I have only just thought about it, too."

Gillian shuddered, feeling as though the ghosts of all the
170

dead miners of the valley were marching across her grave
in their pit boots.

22

DERI SEEMED strangely unconcerned when Eira, back from
her London visit, told him that a promising young "Juv",
with but an average voice, but acting ability above it, was
taking over 'Marcel'.

"There was nothing I could do about the decision and
believe me, I tried."

What use was it telling him of the tough hour or more
spent in argument? How she had been goaded to the edge of
losing her temper at each stone-walling remark by the others
concerned. Always it had come back to the same general
argument. Deri Rhys had broken his contract from the moment
he had walked out of that provincial playhouse. No national
emergency justified such outrageous behaviour. (Eira recalled
having murmured, 'Not even war?'). The gist appeared a
resolution to "leave mining to the miners and the theatre to
the players". There was no doubt in the mind of Mr. Wingtangle, who had come to London especially to discuss the
matter, that the theatre—in block capitals—invariably came
first.

Deri stared at the rain spattered window above the bed
opposite to his own. He was thinking of Goronwy Evans that
morning being moved by ambulance to the biggest hospital in
the South Wales region. Three specialists were to assess the
chances of still saving his leg.

Therefore Eira's quiet explanations scarcely registered.
She had no way of telling whether or not Deri minded not
going back to *Madelon.*

"Something else will turn up, my dear," her tone was
soothing.

He made himself look at her, his attention collected from
a distance.

"If I wish it to," and gave a smile she did not like to see.

171

With apparent innocence as to his intentions she asked:
"Have you any doubts about returning to the stage?"

"Quite a lot! In fact I'll probably stay on here in Wales."

Her hands gripped the strap of the small bag in which she had carried delicacies for Deri. Even now she could not believe him to be serious, though Gillian already had hinted as much.

"Have you thought what you would be asking of Gillian?"

" 'To love, honour and obey'." Again there was a flash of that disturbing sarcasm. Eira hoped he had outgrown that attitude.

"I wish I understood you, Deri. I have tried so often—so hard. Yet I always seem to fail."

"I am sorry, Eira. I suppose it is a lousy way of repaying you for all your interest in me."

"Oh that!" She made a hopeless gesture, looking away a moment to where Staff was arranging flowers brought by one of the visitors in a central position in the middle of the ward. They were not expensive shop flowers but doubtless grown in one of the small local gardens. Eira felt a sudden sadness.

He began speaking again.

"I thought I was doing the right thing in leaving Garreg Wen. I am no longer so sure."

"Has the mining position improved, then, Deri? From all I have read in the papers, I would have thought exactly the opposite."

"Goronwy isn't likely to go down the pit again."

"No. I—I was sorry to hear about him. It is bad luck on Rhiannon, too. That girl has great strength of character."

"More than Gillian should you say?"

"I would not like to make the comparison," Eira answered truthfully.

"How would you feel—in Rhiannon's place?"

"I would do my best to make Goronwy happy."

He leaned over on his left side, studying her face with sharpened eyes. "But you wouldn't know, would you, what it is like to love someone?"

Eira could not begin to answer that. She only stared down conscious of hot, shaming colour coming into her pale face. 'Oh, God,' she prayed, 'let him go on being obtuse.' But Deri seemed suddenly gifted with a keener perception than

172

ever he had shown; due, perhaps to his recent closeness to danger—even to death.

All at once the answer came to him why this woman should have fought all these battles on his behalf. She had called it his "voice". Put a nice, safe label upon the object of her feelings. It was not Deri the man in whom she had been interested, oh, dear no!

Little things began to come back to him. The fleeting surprise and gratification when for some reason, now forgotten by him, he first had kissed her. Her birthday had it been? Then later—much later—when they were rehearsing 'Marcel's' lines and she had made him act up to her. Again they had kissed. There had been response in her lips. And, as it seemed to him now, a hunger.

He wondered why he had never thought of Eira in connection with loving. It was not that she was too old or too plain. He was not good at guessing women's ages but imagined her to be between thirty-five and forty.

'It's because she's always so *collected*. I suppose I've mistaken that for lack of feeling.'

She was controlled. There had been very few glimpses of the real Eira beneath that veneer of business efficiency.

He experienced deep compassion. Poor, gallant Eira hiding her ordinary, mortal weakness! It occurred to him that if only things had worked differently for the two of them Eira would have made him the ambitious wife, which, with his easy-going nature, he needed. From her he would have had the driving force to make him go on with his singing. Gillian could not provide that. She was too subjective.

'If I could have fallen in love with Eira it all would have been so easy.'

Yet he could no more imagine himself being in love with her than with any other unapproachable being.

'I suppose I regard her as a nicer sort of school marm.'

He was fond of her—more, possibly, than he realized, yet a lot of fondness and good intention did not create the sort of love a man needed to have for the woman he meant to marry . . .

It was to his credit that he held his silence over the discovery.

The staff nurse picked up a handbell and began to ring it. This was the signal for visitors to start saying their goodbyes.

Sometimes, if Sister was not in the ward, there would be a little latitude between the first and final bell.

Eira rose, collecting her things. She made herself speak with returning cheerfulness. "Gilly will be coming on her own this evening. I don't know whether I shall be in again. I have to return to the office. I am really only hanging on to see whether or not Gillian wants to come back with me. Any idea how long they are likely to keep you in here?"

He said that whilst his arm was mending well he still had a good deal of intermittent pain with it. He imagined he would be in St. Donat's at least another week. He was drawing sick pay. What would happen after that he was not sure.

"But whatever I decide I'll honour my debt to Shearme's, if it takes me the rest of my life."

Did he really have to think of money just then?

"Only you can decide about the future, Deri." She was determined not to try persuasion. She had done that, in the past; placed him in bondage to Shearme's Enterprizes Ltd. Much less could Eira drag in the one name which still might have influenced him. That of the late Maestro Andres.

The bell rang again and the nurse began to shoe the visitors before her, as if they were chickens being chased out for food. Eira wondered if the girl were from the country.

"In case I don't come again, Deri." She held out her hand. With one of those uncharacteristic, gallant little gestures which perhaps marked the transition from miner to musical comedy lead, he took Eira's hand in his good one and raised it to his lips.

Gillian came out from her evening visit, frowning. Eira asked no questions; just leaned across and opened the car door. They proceeded in unbroken silence to the Gwent Arms. On arrival, Gillian asked almost apologetically whether a drink might not be a good idea. What is more, she chose "a horse's neck" instead of her accustomed gin-and-something. Deri, she said, was persisting in his idea of remaining in Wales. At least until he had made up his mind what he really wanted to do with his life. Gillian, who had never previously issued an ultimatum, had made it clear that she had no intention of sharing "Cartref" with Mrs. Rhys and Deri, as Rhiannon would have done, had she become his wife.

"It would be spiritual death," agreed Eira.

174

"I couldn't live in Garreg Wen and know he went down that awful Prydwedd Road Mine every day. One has to be brought up to such acceptance. I should keep on being afraid for him. We have agreed upon—I suppose one would call it a referendum. Or is that quite the right word? Anyway, I am coming back to town with you, Eira."

The older woman snuffed out her cigarette with brutality.

"Has it occurred to you, Gilly, that by standing firm there may be a danger of your losing Deri altogether?"

"That is a risk I have to take," was the sober answer.

Back in London Eira immersed herself in work, putting in long hours and doing all she could in a personal way to extend the business. Without much heart she went to the London first night of *Madelon*, finding it a depressingly nostalgic experience. She downed whiskies in the intervals, talking to backers, critics and celebrities with brittle wit.

"Shlanta," she raised her glass to Conor O'Hegan, London representative of one of the Irish dailies.

"Not another *Oklahoma!* should you say, Miss Shearme?"

"That is hardly its intention, surely? If it's another anything—which mind you, I don't admit—then surely it's more on the lines of *Irma la Douce*."

"What happened to that Welsh tenor of yours? The one that made quite a success over with the Ballykenny Operatic Society. I thought he started with a show?"

Eira said that was a long story but presented it in outline. Young O'Hegan blinked shortsightedly at his sherry.

" 'Tis a great pity."

"Naturally I think the same."

Madelon only ran six weeks. Eira did not delude herself into imagining that Deri could have given it any longer life. Unless, of course, his voice had become a vogue—as had happened with Tauber after the first night of *The Land of Smiles*. She faced the truth and that was that for all its bright hopes, *Madelon* was very far from being a second *Irma la Douce*.

Still the piece was going on another short tour after which it would be released for amateurs.

Other people also enquired about Deri Rhys. His agent, Brad. Stern, rang twice and Eira could only repeat that she had no news. The best thing was to apply to him personally in Garreg Wen. The agent said that he had done so. Coming up with the offer from a company anxious to take out yet another new version of *Die Fledermaus*. This time it was not to be called *Gay Rosalinda* or even *Pink Champagne* but *The Nightbirds*. They were putting in a big ballet, having the young Prince 'Orlovsky' played by a boy and generally pepping the piece up, as it were.

"Pray tell me no more," pleaded Eira.

"You will admit that young Rhys would make a good 'Alfred'?"

She said she had serious doubts whether he would make a good anything—and by that she really included the word 'husband'.

"Oh, well, I'll keep pressing on," promised the agent.

Another 'Alfred' was all too easily found.

Next time it was for a few performances of *Hiawatha* at a British Spa Festival. Eira could only make the same reply. She had no idea what Deri Rhys intended to do about his singing.

Gillian was going about the office with what Mr. Birdsall called 'stoicism'. Roger-the-Dodger put the matter less succinctly, suggesting there was nothing an evening out with him could not have cured.

"Sure you don't mean 'night'?" Liz interrupted.

He gave an unrepentant grin without answering.

"We all know Gilly is carrying a torch for Deri Rhys," went on Liz, since the object of their remarks was fortuitously out of the office.

"Which is singularly unhelpful when it comes to work," Mr. Birdsall snapped.

Gillian carried out her duties, her mind mostly on something else and only her personal friendship with Eira saved her from being reported for inefficiency. Mr. Birdsall did issue a mild warning, showing her a letter typed with no fewer than five mistakes.

"Don't think I'm being too hard on you, my dear."

She knew she deserved the nicely rendered rebuke.

Eira took her out once or twice to a meal and a theatre and even sent Gillian round greater London on amateur revivals of Shearme releases. That the South Westerners A.O.D.S. were doing *Princess Paula* Eira thought it best to ignore.

Gillian had one letter from Deri not long after he left hospital. It enclosed a cutting from *Y day* (in Welsh) accompanied by a picture of Rhiannon being married to Goronwy in the hospital ward where he then was.

"Isn't this just great of her," Deri scribbled at the top of the paper.

Gillian knew it was grand, unselfish and was typical of the girl's character.

When Gillian took the cutting through to Eira's office, the latter sighed. To Eira there was almost unbearable poignancy about a smiling bride standing beside her groom-in-a-wheelchair. (How paltry Gillian's early jealousy of Rhiannon had come to seem!).

Since neither of them could read Welsh they missed the detailed account of the ceremony. Deri had written that he had been at the wedding but for some reason had not thought it worth mentioning that he also had sung (to the accompaniment of the hospital's harmonium) "the Song of Thanksgiving", which fervently thanked God for love.

In fact Deri hardly could have said less about his doings. Of his thoughts and feelings, he made no mention whatsoever.

"So Rhiannon is married," Eira commented briefly.

"Yes, Rhiannon is married all right." Gillian sighed, for she was beginning very much to wonder whether she herself ever was going to be.

23

DERI HAD gone home to "Cartref" without taking back his old room.

"You keep it, man," he told their lodger. It was possible that Deri did not want to give an impression of permanency. His mother accepted his presence in her undemonstrative fashion, though it was noticeable that their daily menu contained the dishes he liked. He only had to whistle and say "not plum duff, Mam?" to win her wavering smile. Financially things had improved now that she had two men in the house, although Deri's work was intermittent. Sometimes he was down the mine, then had to be on "short time". Next he had been temporarily laid off for two or three weeks during which he went "on the dole", as unemployment benefit was still loosely called in those parts.

When he earned, he set aside all he could to post, in a registered envelope, to the Shearme accountant. Whilst acknowledged, there was nothing in any sense personal about these transactions. It gave Deri a kind of perverse pleasure addressing these envelopes, because by the terms of his agreement he was not bound to pay money other than a percentage of his theatrical earnings.

He saw Rhiannon quite often. She went on working at the greengrocer's, just as she had done before her marriage, but for fewer hours. She lived with Goronwy's family, sharing the back bedroom with him. Already he was learning to do more for himself and eagerly talking about when he could begin fittings for his "National Health leg".

Rhiannon preserved her outward serenity. If she were occasionally unhappy or disappointed in life, Goronwy was never allowed to guess the fact.

Deri came into the shop one Saturday afternoon, humming as he so often did, gave his order and watched her weigh it out for him, then tip the vegetables into his mother's straw basket. Leaning conversationally across the counter, he inquired:

"How is the world treating you, Rhiannon?"

"I have no reason to complain."

He pulled out a handful of small change, tossing the last coin into the air. As it landed, he saw it to be Irish—possibly a penny someone had forgotten to change before reaching Fishguard.

"They want me to sing 'Jim' in their *Rose Marie*," he announced casually, having just been asked to do so by the local amateurs.

"Surely you won't do this?" the young married woman exclaimed, slipping the money into a drawer. They did not run to cash registers in Garreg Wen.

"Why not?"

"Well, I thought you had turned into a professional singer, Deri."

178

"I don't really know what I am any longer and that's the absolute truth."

Because Rhiannon was still the person with whom he could talk most frankly, he explained all the miserable uncertainty of his present position. Though it had not been openly mentioned in his presence, there was a feeling down at the mine that with the present national contraction of the industry he was doing another man out of a job.

"A chap who has no chance of different employment because he has been trained for nothing except how to hew coal out of the earth."

Rhiannon had heard the actual talk. She knew that it lay in her hands to influence him and most of all she wanted to use that power in the right way. She had never quiet forgotten that he was her first love. The protective, almost maternal feeling she had for lamed Goronwy was quite different.

When he came out of hospital she had had to undertake such crude duties as changing the dressings on the stump of his leg, amputated at the knee. There was a degree of passion and of mutual reliance, one upon the other. But it was not a union where romance played any part. Deri had been the man of her dreams who had carried her—in imagination only—beyond the blue beauty of the Welsh hills.

Therefore Rhiannon acknowledged that she had heard the men's talk. Deri had been a bit of a hero after the way he had helped in the rescue work. They wanted to do the right thing by him.

"Meaning they took me back as a kind of charity?"

She shrugged slightly, twisting the platinum wedding ring round on her finger with thoughtful frown.

"Miss Shearme thought a lot of your chances as a singer, didn't she?"

"I guess so," and he kicked a stray onion across the soil-strewn floor of the shop, free from customers because a special sports event was on the T.V. at that time.

"I would have thought you owed her something for all the trouble she has taken over you, Deri."

He did not answer because in his secret heart, as Noel Coward termed it, he acknowledged this fact.

"And Miss Lechmere," the speaker went on in her quiet way. "Are you being very fair to her? I know how—cut

179

off from you she must be feeling. Do you ever write to her? I thought not . . . Remember I *know*. I went through it all myself. Before—Goronwy, I mean."

He reddened in discomfort, never having imagined that it would be Rhiannon who would bring him to his senses.

He was very silent during supper and spent most of the evening scratching away with a steel-nibbed pen on cheap writing paper. Sighing heavily he went out to the post office, which was quite near Glendower Road and slipped the letter into the box. As he walked back, he fell to thinking of the day of the disaster and how, when he had come up to the surface, his first desire had been for a cigarette. The ambulance attendant had offered him one—those were scarcely moments for rules to be too closely observed. Deri had taken a couple of draws, coughed, and been unable to finish the cigarette, so horrible had tobacco tasted after months of abstinence.

He could have done with a cigarette just then, too, only he was sure it would have been no different to the last. Shutting "Cartref's" heavy front door he mounted the stairs which were immediately opposite it and knocking, went in to say goodnight to his mother.

Mrs. Rhys looked oddly different in bed, with a few clinging wisps of grey hair on her rapidly balding head.

"You are going back to London." This was a statement rather than a question.

He had long accepted her instinctive knowledge of such things. Without answering he sat on the side of her bed, which was covered with a thick Welsh tweed blanket.

"Shall you mind, Mam?"

She did not pretend indifference. "You must do what you think best, my son."

"Rhiannon it was who made me see—"

"Rhiannon is a very sensible girl. The one you should have married, Deri."

"Perhaps," he smiled, not wishing to argue.

He was certain that his mother had no active dislike of Gillian. It was simply that the two women lacked a point of contact. Perhaps he could try to teach Gillian a little Welsh, but he knew it to be a hard, jaw-cracking language for those who had not been brought up on it, as he had.

Rising, he bent to kiss the old lady's wrinkled forehead. His hand on the light switch behind the door, he smiled indulgently at her second best hat, ready on the bed post for any nocturnal emergency.

Eira was surprised to receive Deri's letter not only because he had chosen her in preference to Gillian but because he had written at length. She knew how bad he normally was at expressing himself in written words. Such a letter must have taken a great deal of time to compose.

In essence it said that he had been made to see his irresponsible behaviour. He knew now that already he had been out of mining too long. Rather touchingly he stated that instead of being brave, he had been very frightened when he had gone down again after an absence of many months

> "I had learned what it was to fear.
> In a miner that is not a good thing."

In the general heart-searching he gave the impression of having carried on with the rescue operations simply by clenching his strong white teeth and making himself go forward with his friends.

> "That I injured my arm was in part my own
> fault, too."

He wrote that he had been "bloody obstinate" about the conduct of his singing career.

> "I saw myself staying in Wales.
> Doing the man's job for which I
> had been trained."

Then he had begun to be redundant and aware of keeping others out of work.

> "They wouldn't sack me outright
> because of an exaggerated notion
> of what I had done to help bring
> the trapped lads to safety."

But short time and being laid off had told him better than anything the true position which the loyalty of his mates

181

had tried to conceal.

> "You can tell Gilly I have missed
> her like hell. It isn't just 'sugar
> for the bird', as you once called it,
> to say I've missed you, too, Eira."

He gave the impression of the man who taken out of his environment had then grown from it in the process of transplantation. He has seen other places; lived in big towns. Even, as he wryly put it, begun "to scrape together a bit of culture".

> "Truth is, Eira, I am a misfit
> any place but a bit less noticeable
> in London . . . "

He very humbly placed himself once again in the able hands of Shearme Enterprizes Ltd., and the agent chosen by them.

> "If everyone isn't fed up with me."

He brought in the maestro, too, saying it had been a poor return for all the old man's interest in his voice.

> "Rhiannon has said I can do more for
> Wales with my voice than with black
> hands down a mine. Maybe it is true.
> I only know I am homesick for London,
> for Gillian—if she will ever speak
> to me again—and full of humbleness
> towards your self."

He signed himself hers "faithfully". This brought a momentary smile to her face. She was glad the letter had come to her private address and that she had been able to read it when she was by herself. With a child's gesture she brushed a tear from the corner of each eye and next minute was humming a bar or two of a current "Pop" number heard over the radio.

She entered the offices at 10.30 that morning with an air of triumph, demanding to know whether Gillian was busy or not. Mr. Birdsall said that she was available. Gillian came into Eira's office to be told to "catch". Some of the leaves of Deri's letter fluttered to the ground.

"Was ever such a man?" Eira observed, laughing with a light-heartedness she had not felt for many weeks.

Gillian reached the end of the letter at last, folded it neatly and handed it back to the recipient.

"Who do you think responsible for making Deri so sensible. Mrs. Rhys?"

Eira shook her head emphatically. "If you ask me I would say it could have been Rhiannon. Well, child, I had better call up that agent of his."

"Oh, you don't know how relieved I am!" Gillian cried. "I was almost thinking I should have to give in and try to become a good little mining village wife."

"You aren't cut out for that," Eira sounded most definite. "From now on we must both be strict with Deri. He is going way, way up to the top, if I have to push him up every blasted step of the ladder by myself."

"You won't because I shall be there to help." Gillian's eyes danced and so did she. Three whole waltz turns round the office.

24

Deri returned to London not quite certain of his reception. However his crestfallen air did not last long. Any initial coldness on Gillian's part seemed melted by the sight of his dark curls, his wide smile and questioning eyes, whilst Eira, beyond a mild "you're a nice one, aren't you?" seemed equally forebearing with him.

However things were not altogether the same as they had been. For instance he could not go back to his old room. This had been let in his uncertain period of absence, so it had to be a men's hostel recommended by the Y.M.C.A.

One of his first actions was to go on a strictly personal pilgrimage to the Catholic Cemetery where the maestro had been buried. There Deri laid a few flowers on the turf, wishing above all else that the old man could have been spared longer to him.

When Deri reported at Shearme's Eira was friendly and, he was grateful to say, uncensorious.

"I suppose you had to work it out of your system, Deri." At the same time she made it clear that he must not expect to walk straight into a job. Was he all right for money?

"I can manage."

Abandoning her business-manner, she leaned her chin on her hands and regarded him with serious eyes.

"These months haven't been too easy for Gillian. Whilst it has been no direct concern of mine, I could not help knowing how uncertain and unhappy she has felt. You hardly ever wrote, did you?"

"There was nothing to write about, Eira."

"How like a man!" but she smiled as she said it. "Do you know what my advice would be to you both? Go off and marry! Take a short honeymoon and then we will see what can be done in the way of finding you professional work again. Remember, Deri, no management likes to engage a contract-breaker."

He flushed, promising to see what Gillian's views might be. When he tried to make the idea seem a spontaneous suggestion of his own, she had an immediate suspicion of the truth—but prudently she kept it to herself. Even if Eira were behind the scheme—did it matter? Already there had been too much apartness between the lovers.

"Yes, Deri, I would like us to be married just as soon as the banns have been called."

Gillian did not want a special licence scramble. She owed it to her parents to have a more or less quiet wedding from their home. It was still Mrs. Lechmere's idea that every bride should wear white, but Gillian was against this, having an idea that there would be bad luck attached to that. Her marriage to Alec was to have been a white wedding. The dress had been ordered and finally fitted. Then he had died and it had remained unworn by her. Mrs. Lechmere understood and did not press the matter, though in her opinion it remained a pity that her only daughter should want to wear a coloured ensemble.

Deri was alarmed at finding what he had taken to be a

small-scale country event was assuming almost the proportion of a society wedding. Eira told him that on that day at least he would be quite unimportant. Provided he wore a morning suit and top hat he would not disgrace Gillian too badly. He went to the hire firm to which he had gone before for dress clothes and was gratified at finding the present requirements equally easy to arrange. Only a few people were coming up from Wales to see him made Gillian's husband. His mother bought a new hat for the occasion. Though she was not good at talking to people, she certainly did not let him down in any way. When the small reception reached the point where bride and groom should be departing, Mrs. Rhys embraced Gillian as well as Deri.

"Be good to him," the old lady whispered.

"I'll try," Gillian promised, with acute embarrassment.

Eira, one of the smartest people there, kissed the young bride and was about to touch Deri's cheek briefly with her lips only to be told by him that that would not do at all. He kissed her properly and afterwards, in the car taking them to the station, Gillian said:

"That was nice of you, Deri."

He looked at her in momentary surprise. Surely she did not think he had needed prompting? Had not Eira done more for them than anyone else? Indeed it was on the wedding cheque that she had given them that they were able to stay at the Leinster Hotel, near Lismore, a good centre from which to resume their acquantance with Ballykenny and to see a little of Gillian's relations near Cork.

In fact, Deri was surprised to find how well remembered he was around Ballykenny and the interest they took in his marriage. Such an event called for celebration and in Southern Ireland that meant keeping it up far into the following day.

They flew back to London from Shannon to the home which Gillian formerly had shared with Liz and her friends.

Eira had the key. Not only had she been over to lay in a few necessary articles of food, but the place was freshly dusted and flowers welcomed them in all the available vases.

"Sometimes I wonder what we've done to deserve such a friend," Deri remarked, suddenly very still and serious.

It must not be assumed that Deri Rhys rose to immediate stardom in London, or that he was necessarily compared with

185

Caruso, Tauber or de Lanza—according to the generation of those who remembered those three great voices.

Even with his exceptional gift the first years of a singer were ones of struggle, with Gillian retaining her job and neither of them feeling altogether justified in starting a family. The work which came his way varied. Sometimes it was no more than a few concerts, eked out with the odd date on the B.B.C.

Then for three full, happy months, he went to a small Arts-Council-cushioned company which produced one act operas for shoe string casts. He had the pleasure of appearing in such delightful works as Offenbach's *Fortunio's Song*. Another lucky break was a tour in *Chu Chin Chow*, where, as he said, he felt rather under-dressed as the tenor serenading his Eastern sweetheart.

Sometimes Gillian was able to join him for a while, but it was not always financially possible. Then she would have a great orgy of cleaning and decorating the flat against the date of his return.

The second year of their marriage he had a whole summer season at Llandudno. Eira arranged a temporary release from Shearme's so that Gillian might live in North Wales with Deri. What was more he was able to invite his mother for a holiday with them. She could not remember having had one since she became a widow.

During these two months Gillian came to know her mother-in-law as well as she was ever to do. Even then the old lady was never seen hatless. This particular secret remained Mrs. Rhys's until such time as Gillian went to Garreg Wen and saw her laid out in the front-bedroom upstairs. A moment during which Gillian regretted the jokes which she and Eira had made about the hats.

'I am glad now I never asked Deri about it,' Gillian thought

"Cartref" was not his to keep. It had to go to another miner's family, though he would have liked it to have been offered to Rhiannon and Goronwy, with their two small boys.

"It wasn't possible, I know," she said to Deri, understanding as always.

When he saw her two boys be began to wonder whether he and Gillian were doing the right thing by avoiding parenthood on economic grounds.

186

"Damn it, Deri *bach*, a marriage isn't any marriage at all without kids," Goronwy pointed out, walking—so Deri thought—very well on his artificial limb. The N.C.B. had found work for him "on the surface" and he was able to ride a motor bicycle over to Prydwedd Road Mine.

Deri said nothing to Gillian about what had been said. After all, it was men's talk and he was not, of course, aware that Rhiannon had put forward much the same advice.

"No, it isn't that we aren't able to have a family," Gillian admitted, reddening, "but we can't afford one just yet."

"My Mam brought up four of us on —" and Rhiannon named a staggering pittance of money. "True we had free coal and grew our own vegetables in the back garden."

Not only did Gillian feel sad, but a little selfish into the bargain . . .

When Deri did have his chance of a London lead, they had so far lost hope as not quite to believe what Eira had just told them about the result of the audition.

"This time it *is* your big chance, Deri, and it is up to you what happens. But if you go rushing off to help at a mining disaster anywhere between Land's End and John O'Groats, I wash my hands of you for ever."

He smiled and gave his word.

Rehearsals were relentless, for the piece was under American direction. Just as they had shown what could be done in the way of turning Scotland into a musical with *Brigadoon* so a later inspiration had made a high-powered group of composers, librettists and lyricists in turn consider Wales. Apart from the last act of *Florodora* the territory was apparently unexplored.

A call had gone round the theatrical agents to send along anyone who even looked Welsh. If the real thing could be found, so much the better. They must be able to sing, and if possible be prepared to do some of it actually in the Welsh language, for which tuition would be provided by a special coach, if necessary. So when Deri, an ex-miner with a superb voice, was auditioned this was more than the ambitious promoters had hoped to find.

"And he looks all right, too," one of the backers had gasped, expecting, Eira wondered just what!

She stopped into one or two of the rehearsals and had to admit that when it came to slick presentations the Americans

187

won on easy terms. Whilst she thought *The Land of the Leek* lacked that intrinsic fey charm of *Brigadoon*, she had an idea that it might be in for a marathon of a run—unless, of course, it turned out an un-deserved flop such as *Candide*.

"I feel as though our whole future depends on this show," Gillian admitted.

"You two have had quite a tough time one way and another, haven't you?" they were lunching together at the time of the conversation. "Has it been worth it, Gilly?"

"Of course."

Eira smiled without speaking.

They approached the first night in a spirit of united hope but for divergent reasons. Financially Eira would welcome a twelve month or two year run, since Shearme's already had taken over the amateur rights. A successful West End premier made a great deal of difference to their ultimate worth. On a more unselfish level she wanted success so that Deri and Gillian might have that lucky break they seemed to Eira to deserve. For Gillian it was simpler still.

'If the libraries do a good deal I'll feel justified in having a baby.'

The Land of the Leek opened before a somewhat sceptical audience. To tell the truth, people were a little tired of assured American successes. But when they found in place of noise and gusty tunes the inter-woven musical themes of Welsh traditional airs, they began to relax.

Deri had never sung better except, perhaps, that very first time Eira had heard him in Ballykenny. Or was it that no subsequent impact on her could be precisely the same? Fascinated, she could tell the similarity of his effect upon the present audience. He was moving them, as he had moved her—then.

Even Gillian who had never felt quite the same musical response to Deri's singing as Eira, found her eyes moist. Eira reached across the arm of the seat and gripped her hand hard. Then the applause broke.

"He's there, Gilly. There at last," she whispered. The show was halted until he had sung again and yet again.

In the interval the head of one of the big ticket agencies said they were prepared to sign a big deal on the strength of the reception.

"It will be the biggest we've risked since *My Fair Lady*,"

he confided, adding, "That young tenor has a fine voice."

"And I was the one to discover him," Eira answered, laughing and briefly related how she had come across him in the first place.

"No idea you were such a good talent scout, Miss Shearme."

"I was on *holiday*," she pointed out, as if that made all the difference.

The bell went and her friend, Conor O'Hegan, of the Irish press gave her a thumbs up sign from across the foyer.

The tumultuous enthusiasm of the final curtain must have dispelled any doubts still held by the most pessimistic of theatregoers. As Eira and Gillian subsequently made their way back stage, Eira said:

"You know, I rather think this is where I came in, Gillian!"

Whereat Gillian laughed, knowing that both were thinking of Ballykenny and the Irish holiday that had taken such an unexpected turn.

THE END

A CAMEO ROMANCE

Doctor Simon's Secret

By KATHLEEN TREVES

Deborah Markham had just arrived from France to
start her nursing training at Sappington General
Hospital when she met Langdale Simon. Met him
and fell in love, little knowing that he was the
R.M.O. at the busy East Anglian hospital where
she was working.
But loving Doctor Simon was not an easy matter.
His life was shrouded with mystery, and a hospital
is not an easy place in which to keep a secret.
Where did Dictor Simon visit every Thursday?
Why did he have such strange friends, and why
was Lady Allisande Pendrigh so hostile
towards him?
With Deborah torn between love and fear, trust
and uncertainty, her friends decided to take matters
into their own hands — with surprising results for
everybody.

25p

WORLD   DISTRIBUTORS   (Manchester)   LTD

A CAMEO ROMANCE

Spotlight on Susan
By LEILA MACKINLAY

All her young life Siobhan Jacquet, daughter of an
Irish mother and a Durham ex-miner father, had
always wanted to act and she won medal after
medal at music festivals up and down the country.
Then she won a year's free tuition at the Theatre
Training Centre. Here she remet Gareth Muir, a
man of about 36, who had been an adjudicator at
her last Festival and friendship grew up between
them. During the year Siobhan (whose stage name is
Susan) also met and fell in love with handsome
young Roderic Raven, ex-student of the Centre and
now juvenile lead in a West End play, but finding
that marriage was not in his mind she accepted
Gareth when he proposed to her. His work and her
stage commitments often parted them, and Susan,
the actress, found her job plain sailing compared
with the other – as Siobhan the wife – before she
finally found happiness. . . .

25p

WORLD DISTRIBUTORS (Manchester) LTD

A CAMEO ROMANCE

Destined for You
By KAY WINCHESTER

Kerina Chandler's young sister, Stevie, shows
promise of becoming a violinist and both Kerry
and her father sacrifice almost everything to further
Stevie's future. But when Kerry persuades her father
to open their beautiful country home to paying
guests and the first visitor, Marcus Neame, comes to
The Maltings her whole world is turned upside
down. Marcus is almost blind through an accident
and in his wake comes trouble, mystery, and a new
emotion that Kerry has never found in her
relationship with young Dr. Peter Graham, who
loves her.
There is the development of the mystery behind
Marcus; there are the troubles caused by the other
guests at The Maltings and spoilt Stevie's
disturbances: ingredients enough for mounting
tension and strained emotions before a poignant and
absorbing climax.

25p

WORLD DISTRIBUTORS (Manchester) LTD